MAN AND BOY

Hardin Buck had everything a man could want—the love of women, the friendship of men, the satisfaction of good work well done. But there was one thing his rich and full life lacked. A son.

Jeff Beecher returned from college to Oklahoma to discover why his father had committed suicide, even though this meant digging up buried shames and scandals. Soon he found himself lost and alone in the country of his childhood, his memories of the past shattered, his dreams of the future clouded.

There were no ties of blood to draw Hardin and Jeff together. There was only deep and desperate need . . . and something that both would have been too embarrassed to call love . . .

GENERATIONS
OF
MEN

BY JOHN HUNT

CURTIS
BOOKS

NEW YORK, N.Y.

For My Mother
Elizabeth Palmour Mathews,
whose love and courage created
an unforgettable example

and in memory of my
grandfather, J. C. Hunt,
a fox-hunting man

PART ONE

I long ago lost a hound, a bay horse, and a turtle-dove, and am still on their trail. Many are the travellers I have spoken concerning them, describing their tracks and what calls they answer to. I have met one or two who have heard the hound, and the tramp of the horse, and even seen the dove disappear behind a cloud, and they seemed as anxious to recover them as if they had lost them themselves.

Thoreau

CHAPTER I

☐ Chetopa county is a bleached expanse of grassland and blackjack trees, thinly peopled and still belonging to the natural domain of sun and wind. Its weathers are various and ever-changing, yet really no more than modulations of the dominant natural keys. It is a country where the skies are watched, talked about, despaired of, but never forgotten.

Anciently it had been an inland sea and now it was prairie, a long series of waves of bluestem grass where white-faced cattle had replaced the buffalo. Beneath circling hawks, coyotes hunted the ravines; rattlesnakes curled in the cool of the limestone ledges. The earth was silent, deeply and intensely still, prostrate before the black violence of tornadic winds or stunned by the heat that hammered against the surface of the yellow roads. In this place a man stood close to himself, carved out in isolation against the sky, and there was a nearness to the land and all its seasons which once felt could rarely be satisfied elsewhere. Maybe it was simply that here the wind blew always and that a man grew accustomed to hearing its song in his ears. This was the way it had seemed, at least, to Hardin Buck.

These thoughts, or something like them, had been in his mind when he had returned to the county more than thirty years before, but on this September afternoon he felt them again with a keenness which struck to the bone. For these grasslands of Oklahoma had been his home, the

9

skies and the weathers which ruled them were in his blood, and now death had hunted him down. The years of his life had faded behind him and there was not much time left, and as he stared out across the light-emblazoned surface of the plains he seemed to hear the grim and implacable padding of death's pursuit, following him as a lean coyote might follow the trail of some wounded and dying buffalo bull.

Buck was sitting on the far point of the ridge, his back against a lightning-split blackjack that flowered against the sky like some giant candelabra polished to ivory by the incessant wind. This was the tip of the wedge of up-thrust earth on which he had built his house, and behind him blackjacks and sumac and buckbrush and oaks formed a panoply of shade above the faint path that threaded back through the sandstone slabs to the rock house. Before him was the prairie contained by the familiar limits, the dark line of distant sky on the west, the crooked sprawl of trees following the creek southward, and to the east, another ridge much like the one on which he now sat. From time to time he raised his head and narrowed his eyes toward the horizon and then he looked back to the pistol that he was cleaning. His hands, strong and brown and long-fingered, worked upon the gleaming steel with assurance and when his face rose to the light the hands worked on deftly, rapidly, and yet without haste. Buck's face was brown, too, fired by sun and wind to the color of a saddle, and like his body it was long and bony and spare. A ragged scar ran above one eye and across his temple to where his clipped hair was a severe gray against the leather of his skin. His nose was flattened at the bridge where he had broken it twice and when he smiled his teeth were big and uneven and tobacco-stained, and yet in his quick eyes there was something so wild and free that the chief impression he gave was one of grace, a high-strung, wiry, thorough-bred grace that attended his movements even when he sat as he did now, his back against the cracked trunk of the tree, his whipcord-clad legs stretched full length before him, his crossed boots filmed with a faint layer of dust.

But there was a shadow in his eyes this afternoon and a frown upon his brow as though he were listening to something or thinking about things which he had not thought of for a long time. He ran his hand hard across his forehead where the wrinkles lay deep and shadowed, and for a moment his hands ceased and he listened again. At last he tightened his jaw and turned abruptly back to the pistol, and after a few more minutes' work he was done. When he had reloaded it, he twisted the shining barrel in his hands and nodded with satisfaction. He raised his arm and sighted on a fence post down in the draw and then a movement traced across his vision and drew his face sharply upward. There were two of them, turkey buzzards, wheeling the vast sky above him in lazy, effortless flight. He rose quickly and found the thin, vertical sight against the black silhouette and fired twice. Then with the gun still smoking a little against his leg he stood there staring into the sky, swearing steadily and coldly while the apparently unruffled buzzards ascended in tightened circles until they seemed not much larger than the sight which he had held upon them.

He had returned only that morning from the clinic in Kansas City, where the doctors had put it to him bluntly. If he were moderately careful, he had a year, maybe two, to live; if not—they had simply shrugged their shoulders. They had seemed disgusted, almost angry at the way he had ignored the warnings, the labored breath, the terrible grip of pain in his chest. Too many mountain trails, they had said; too many nights in the rain for a man of sixty. Too much beef and Scotch, too much chopping wood; in short, too much of everything which he had loved. He had known it, of course, and he had thought of death, and yet it hadn't really mattered to him before. He had decided about these things as a young man when he was flying a baling-wire crate of a plane in the first war, and he had never found reason since to change his mind. And

11

now as he grew old and he could hear death closing in on him, he found himself remembering deer which he had shot in the mountains of New Mexico, how life had fled in one terrible, splendid moment, and how there had been something sacred in such a death with the bright blood staining the earth which lay cold and darkening in the mountain shadows. It was the feeling he still got while quail hunting in the last brief flare of autumn, and he thought sometimes that it seemed a good kind of death because there was so much life in it, being at once the dying of the fire and the ashes from which life would spring. He had decided long ago that when his time came he would go out clean and hard and, if possible, in his own way, carrying his life in his hands like the precious thing that it had always been to him.

The sound of a car door slamming was muffled in the heavy afternoon air. Buck heard it and felt immediately the quick sense of annoyance that always came over him when he saw or heard a car approaching the ridge. He slipped the pistol into his pocket and walked rapidly toward the house, but his anger was gone by the time he reached the gate of the yard. It was John White Eagle's car, an old red pickup truck with the right fender missing, and it sat there with a kind of sag in the middle, looking tired and misused like a hard-ridden horse. When he came around the side of the house, he could see White Eagle stretched out in a chair, leaning back against the elm tree which shaded the side yard. The old Indian was dressed as he always dressed in summer, in heavy dark trousers and a white shirt, and his face was shaded by an uncreased, broad-brimmed hat. His eyes were concealed by dark glasses, and short, thick braids of black hair hung to his shoulders. He raised his hand in greeting when he saw Buck.

"Hello, Little Owl," he said. He spoke in the language of the Chetopa, and his voice was heavy and guttural.

"Hello, John." Buck sat down at the table. "How's everything?"

12

White Eagle shrugged. "The dance was bad; fewer young men there than the last time. But the dances are always bad now." He spoke quietly and slowly, somewhat formally, and his hands, brown and wrinkled and vein-crossed, lay motionless on his knee. "You have been gone."

"Yes," Buck said quickly, looking away. "Kansas City. It's a long way and it takes too much time."

"I have never been there." White Eagle pulled a toothpick from the breast pocket of his shirt and began picking his teeth. "My boy Paul goes there—he and his friends. From seeing them when they come back and hearing their talk about it, I have never wanted to go."

Buck nodded and sat without speaking. He watched White Eagle remove the dark glasses and fold them and put them carefully into his shirt pocket, and he knew then that the ritual of greeting was over.

"This is one bad place for a man to be in summer," White Eagle said.

Buck smiled. "Summer's about gone."

"Maybe, but the sun's still here. Can't buy a bottle of beer in town. Run out every place. Pig Stand was dry by ten o'clock last night, and I can't keep a bottle around the house."

"You've got too many thirsty friends," Buck said, getting up and going to the kitchen. He was carrying a little wooden tub filled with iced beer when he returned. "This is what's left over from the last time you were here."

White Eagle was looking out over the prairie toward the east ridge. He watched Buck for a moment as he opened the beer and then he looked back out toward the long waves of grass. His eyes grew narrow, seeming to sink back into the hollows of his wrinkled face, and his heavy features had the molded silence of a funeral mask. He untied the white handkerchief that lay knotted around his neck and wiped his face with it and tied it again, the knot resting just in the hollow of his throat.

13

Then he reached for a bottle of beer. When he had taken a long drink, he held it where he could see the foam bubbles rising. "You know, Hardin, this is a good place you got here." He gestured toward the house with an easy movement of his hand. "You got good grass here, shade trees—you made a good choice."

"I've never regretted it," Buck said. "I would have liked more water than what I've got, but then I guess that's too much to ask."

"You're high and you get the wind; you can't expect water. And this is dry country. I remember my father saying that in Missouri in the old days there was much rain, that there were many ponds and that the creeks ran full. Oklahoma is dry; you have to like wind and sun and dust to stay here." He was silent then, and he sat looking again toward the east ridge. After a while he lit a cigar and set his bottle on the ground beside him. When he spoke he did not look at Buck but continued to watch the slender finger of trees in the distance. "We will be dancing again soon, Hardin. I want you to come. We will be dancing at Rock Springs, and I would like for you to be there. This may be the end of the dancing now."

"There'll be more." Buck growned. "You have young men in the tribe."

"No," White Eagle said, shaking his head. "Sometimes I think that after me there will be no more. There is a sickness among the young men; they will not dance. They have turned their eyes away from the earth, and it is no longer their home. They are like white men now. Paul, my boy, he is a stranger to me; more like a white boy than my own son. But you must come because this may be the end of it all, and I want you to have seen it so that someone will know—" He moved his hands with a sudden, abrupt gesture of difficulty and his face stirred with pain before settling back into impassivity. "It is a bad thing to think that all of the old ways are dying."

Buck nodded. "I have always said that, and that is why I worked to build the museum. Then there will be a record, something which will say these people lived, and that they were here once, too. There will be something for the memory to hold to." He spoke carefully, molding his thoughts into the repetitious formality of the Chetopa tongue.

"The old ways cannot live in that museum," White Eagle said, lifting his fingers to his chest. "They live here or they do not live at all. Building the museum was only building the long pine box."

Buck's eyes were tired and wrinkled in the corners as he squinted across at White Eagle. "Things are different, now, John; the young ones have to change. Your son and the others have to live with the white man—live in his kind of world."

"All right," White Eagle said. "The old life is past. I know that because many of my friends are gone and one of these days I will be gone too. But I do not want the old way to be forgotten; if it dies, my people will have nothing. Because even if they wear glasses and get drunk and run after money they are still Chetopa and not white. White ways are no good for us."

"You let me know about the dance," Buck said after a while. "I'll be there." His eyes were quiet and preoccupied and he rubbed his hand slowly along his jaw.

White Eagle lit his cigar again and then nodded through the smoke. "That will be good," he said.

Presently John leaned forward a little in his chair and turned his head, listening. "Somebody comin'," he said after a moment. And then Buck heard it, too; the clopping of hoofs and the steady creak of leather. "Must be Sam," Buck said.

The sound came closer and stopped, and they heard the jarring of the gate. Even before he came around the house, Buck could see him as he had seen him countless times before, a tall man, lean, bent in the shoulders, dressed in overalls which were long past the age where they were strong enough to wrinkle, in shoes that looked as blunt and as permanent as stone, in a shirt that was

15

paper thin and the color of spring water, and always the straw hat, creased and sweated and ageless. At the corner of the house Sam stopped for a moment, looking at them, and then came on. As he sat down, he tossed his hat on the table and emitted a long whoosh of breath.

"It's a sonofabitch for hot, ain't it," he said. He wiped at his forehead which was a brick-red series of wrinkles and creases suddenly becoming white where his hat had protected his head from the sun. His hair was wet and disheveled and stuck close to his skull. "Well, are you gonna pour me one or should I just help myself."

Buck laughed and gestured toward the beer. "I was afraid maybe you'd be starved before I could get back and give you something to eat. Hasn't your corn burned out yet?"

"Burnt out?" Samuel said, taking the opener and pulling a bottle from the wooden tub. "Why Hardin, that corn's so tall I have to take a step ladder to get at the ears. Why there's so much corn out there that—"

"I know about that tall corn of yours," Buck said. "How'd it happen you could take an afternoon off with so much to look after?"

Samuel set his bottle on the table and began rolling a cigarette. "Hardin," he said, "listen. What's planted is planted—what's gonna grow is gonna grow. The rest is up to the good Lord and the weather and they's not a blessed thing I can do about it. Farmin's just like shootin' dice, and I can hope just as hard over here as I can sittin' on my front porch. But what in the hell do I care about a bunch of scrub corn, anyway; I'm what the boys in Grey Horse call a retail merchant."

Buck laughed again, shaking his head, thinking of the old Dodge which Samuel used on his route, the back end loaded with chewing gum and shoe laces and tea and suspenders and all the other products marked Higgins. A kind of portable general store, bumping along the back roads, the trunk made into a kennel and always occupied by a couple of long-eared, sad-eyed hounds so that there

16

was always the possibility of a trade or a hunt or just company.

"Don't come around my place with that store of yours," White Eagle said. "We ain't got rid of that last load you left there." He was speaking English and his words sounded abrupt and disjointed in their alien rhythm.

Samuel took a piece of board from his pocket and began to whittle it down to a point. "But talkin' about weather," he said. "You know, I don't give a ring-tailed damn about summer. I'd just as soon go without it, and have a fall that was twicet as long. Man, that's the time of the year for me. Ever' night, runnin' them hounds. Hear 'em all over Chetopa County on a clear night when it'll carry."

"Chetopa County, hell," Buck said. "They can hear that pack of yours clear up to Caney. First time I ever heard of a man incorporating a grocery store with a bunch of hounds as stockholders. I can see a man being land-poor, even horse-poor—but hound-poor!"

Samuel looked at him a moment and then smiled. "Hardin, that would be right 'cept for one thing—you got it just backwards. It ain't that I'm hound-poor—I'm fox-poor. There just ain't enough fox around here to keep me busy, so in between times I have to run that dad-blamed store."

The talk rolled on, down the afternoon and into evening. And when the cool came in, stroking ever so lightly the grass at their feet, they sat silent, hearing about them the faint rattle of blackjacks in the wind. White Eagle's fingers drummed slowly on the rusted top of the old metal table, and at Samuel's feet were the curled remains of the board. What was left of the sun lay glistening in the treetops on the east ridge.

Finally Samuel sat up erect and reached into the breast pocket of his shirt. "You people talk too much," he muttered. "I might'n near forgot what I come over to tell you. I got me a letter this mornin' from the East—from

17

my grandson, Jeff. Boy's plumb growed up on me—he's close on twenty-eight or nine. Course I ain't seen him since he used to come down to the farm in Tennessee— all the way from the East." He spoke hurriedly now, looking at them over the letter. "Name's same as mine— Beecher—Jeff Beecher. Son to my oldest boy, George. George's dead now."

"What did the letter say?" Buck was carefully tamping his pipe.

"Read it," Samuel said. "Read it out loud, Hardin. See what you think."

Buck read it and then handed it back. "All he says is that he wants to see you and that he's coming out."

"Yeah, I got that," Samuel said. "I got that much. But what's botherin' me is that he never said what he was comin' for. He never said what it was he wanted."

Buck shrugged and set his empty bottle on the ground beside him. "He says he's coming out to stay with you awhile, that's all. Maybe he's on vacation."

Samuel shook his head. "I just couldn't rightly say. Haven't heard from any of 'em in a coon's age. And who the hell would want to come here for a vacation?"

"How long has it been since you've seen him?"

"Oh, fifteen years and better. He used to come summers down to the farm. But his mother—she was the one from the East that my boy George married—she didn't like it any too good and made him stop comin'. Claimed she couldn't get him back into shoes in the fall cause his feet'd spread so much from goin' barefooted. But he wouldn't be comin' all this way just for a visit."

"Why not," Buck said. "There's nothing so out of the way about that; it's perfectly natural."

"Not any more, Hardin," White Eagle said. "You don't have a family, but I can tell you. When your boy knocks on the door now, you wonder what's the trouble. When he taps you on the shoulder, you reach for your billfold."

"No, I have no son," Buck said simply. "Perhaps you're right."

"That's true," Samuel said. "But then Jeff's a good boy. That is, if he's anything like he was when he was a kid. Besides, I wouldn't be surprised if he wasn't just homesick for them hounds." Then he had to raise his voice above their laughter. "Just wait and see. He used to be plumb crazy after hounds when he was little."

"Well, there's one thing about it," Buck said, smiling briefly as he got up. "We don't have long to wait. He should be here in a couple of days, according to the letter. Now what do you say to some dinner?"

"Wants to rain," White Eagle said.

Samuel was gone, and Buck and White Eagle sat at the table, finishing the last bottles of beer. Around them the twilight had come in suddenness and silence, merging into dusk everything save one crimson cloth of high and westward cloud. Down in the pasture a steer bawled, a series of short and breathless bellows in the night. And behind the thin grate of crickets bumped occasional rumbles of thunder, shaking open the sky to reveal gray shreds of cloud.

"Yes, but it won't," said Buck. "It's just the heat."

"Yeah. You could smell it if it was comin'." The match White Eagle had struck carved his face from the darkness. The flare of light rose, trembled, and then was gone, leaving behind the large, orange glow of a cigar. "I never thought nothin' about Sam havin' people. Never thought about it that way at all. I guess it just seemed natural, him bein' alone like he is."

Buck knocked out his pipe and settled back in his chair. "He told me about himself once. Oh, more than once I guess; we've gotten around to it on nights when the trail was cold, and that's many a night around here. I just kind of pieced things together, little things he'd say now and then. From what I could gather, it seems he came out here from Tennessee; he'd tried all kinds of work back there, but he had what you might call an attachment to bankruptcy. He just couldn't stay away from it. Course it didn't cut into his fox hunting any; I know for a fact that he paid five hundred dollars for a hound one time that came into the station dead. In between hunts he got himself a family and—"

"Wait a minute," White Eagle said. "How come he couldn't get his five hundred back?"

"It was a prepaid deal," Buck said. "He wouldn't open the crate at the station because half the fox hunters in Tennessee were there, waiting to see what he had paid for. He wouldn't even admit the dog was dead until he got home by himself and then there wasn't any proof. Well, the family—it was all boys. One of them even got to college—married a woman from Boston and did well in the insurance business. I believe he killed himself although I'm not sure of that part of it. Anyway, it was his son that Samuel was talking about tonight. And when Sam's wife died—I imagine that she was one of those thin, silent, suffering kind—after she died, the boys apparently got together and decided that they ought to do something about the old man—give him another chance was the way they probably put it, although they should have known better by that time. One of them came out here and made all the arrangements and they set Sam up in the grocery business. You remember how it was then with the oil—a man had to go some not to make more than he could spend. Well, Sam went bankrupt three separate times and the boys gave up. This time he was spending all the money he could rake together on importing foxes—seems he couldn't find any foxes around here so he had to bring 'em in from Tennessee. So the boys did one last thing. They bought the farm, paid for it, and gave him the deed. They were through. That was when I still had the bank and they worked through me— that's the way I got most of the details."

"Yes," White Eagle said. "But the boy, the one that's coming out?"

Buck put his hands behind his head and leaned back. "I don't know," he said quietly. "I just don't know. It's been

20

a long time; maybe Sam doesn't realize how long. And people change. I hope he isn't counting on it too much."

It was full dark now, and in the pasture the fireflies were making the night glimmer. White Eagle straightened his hat on his head and got up. "I guess I better be gettin' back home," he said.

When they got to the gate he stopped and looked at Buck. "Listen, Little Owl. Is there somethin' in the wind for you?"

"No," Buck said, smiling and putting his hand on White Eagle's shoulder. "Nothing important."

White Eagle nodded and looked up at the sky. "I didn't know," he said. "You won't forget the dance."

Buck shook his head. "You let me know about it. I'll be there." He watched the red glow of the taillights disappear down the road, and then he went back to the house. As he undressed, the thunder rolled threateningly through the sky, and the sighing of the blackjacks seemed a whisper of despair.

CHAPTER II

☐ It was a hot afternoon in late September when Jeff Beecher drove into the main street of the little Oklahoma town. The tires of his car slicked wetly along the sodden asphalt and he blinked his eyes against the sun that pierced the windshield like a blade. His hands and legs were stiff from the long drive, his face felt coated and waxen, and as he eased back against the seat he rubbed his hand across his neck, thinking with pleasure of a bath and a change of clothes. And yet now that he was finally here he was aware of a faint reluctance, an anxiety uncomfortable as the sweat which worked its way down along his ribs.

The street he was following was arched by branching elms which stood motionless and gaunt, their leaves withered and curling around the edges, hanging like dead flags on a windless day. Behind the trees were rows of identical frame houses, stark and silent in the glare, houses whose people seemed to have fled before the sun, abandoning tricycles and cars and porch swings in their flight. Then the trees left off and he found himself in the business district which lay across the town like a centipede. A scattering of cars stood diagonally along the street on either side, and men with one foot pulled up behind them for support leaned against the buildings in rectangles of shade. Three small Negro boys walked slowly along the sidewalk, pulling behind them a faded red wagon in which a baby sat mouthing a popsicle. And

23

this was Grey Horse, prone and sleepy and still, with cars moving desultorily through the square around a tall and rather precarious brick building set like a flatiron in the center, and men sitting along the curb on the shady side of the triangle, whittling and chewing and talking among themselves. To Jeff the town seemed strangely silent, almost lifeless, as though it had been struck at the base of the skull by the sun.

Extending out over the far corner of the square was a peeling and bulbless electric sign reading *State Hotel*. Jeff turned into a parking place and when he switched off the ignition, he was aware even more of the silence which seemed somehow augmented by the raucous chatter of sparrows fluttering in the dust. After a moment he got out of the car and stretched. He wiped the sweat again from his face and crossed the street and went up the steps of the hotel. A little group of old men sat there talking in the shade and as he passed them they became silent, looking at him from under large-brimmed straw hats, their faces creased and leathery and suddenly bristling white where a swath of sun lay across a jaw. They all sat quiet and motionless save one, who leaned slowly forward toward the sidewalk and spat.

Beyond the screen doors it was dark and cool. When his eyes had become accustomed to the shadows, he saw that there were a few shabby chairs scattered around a large, bare lobby. On one side, two broken sofas flanked by spittoons faced each other before a window that looked into the street. And from the far end of the lobby he heard a high and mournful voice, whining a song that was neither love lament nor hymn but somehow compounded of both. Behind the voice and echoing it grotesquely was the metallic clangor of a steel guitar. He walked down to the desk, the voice loud in his ears and the guitar strumming harsh and thin in the shadows. Then suddenly the song ended and the voice was talking about hog mash. Jeff drummed his fingers on the top of the desk and coughed and finally said loudly, "Anyone

24

there?" raising his voice above the noise of the radio. There was the creak of someone rising from a chair and then a tall, grizzled old man was standing in the doorway behind the desk. Wide suspenders rode up over his bare and sloping shoulders and his skin was the pale yellow color of his undershirt. He held a pipe loosely in one hand and he regarded Jeff without much curiosity over a pair of small, steel-rimmed glasses that looked as though they had been fitted for him at Woolworth's.

"What can I do for you, mister?" he said.

"I'd like a little information," Jeff said.

"You bet."

"I'm looking for Samuel Beecher. Know where he lives?"

"Sam Beecher—fox hunter? Sure, I know him. Come to think of it, though, I'm not just for sure where he lives at." He rubbed his chin and thought a moment. "Did you see them people settin' out on the front steps when you come in? One of 'em will be able to tell you—you can always count on them birds. You ain't sellin' anything, are you, bub?"

"No," Jeff said, smiling. "Sorry to trouble you—I'll ask someone outside."

But when he got to the steps the men were still sitting in silence and he was hesitant about asking them. There was something about their quietness which made him feel that they were studying him, though none of them was looking at him directly. Then he saw a taxi parked at the curb.

"Samuel Beecher? Lemme see. He's the one that has that Higgins route, ain't he?" The driver was a small, narrow-eyed man with a pocked face and heavily oiled hair. He was working hard at his teeth with a toothpick. "Sure," he said. Leaning over to the opposite window he shouted toward the men on the steps. "Hey. One of you boys tell me where at Sam Beecher lives?"

The man nearest the cab got up and came over to the window. His lank body moved with slow and deliberate

25

dignity and when he got to the curb he stopped, not stepping off but merely leaning forward a little toward the outstretched face of the driver. "Who was it you was askin' about?" he said slowly.

The driver indicated Jeff with a movement of his head. "Fella here lookin' for Sam Beecher."

The man nodded. "Shorely." He stepped off the curb and looked over toward Jeff, blinking his eyes a little in the sun. "Afternoon," he said, touching the brim of his hat. Then he looked back at the driver. "Sam lives north about eight miles out on the Cherryvale road. House sets up on a little hill just 'fore you cut down toward the creek. I don't reckon you can miss it—them hounds will let you know when you're there, like as not. They's usually a pack of 'em layin' around the yard."

"I think I know where it's at now," the driver said. "Just before you come to that bridge on the Cherryvale road. Much obliged."

The man nodded and touched his hat again before he went back to the steps. As he turned, Jeff could see the tendons of his neck standing out prominent and hard beneath the sun-baked skin.

The driver explained how to get onto the Cherryvale road and Jeff thanked him and returned to his car. He drove quickly through a few blocks of white frame houses interspersed with occasional brick or stucco dwellings and was soon jolting along a dirt road that led away from town. The road was yellowish and ribbed with iron ruts that bounced the car from side to side, and behind him as he drove along rose twin funnels of dust, twisting furiously and then going limp, fanning out to powder the trees and grass beside the road. Jeff was relieved by the slight breeze which cooled the perspiration on his forehead and he looked with interest at this land which was so strange to him. For the most part it was open country with only occasional trees clumped together on the ridges where they formed thin, dark

26

islands in the vast sweeps of grass. It was grazing land and as the car went by, white-faced cattle lifted ponderous heads and stared. With their wide-set eyes and their steadily moving jaws, they seemed to fit perfectly into the landscape, at least in character, as though nothing more active or sensitive could survive the intensity of the heat and the emptiness. The land seemed to Jeff almost incredibly empty—just endless grass stretching to the horizon and the sky a merciless blue enclosure, bright and hard as steel. There seemed neither sound nor movement, for the wide circling of a hawk poised high above the prairie was less movement than merely emphasis of the deathly stillness of the earth. And the sun, close and fiery and hugely dominant, seemed to cut trees and fence posts and rocks away from the surrounding air and leave them harshly clear and isolate, outlined as though by acid.

Finally the land began to rise and Jeff could see a one-story frame farmhouse set back from the road at the top of the ridge. He drove up to the gate, bumped across a cattle guard, and stopped below the house. A screen door slammed in the stillness and as he squinted through the glare toward the shadows of a long porch he saw his grandfather standing there, looking down at him. The old man waved his hand in greeting as Jeff got out of the car.

When Jeff got closer to him he could see that Samuel had not changed much through the years. His face was dark red, sprinkled with a white stubble of beard, and his lower lip still stuck out a little as though he were looking for a handy place to spit. He no longer seemed as tall as he had when Jeff was a boy and he was thinner now, his Adam's apple jutting sharply from the cords of his throat. But he smiled in the same way and his eyes still had a lazy, humorous gleam which made him seem young in spite of the deep vertical wrinkles down his cheeks and the hard gray of his thin hair. He stood at the bottom of the steps to the porch, nodding a little and scratching his head and then Jeff, seeing what seemed like embarrassment in the old man's face, realized how long it had been.

"Hello, Pap," he said, setting his bags down.

"Hi, boy."

They shook hands, and as Jeff felt the strong old fingers gripping his own, he knew for a moment an inexpressible sense of pride and belonging as though in the very strength of that rough and bony hand there were feelings too deep ever to be voiced.

"Well, you finally got here, didn't you." His head was cocked to one side and his eyes roamed eagerly across Jeff's face.

"Did you think I wouldn't make it?"

"Aw, I don't know—it had just been so long." Then Samuel reached down for a suitcase. "Give me one of them bags and lets us git out of the sun."

They walked up through the bright heat into the shade and then Samuel held the screen door open.

"You can put your bags away if you want to," he said. "This bedroom right here'll be yours."

And when Jeff entered it, he was at once aware of a memory that was almost a tangible presence. It had something to do with the odor of the room, the faint old smells of cooking and of dust and of lumber and of a room that was not much used; but it was more the bare, clean simplicity—a thin white coverlet shaping the bed in the faint obscurity of shadow, a tall, perfectly spare dresser topped by a filmed mirror, and in a corner one thin-limbed, round-backed chair, focusing the room in its empty and somewhat solemn grace. There was one window that looked out toward the small valley below the house, and through it the light came dimly. Jeff set his bags down and then in the silence he could hear a faint droning. Following the sound, he saw high in the corner of the room a rounded daub of mud.

"Them's yellow jackets," Samuel said from the door. "Won't bother you none."

Jeff looked at him and smiled. "It reminds me of the place in Tennessee. This room's just about like the one I used to have on the farm, isn't it?"

"Do you still remember that old place back there, boy?" It seemed to Jeff he said it almost hopefully.

"Sure, I remember it." Then suddenly he felt uncomfortable; the room seemed close and he needed to get back out in the air. "I'd certainly like a drink if you have some water around."

"You bet. I got good water here, Jeff—that's one thing I can say for the place. Got good water and a good south breeze at night. Come on around to the back."

They went down the hall and out the kitchen door and then Samuel pulled up the bucket from the well and gave Jeff the dipper. It was rough against his tongue and the water was clear and tasted a little of rock. He felt better here in the open even though the sun burned on his face, and he looked around while Samuel drank. In back of the house was a large pen put together of chicken wire and crooked posts. It was filled with hounds, most of which lay stretched out in the dust in whatever shade they could find. They had long, narrow faces and ears that hung down like flaps; their sides moved quickly in and out in the heat. One of them got up and walked slowly to the fence and then stood there, his head lowered and his tongue out, looking at Samuel. At the side of the house was a barn which slumped rather than stood, its sides unpainted and weathered and the roof bent as though warped. Two horses were eating noisily in an enclosure which adjoined it, their bodies heavy and shining and their tails flicking back and forth across their flanks.

"I guess it ain't much of a place when you get right down and study it." Samuel was standing there, the dipper still held in his hand, looking out toward the barn. "Not much more'n a forty acres an' a mule an' sweat it out kind of a proposition."

Jeff looked at him, smiling. "I like it. Don't try and

29

talk it down now, because this is what I've been looking forward to for a long time. Plenty of room, quiet—it's just the way I wanted it."

"Yeah, they's plenty of room, I guess." Samuel hung up the dipper and lowered the bucket into the well. "I can't kick on that account." And now he looked over at Jeff, his eyes squinted a little as though in question. "But sometimes it just seems kinda poor-like. They's one helluva lot of sun, and the dust blows, and you can go a whole summer without water enough to wet your hair down with. I mean it ain't easy to get a livin' out o' the ground lessen it's oil you got or cattle."

"How'd you happen to leave Tennessee then, and come out here? That was a good place you had back there, as I remember it." Jeff reached for a cigarette and offered Samuel one, but the old man shook his head.

"Aw hell," he said smiling. "That was so long ago I've damn near forgot. Let's go on around to the porch where there's some shade."

From the porch they could look down on the road which angled sharply toward the creek and then disappeared in the trees, reappearing briefly on the hill that lay to the northeast before finally bending out of sight. It was a small road, its center packed hard with gravel and its edges soft and indeterminate in the yellow dust. It was like a bright and glistening snake winding down to the deep shadow of the creek bottom. Jeff was looking at it, frowning a little as he sat there in the cane-bottomed rocker. Like Samuel he was tall and rather loose-jointed. His arms and face were evenly tanned and his clipped hair was bleached yellow by the sun. There was the appearance of ease in the way that he rested his feet on the railing of the porch, trailing one arm down toward the floor, and about his body there was a hard, smooth cleanness like that of a stone washed by the sea. The skin was tight on his face, making more prominent his strong, slightly arched nose and the cheek bones that lay wide and flat beneath his eyes. The eyes themselves were gray with just a trace of blue as though the original color had faded from too long exposure in strong light. He wore a pair of limp khakis, a thin denim shirt with the sleeves rolled up high above the elbows, and sneakers stained the color of rust.

Samuel was sitting in the swing and its chains creaked rustily through the monotonous drone of the yellow jackets. "Well, it's been a long time, ain't it." He pulled a small sack of tobacco from his shirt pocket and began rolling a cigarette. "You was speakin' about that place in Tennessee. I was tryin' to think how many years it was since the last summer you spent down there."

"Wasn't that the summer I caught that big gar and got mad when you wouldn't cook it for me?"

Samuel was silent for a moment. Then he grinned and scratched a match across his pants leg and lit his cigarette. "Naw, that wasn't the time. That was before. I believe the last summer was when your daddy bought you that little ole spotted pony. Remember? You was always runnin' him up an' down the road in front of the house."

"That's right," Jeff laughed. "I thought a lot of that pony—wanted to take him home with me in the fall. What did you ever do with him after I left?"

"I don't rightly recall," Samuel said. "I guess I probably sold him. But that must have been fifteen years ago or better, wasn't it?"

"It must have been. I think I was about eight that summer—nine maybe."

"Long time." Samuel reached down and loosened his shoes and when he had pulled them off, he held his feet out in front of him and slowly moved his toes. "Tell me about what you've been doin'. I never get any news 'less somethin' legal's connected with it. Wasn't you across in the army? Seems like somebody told me somethin' like that."

"Yes," Jeff said. "I was overseas for awhile, in the Pacific." He removed his feet carefully from the railing and leaned forward in the rocker as though he were watching something down on the road. The lines around his eyes converged in concentration; he began once to speak and then stopped as though he had lost the thought. Finally he put his cigarette to his lips and tossed it abruptly into the yard. "I guess the main thing to tell you is that Mom died two weeks ago." His voice had gone suddenly quiet and his face was without expression.

The old man turned and stared at him for a moment and then looked back out toward the sunlight. "I'm mighty sorry to hear that, son. What was the trouble?"

"Doctor said it was cancer."

"Yeah?"

"It was good in a way, I guess. Her health had been poor for a long time. She drank some, you know." He looked fixedly at the road and his hands tapped lightly against the sides of the chair.

"It's been a good many years since I last seen her," Samuel muttered.

"I'm not sure you would have known her," Jeff said, his words strangely cold and deliberate. "She changed a lot toward the end."

Samuel turned and looked at him again. Neither of them spoke for a while. Then Jeff sat up and reached in his pocket for a match.

"What about you?" he asked when he had lit the cigarette. He was smiling again as though he had forgotten the words he had just spoken.

"There ain't nothin' much to tell," Samuel said. "I come out here pretty quick after your grandmother passed on. Had me a grocery for awhile but it just looked like me and that store wasn't an even match—least I wasn't much of a match for it. Man needs to be there ever' day to do any good and I had other things on my mind." He rubbed his jaw and looked over at Jeff and smiled. "So I fixed it up so's I could do things the way I wanted—I just kinda transferred that grocery to the back end of my car, you might say. I got me a Higgins route

32

—you can go with me tomorrow if you want. Then the boys got me this farm and I've just more or less been here ever since."

"I'd like very much to come," Jeff said. "I've never seen this part of the country before."

"Well, they ain't a whole lot more to see than what you can see from right here," Samuel said, gesturing toward the fields and low hills that lay beyond the road. "And things is kinda burnt out now—you picked yourself one helluva hot summer. But you ain't told me how you happened to decide to come out." He seemed almost insistent, as though he were suspicious of what Jeff had come for.

Jeff frowned and ran his fingers stiffly through his hair. "I don't know—you might almost call it homesickness. When Mom died, you were the only one left outside of my uncles and I've never been around them much. And then I've been looking after her, too, for a long time." He looked over at Samuel questioningly and then he turned away and went on, his voice low and troubled as though he were ashamed of what he was saying. "I felt like somebody had to be there, and there wasn't anybody else to do it. It got to where she was coming down stairs every night about eight, all dressed up and talking about who was coming to dinner that night and raising hell because there didn't seem to be any servants around. Then she'd brighten up when I mixed her a drink and we'd sit there in front of the fireplace in that big empty house. When she died—well, I just wanted to get away from the place for awhile." He stopped again because he did not know how to say just what he had come here for, at least not now in the full silence and glitter of the sun.

But Samuel had apparently noticed nothing unusual. "Sure," he said. "I was mighty pleased to get your letter. But you know somethin', I was wrong a minute ago. I'll tell you when that last summer was—it was the summer your folks sent you that BB gun."

"You mean the gun I lost off the back of the wagon," Jeff said.

"Yeah. We went in to get it on a Saturday mornin', remember? We musta been gittin' groceries because it was late afternoon when we started home. You was settin' back in the bed, holdin' the box in your hand—hadn't even opened it yet. You musta got up in the seat with me, or maybe you went to sleep. Anyway, when we got home, the gun was gone. Couldn't find it no place. I remember you never said a thing, just went in on the daybed and laid down and wouldn't touch a bite to eat—just laid there real quiet. I went out after supper and I'll bet I covered ever' inch of that road, and there just wasn't no gun. And then when I got back to the barn about sundown, I could see that old Indian riding up to the house on that little brown mare of his. Funny how I can remember that horse and I can't think of that Indian's name at all. But he had the gun, right across the saddle in front of him. I called you out of the house and he gave it to you—said he found it lyin' in the road."

"I had forgotten about that. He was the one I used to watch spearing fish down at the creek."

"That's right."

"Sure, I remember it now. We got those targets and tacked them up to one of the columns on the porch, and every evening we'd have a shooting contest. I used to practice up on the hogs."

"That was the time," Samuel laughed.

The shadow of the house lay long and pointed and thin now across the road. The hilltops were still bright, but the light was fading from the rest of the land.

Finally Samuel pulled on his shoes and got up from the swing. "Gittin' about supper time, I reckon. You say here in the cool while I go down to the field and pull some corn. It growed purty well this summer, rain or no rain. Weather was dry even for here, but then this has been quite a summer in more ways than one."

Jeff watched him cross the road and crawl through the

fence into the cornfield. Then he could see the stalks shaking as Samuel worked down the rows, pulling the corn, and suddenly the remembered familiarity of it all made his throat ache. It had been so many years, and now he was with Samuel again and there were questions that he must ask him, ghosts that he must bring back to life. He was thinking of how he had sat with his mother that long, silent Sunday afternoon before she died. It had been almost as though the intensity of the pain had cleared her mind a little, and he recalled how she had looked with her teeth pressed against her lips, her hands opening and closing before her on the coverlet, how she had talked so slowly that he could not believe that she would ever finish telling it. The cry of locusts had made the afternoon seem hotter than it was and her fingers, scraping against the sheet, had been pale almost to blue. "You see, my dear, he made me promise. That was like him. I mean to talk about it ahead of time like that. The promise was because he was crazy over you. Whenever he was going to do something that would hurt me in some way, he would always tell me about it first. Tell me and then just stand there, watching my face." Her voice was low and hoarse and he had strained forward in his chair to hear her. "He seemed to get a funny kind of pleasure from it. Sometimes he would do whatever it was, sometimes he wouldn't. But he had a cruel streak, your father did. He liked to upset me just to see how I'd act. Not exactly threaten—I wouldn't call it that; he played, a cat-and-mouse sort of thing. I suppose it was exciting in a way when I first knew him. He never was sweet like other boys. No, he was mean. He slapped me more than once. You might as well know it because you're like him in lots of ways and I suppose this is the time when a person ought to be telling the truth. He'd get so jealous—at parties and dances. I always told him he took things too seriously and he never liked that, I can tell you." She laughed a little and then coughed, holding her hand against her throat. The eyes that shone in her white face were bright as ice. "But he made me promise not to tell you. He would talk about it until I would think I just couldn't stand it another minute and then he would take me here by the shoulders and he would shake me until I'd say yes. I suppose I thought it was just another way he'd found to hurt me. He talked about it so much that finally I didn't even get scared anymore." She paused for a moment and raised her eyebrows, almost as though she were inwardly amused. "Then one afternoon —you were ten that summer and he had sent you down to the farm—he said he was going to clean his gun. He went out to the garage and I heard the noise—like an explosion way off somewhere—and when I got there it was too late. Why did he do it, you say?" She straightened the covers carefully and smiled a little. "If I had to answer it I suppose I would say spite, but then that would never satisfy you. I don't guess anyone could satisfy you, really, unless it would be your grandfather. The old man never would talk much with me, but he'd be the only one who might know. I promised I'd never tell you; I don't suppose it matters much now."

"You better be hungry," Samuel was calling as he came up from the road, his arms filled with corn. "I got enough here to feed an army."

"Has there ever been a year when you didn't have a field of corn planted?" Jeff said as he got up to open the door for him.

"Man, you can boil it, roast it, bake it, fry it, drink it, and feed it to stock. When the good Lord made him a world and wanted to put somethin' in it to eat, he put corn. Come on inside and we'll shuck it and trim us off a few slices o' ham. This is hog heaven for a beans-and-fatback man like me."

After supper, Jeff returned to his chair on the porch and when the old man came around the side of the house, he had one of his hounds with him. "He's too old to do much huntin' anymore," he sighed as he settled into the swing. "But he was a goer and a stayer in his day."

It was dark now and the road was a faint trace of shadow through the night. The hills were black and shapeless beneath the stars, and from the creek bottoms came the poignant, rhythmic cry of a whippoorwill. The fields beyond the road flickered with lightning bugs and in the trees the cicadas made the air ring with their heavy, pulsing chant. One of the horses snorted and the sound was abrupt and loud above the steady music of the night. Occasionally the hound thumped its tail against the porch and Jeff could hear its light and steady panting, and looking over toward the swing he could see the gleam of Samuel's knife as it went back and forth along a piece of board. He looked over toward him for a long time in the darkness, and Samuel's voice seemed sweet and distant as though it were echoing forth from a dim but cherished past.

CHAPTER III

☐ The sun was slanting sharply through the bedroom window when Jeff awoke the next morning. In the long shaft of light he could see the dust motes spinning slowly upward, while out beyond the window were the hills, humped darkly thin and clear against the bright blue air. It took him a moment to remember where he was, and then when it came to him he relaxed against the bed, looking out toward the unblemished sky and letting memory move slow and fragrant across his mind.

It was not long before he heard the sound of a skillet on the stove. He got up quickly and walked back to the kitchen through the shadowed coolness of the hall. Samuel was standing before the range, barefoot, wearing faded overalls that had the look about them of rubbed-down wood. His shirt was fresh and white and the sleeves were rolled midway up his forearms. He was cutting slices from a large side of bacon and putting them in the skillet.

"Mornin'," he said, looking up at Jeff. "Sleep good?"

"Fine," Jeff said. He yawned and rubbed his fingers through his yellow hair. "Just fine. I hope it's that cool every night."

"Oh, the nights are cool enough. Breeze comes pretty steady, cain't complain about that. I put a basin and a towel out back for you to wash up with."

"Good," Jeff said. "I'll be through in a minute."

He stepped gingerly out of the back door onto the

large, mossy stone that served as a step and walked on across the hard ground to the well. The dust was faintly grainy beneath the soles of his bare feet, and he could feet it settling dry and powdery across his toes. The morning air still had a faint edge of coolness, but almost immediately perspiration began to form across his fore-head and along his legs. He raised the bucket from the well and brushed his teeth and washed his face in the cold, clear water, noticing again the taste that seemed to make itself felt along the edges of his teeth. Around him the farm was hushed in the stillness of early morning. The hounds lay watching him from the shadowed pen and in the lot adjoining the barn the horses stood motion-less save for the switching of their tails, their long, gleaming necks curving down to the still wet grass. The barn itself, weathered and almost fragile in its lines, had a silvery cast about it, a kind of dew-gleam glistening in the delicate, early light. He dumped the wash pan, nar-rowing his eyes a little against the sun, and then before he entered the kitchen, he paused on the stone by the door and brushed the dust from his feet. Inside, the house was warm with the odor of frying bacon. He went back to his room and slipped into a shirt and a pair of khaki pants and when he returned, the eggs and bacon were on the table.

"How about some coffee?" Samuel said, taking up a small black pot from the stove.

"Fine." Jeff sat down and rubbed his hands in anticipa-tion. "It sure smells good."

Samuel filled the cups and put the pot back on the stove and then drew a chair up to the table. "I was thinkin' we might drive over to Four Corners this morn-ing and check on some of my customers," he said, when they had eaten. "I got to sell somethin' ever' now and then just to keep in tobacco and to get some bones for them worthless hounds out yonder. Like to come along?"

"Anything you say," Jeff answered, finishing his coffee.

"Then let's wash the dishes and git goin'."

When they had cleaned up the kitchen, Samuel moved his car around to the back door. The rear seat was missing and the back portion of the car had been turned into a bed for hauling. Into this empty space now they loaded tea, pencils, chewing gum, corn plasters, boxes of spices, shoelaces and many other things which Jeff had no chance to examine because Samuel was pitching the boxes to him one after another from the kitchen door.

"They've all got the same name," Jeff said, leaning against the door when Samuel disappeared for a moment. "You mean to tell me one company puts out all this stuff? What kind of an outfit is it?"

"Crazy if you ask me," Samuel answered, reappearing in the doorway with boxes of combs in each hand. "They don't make nothin' any good, but they make a lot of stuff cheap. That's where the money is, it looks like. Don't make no difference how no-count it is, long as you make plenty of it and cheap. Somebody'll buy it. Why I wouldn't walk across the road to get anything that Higgins made if they was givin' it away."

"Why do you sell it, then?" Jeff asked, looking at the old man with a wry smile.

"It gives me a chance to get out and see people once ever' so often," he said, handing Jeff a box of kitchen brushes. "Christamighty, a man cain't set on his front porch all day long ever' day. Gets tiresome. And then it keeps me in scratch, too."

He came down from the kitchen door and stuck his head into the back seat and looked around. "Looks all right," he said after a moment. "Just one more box of jawbreakers and then we'll take off."

It was eight thirty when they drove across the cattle guard and out onto the county road. From the pocket in the front of his overalls, Samuel extracted a large gold watch that was hung from a piece of twine. He looked at it and announced the time somewhat triumphantly. "Not bad," he said. "Not bad. I'd probably own that damned

41

Higgins outfit one of these days if I had you with me all the time."

Jeff watched the road for a while, and when they were beyond the bridge and beginning to climb the hill on the far side, he looked over at Samuel. "Those dogs ride all right back there, do they?" He was referring to the two hounds that Samuel had put into the car just before they left. "Looks like they'd be awful hot—can they get enough air?" He was curious as to why Samuel had brought them along, for the old man without a word of explanation had simply kicked them up into the trunk. "Yeah, they'll be all right. I got air holes punched through on this side and then that turtle back don't go all the way down. We'll get 'em some water when we get to Four Corners." He reached into his pocket and pulled out a thin rectangular plug of tobacco that had the color and the texture of a composition sole. Gripping it in the hand that held the wheel, he reached into his pocket again and this time brought out a tiny, mother-of-pearl knife. When he opened the blade, it was about half as long as his little finger. Then he very slowly and methodically carved out a square section of the plug and put it in his mouth, moving it carefully around in his jaw until it was settled.

They were well out of the creek bottom now and riding along on level land on the far side. There were few trees here, for it was mainly open prairie stretching flat and distant to a far-off horizon. The grass grew thick and high and was slightly bent from the wind. Taut barbed-wire fences lined the road on either side and the road itself was heavily rutted and covered with a layer of crushed rock that had worn thin in the center of the road and lay white and loose on the edges.

"This is really what you might call the back way to where we're goin'," Samuel said. "We could have gone through town and picked up the highway, but I thought you might like the chance to see some of the country.

This is all the Simpson ranch along here. Pretty good size, too."

"How big is it?"

"Oh, I guess around fifty thousand acres."

"That's a lot of land," Jeff said.

"A helluva lot too much for any one man," Samuel said. "But then I guess they ain't in it for the land."

Jeff lit a cigarette and looked out at the dusty grass on the side of the road. "Didn't you ever think of something like that—ranching, I mean? You were still young enough when you came out here."

Samuel frowned a little and moved the tobacco in his mouth. "I guess maybe I thought about it some, but it takes an awful lot more than just thinkin' about it." He looked over at Jeff and then looked back at the road as though he were puzzled about something. "It's a man-sized business and them boys play for keeps. Closest I ever got to a steer was with a knife and fork."

"Yeah," Jeff said quietly, and there was just a trace of dryness in the way he smiled. He was remembering the things they had always said, his mother and others of the family, whenever they got together and talked about his grandfather. His mother had been contemptuous of the old man, and his father had never seemed to want to talk about him at all. Samuel was not the kind of family disgrace that people could get angry about or declaim against; he seemed rather to provoke only a sarcastic tightening of the lips and a short shake of the head. But Jeff could remember being confused as a boy when his father or uncles would dismiss his questions about Samuel by saying that he was crazy on dogs like other men were crazy on whiskey, that he was selfish and thoughtless and no good, and then before long they would be laughing and telling stories about the old man that seemed to go on without end.

"It was just that I was a little surprised to think of your running a store when there must have been so much going on here, when things were as wide open as I imagine they were. But I guess you were doing what you wanted to." He flipped his cigarette out of the window and held out his hand to catch the breeze. "It's funny the difference between you and Dad; he would have had his hands on a ranch first thing."

"I reckon he would've at that," Samuel said. He did not look at Jeff now, but continued to look down the shining strip of road that stretched before them, his face long, without emotion, quiet save for the occasional movement of the jaws and the slightest lift of the eyebrows. "But then we always did do things different, me and your daddy. There's Four Corners up ahead."

The land had been rising imperceptibly, and the road had followed the rise until now just at the edge of some tight-clustered blackjacks it slanted down across the sloping flank and into a trough of land which lay between the ridges. The dirt road became blacktop and they passed several small frame houses which sat back from the road behind what was less lawn than merely cut-down weeds, straggling and burned out and yellow like the houses. In one or two of the yards there had been an attempt at flowers; dust-colored zinnias drooped away from the sun, isolated in their beds that were protected by jagged fragments of rock or cast-off tires. Women sat in some of the doorways, fanning themselves, looking out at the road with no apparent interest or curiosity.

Downtown, which was a block of frame and sandstone buildings lining the street on either side, the middle of the road was filled with cars parked diagonally beside each other. The newer cars seemed too big for the street and looked out of place, their chrome and metal dazzling in the town's dull decay. Samuel turned in and parked at the end of the row in front of one of the frame stores. In fading letters across the top of the building, just above a down-slanting wooden roof that extended out over the sidewalk, Jeff could read the words *Sands Groc.* Three men sat in the shade on a bench that stood to one side of the double swinging screen doors. They were dressed in what Jeff now took to be the conventional clothing of town loafers—overalls, straw hats, and faded blue shirts. One of the men wore a pair of brown slippers in place of the usual high-topped work shoe. The sidewalk rose a good two feet above the road and on the edge of it sat a fourth man, peeling shavings into a pile at his feet.

"Hyere comes the store," he announced to no one in particular, as Jeff and Samuel got out of the car.

Jeff, looking at the man who had spoken, saw a face that seemed quite without humor, gaunt and saturnine and covered with a black stubble of beard. The bones were prominent and appeared to drive in toward the nose like a wedge, and the skin, more like hide than skin, was stretched tight and dry in a way that made it seem that such a face could never perspire, as though it had been cauterized in the steady and unwavering flame of the sun. It was a face that struck Jeff as singularly bleak, and this, coupled with the man's remark, annoyed him.

"Anything you want to bring in?" he asked, looking over at Samuel.

But Samuel was already getting out of the car, shouting through the window as he opened the door. "And it's a goddamned good thing it rolls, too—else I'd have to fix up some benches and shade for you birds, and git me a stove in the middle of it so's you wouldn't git cold in the winter. I never have been able to figger out who owns this place—looks to me like Virgil just works it so's you'll have someplace to set."

"Got to listen to Sam when it comes to groceries," one of the men on the bench drawled. "He's done run through more stores than most o' the folks 'round here's been in. Ain't that right, Sam."

"I've probably quit more stores than you've seen," Samuel answered, "and by God, I'll take one with wheels. Come on, Jeff—let's git inside 'fore they talk us out o' somethin'."

Jeff left the car and followed Samuel up to the store.

45

The men nodded as he passed; one, the man sitting on the curb, said "Howdy"; but none of them looked at him. At least Jeff did not see them looking at him; yet he felt it, their cold, clear eyes looking at shoes which would be Sunday shoes to them and at khaki pants which they would also wear on Sundays except that they would probably not wear them at all; they would wear pants of heavy cloth, coarse to the skin, and black (they would not even have khakis because they were inbetween pants, and for these men there was nothing between work or shade-sitting and Sunday); and at the shirt, too, white oxford cloth with buttons on the tips of the collar, and at his face which he suddenly realized now, as though he had looked into a mirror, was neither lined nor familiar.

The shadowed store was fragrant with hay and its darkness seemed contained in the very floor and walls, leaving them with the appearance of having been freshly oiled. It was a darkness which lent a kind of dignity to the stacked rows of cans, even to the celluloid case on the counter which held snuff and cigarette papers and which was decorated with the symbol of a bull rampant and an inscription which read *Bull Durham*; it imparted solemnity to the stolid, bellied stove in the center of the floor and to the long, belt-high counter which ran almost the length of the store. It was a darkness which was rich and warm, softly agleam with the glint of metal, a darkness resonant with the small, immemorial sounds of human transactions. The very atmosphere seemed worn smooth by long handling.

"Howdy, Mr. Beecher."

Jeff saw him then, a large slope-shouldered man seated on a barrel in back of the counter. His face was pale and strangely lopsided, as though the tobacco he was chewing had pulled his jaw permanently out of place.

"Howdy, Chester. Virge in?" Samuel lifted the top from a jar of penny candy and took several pieces, motioning for Jeff to help himself.

"Mr. Sands is at his desk, prob'ly," Chester said. "I

46

wouldn't rightly know. He don't come in this part of the store much, jest bellers like a stuck hog. Sometimes he don't even want nothin'—jest takes a notion to beller, I reckon."

"Well, I 'spect we can find him. Thisyere's my grandson, Chester. Jeff Beecher. Name's same as mine. Comes from the East."

Chester muttered something inaudible and then stretched a large white hand across the counter. He looked at Jeff for a moment, squinting, and then he turned back to Samuel. "He came a helluva piece just to see Virgil."

"Oh for Chrissakes, Chester. He didn't come out here to see Virgil. Where's your head at, boy?" Then Samuel leaned across the counter and spoke quietly, almost confidentially. "Tell me somethin'. You been here awhile now —how do you like keepin' store?"

Chester ran his hand across his mouth and slowly shook his head, moving it heavily from side to side so that he looked for a moment like a confused white-faced steer. Then he looked up at Samuel, his eyes small and bewildered. "You know what it's come to, Mr. Beecher? He's got to the point now where he even makes me pay for my pop. Yessir! Cain't even drink a goddam bottle of sody but what I got to mark it up. He give me the paper himself, with a place for me to mark on it ever' time I have a bottle. A goddam little old bottle o' pop. But by God, 'fore I married her I could come in here of an afternoon and drink me a case and he wouldn't open his mouth."

"Chester," Samuel said, "I always said that pop would get you in trouble. You shoulda stuck to beer—he couldn't have waited you out at two bits a bottle."

Jeff was standing a little behind them, waiting. He fumbled in his shirt pocket for a cigarette and when he had lit it he leaned against the counter, feeling somewhat useless and conspicuous. The conversation embarrassed him a little; he felt that he was expected to take part, at

47

least to nod at the proper times. And yet there was nothing for him to say even though he felt that Samuel was doing this for his benefit, almost prompting Chester to talk as one would prompt a child. And then as he leaned there, blinking a little against the smoke that curled up into his face, he heard the voice coming suddenly from the back of the store, a sound flat and straight and sudden and without variation, felt rather than heard like the slamming of a door.

"Chester!"

Chester did not move save to nod his head in the direction of the sound. "See what I'm talkin' about?" he said with weary vindication.

"You got those loafer pals of yours in here again?" The voice was more accusation than question.

"Goddamn it, I'm a-talkin' to Mr. Beecher," Chester shouted, swinging around on the barrel and glaring toward the back of the store. "And one of his kin. Mr. Beecher took some of that there penny candy—you want I should mark it—?"

"Quit that runnin' off at the mouth and tell him to come on back here."

But Samuel had already started, walking slowly until Jeff could catch up with him and then, as they got to the back of the store, leaning back and saying, "Chester just married Virge's daughter and now Virge has got him a handy man that cain't quit on him. He never could keep anybody much over a month before."

They went through a door into the back of the store and found Virgil sitting before a large and cluttered roll-top desk. His appearance was a surprise to Jeff; he had expected someone big-shouldered and burly to go with the voice. But the person he now saw sitting at the desk might conceivably have been taken for a dwarf except that there was nothing particularly misshapen or grotesque about him. When he got up, Jeff saw that he resembled nothing so much as a keg mounted on two stubby legs, his belly being such that his belt formed a kind of inclined ellipse, disappearing somewhere between the tight, rounded shirt front and the legs that seemed to end at the knee. His smooth, bald head glistened even in the half light, and his mouth widened around a cigar that was too big for his face. The rimless glasses that he wore were pushed up tight against his eyes, and as the eyes blinked quickly at him, Jeff was aware that Samuel was making the introduction.

"Glad to know you, Mr. Sands," Jeff said, taking his hand.

"My pleasure, son, my pleasure." Virgil shook hands briskly and then turned to Samuel. "What did you want to stand out there and talk to that damn fool for; you know as well as I do he ain't got a lick o' sense. Sometimes I think he's plumb foolish, like maybe there was screws loose or somethin'." He shook his head sadly, looking up at Samuel. "You know how long I've worked to get this store like it is. Why I'd almost rather burn the sonofabitch than leave it in his hands." Then he turned back to Jeff. "You'll have to excuse me, son, for talkin' this way, but the boy just seems to kinda work on me sometimes and I cain't help myself. Well, that's enough of that. Sit down, take the sacks off one o' them boxes. I got some cheese here if you're hungry."

"Well, it has been awhile since we had breakfast," Samuel said, winking at Jeff.

On the desk, amid a jumble of papers and cigar ashes and a half dozen shotgun shells, Jeff could see a quarter of a head of cheese and a box of crackers that appeared to have been freshly opened. He took a sack of strong-smelling feed from a box and sat down on it, pulling his legs back to make room for Virgil, who was going to the door. And when Virgil shouted, his whole body seemed to recoil with the motion of a battery of guns.

"Chester! Go out to Mr. Beecher's car and get whatever we need. When you come back, bring us in a couple cans of them dime sardines." Then he returned to his swivel chair before the desk, excusing himself as he

49

passed again before Jeff, and began to carve small, neat slices of cheese for the crackers. "Haven't seen you for awhile, Sam. Where you been keepin' yourself?"

Samuel was seated on a barrel with his feet resting on a sack of feed. He had taken the tobacco from his pocket and was now rolling a cigarette with quick, sure motions of his rough fingers. "Had me a little trouble with my dogs, Virge. Couple of 'em got sick."

Jeff saw Virgil's hand stop in the act of cutting a slice of cheese, and then he saw his eyebrows raise just a little above the tight-fitting glasses.

"Sick, huh?" Virgil said. "Well, that's a shame." He finished slicing the cheese and slowly and carefully put it on a cracker. "Now which ones would that be?"

"Don't even think you know 'em," Samuel said. "Couple of pups I ain't had very long."

"Oh," Virgil said, nodding slowly.

It seemed to Jeff from the way he said it that he was relieved about something.

"Rest o' the dogs all right, I suppose." Chester had brought the sardines in and Virgil seemed intent on opening the cans.

"I guess," Samuel said carelessly. "Course you cain't never tell about a hound. You probably heard about the time that Sim Henry came close to sellin' me one that was deaf."

"That surprised me, Sam. I woulda thought you knew more about hounds than that."

"Knew enough about hounds, all right," Samuel said, reaching over to the desk for a cracker. "But I might'n near didn't know enough about Sim. Hardin Buck put me straight just in time."

"Yeah," Virgil said quickly. "Man's got to get up mighty early to catch Buck asleep on anything like that." Then he leaned back in his chair, nibbling nervously at a cracker, and looked over at Jeff. "Well, young man, how do you like this part of the country?"

50

"I only got here yesterday," Jeff said. "Haven't had much chance to look around."

"Well, you stick with your grandaddy for awhile and I reckon you'll see 'bout all there is to see around here. Where're you from?"

"Connecticut." And from the way that Virgil was looking at him, his eyes blinking quickly and shifting a little from side to side, Jeff had the feeling that he was merely making conversation and that something more important was on his mind.

"Come out for a visit," Samuel said.

"Well, that's fine." Virgil nodded. He looked quickly out of the corner of his eye at Samuel and nodded again to Jeff. "Yessir. That's all right. Like to see a man keepin' in touch with his family. Sam here woulda had to learn to bark if somebody hadn't come to see him pretty soon."

Jeff smiled and said nothing. He was wondering at Samuel's silence. The old man seemed to be forcing Virgil to talk by just sitting there, occasionally reaching over for a cracker or paring his nails with the little knife that he carried. Virgil appeared to be nervous, tapping his cigar with his thumb and shifting around in the swivel chair. In the silence Jeff could smell the dead cigar in Virgil's hand and the heavy, sweetish odor of the feed.

"Well, Sam," Virgil said after a while, "I don't suppose you brought any dogs with you."

"Lemme just have one more o' them sardines, will you, Virgil. Much obliged." He put the cracker carefully into his mouth and wiped his hands on his pants legs. "Yeah, I brought a couple along. Man cain't never tell when he's liable to run into a swap. Course these dogs is different— couldn't no swap do for them—I just more or less keep 'em with me for company."

Virgil was leaning back in his chair with his hands held out before him, his fingers just touching. The hands moved back and forth ever so little. It seemed to Jeff that there was something anxious in his face, and yet something resigned, too. "One o' them dogs wouldn't be Ben Patches, would it, Sam?"

"It surely would."

"And Fireball Two?"

"And Fireball Two."

Virgil looked sadly at Jeff, nodding as though faced with some whim of fate that was too outrageous in its coincidence to be believed. "Let's go out and see 'em," he said in a low voice.

Samuel started to protest, but Virgil was on his feet, moving out into the store with a slow and somewhat determined tread as though his legs were being worked by wires. Jeff followed the two of them to the door through the dark, oiled silence of shelves and barrels and harness and worn wood, and just as Virgil reached for the screen, Chester, who had watched them filing past, spoke in a tone of voice which he had doubtlessly heard on the radio or in a picture show and which to him probably signified the ultimate in sarcasm. "Be gone fur long, Mr. Sands? I mean if there's any real important messages shall I tell 'em you're shootin' a great big game of snooker with Mr. Beecher and—?"

Virgil did not speak. He simply stopped at the door and turned and looked at Chester, not even raising his hand. Then he went on through the door and across the porch and stepped off the high curbing into the full light of the road.

The men in front of the store had not moved. They looked up now and one pushed his hat back a little on his head. "Whatcha aimin' to do, Sam?" he said. "Buy him out?"

"Might," Samuel said, jumping down from the curb and following Virgil out to the car.

The man on the curb carefully closed his knife blade and got up and stretched a little. "I always claimed Sam wouldn't be right lessen he was runnin' a grocery into the ground somewheres." Then he walked slowly and somewhat stiffly out to the car, followed by the three men who had been sitting on the bench.

Virgil looked even shorter in the bright glare of the sun. And he still had that helpless air about him, as though he were being moved by some force beyond his control. Jeff stood a little to one side, wondering what it was all about. The whole thing seemed a bit ridiculous, all of these men standing there watching Samuel as he raised the door to the trunk. He looked around him, half expecting to see people congregate from the stores and buildings up and down the street. But there was no movement; the street was empty save for him and the five men and the gleaming row of cars and the huge and heavy presence of the sun. He wiped the back of his hand across his forehead, and then he saw the man who had been sitting on the curb spit and say "Yeah," in a silent and final kind of way. The turtleback was raised, revealing the two hounds, which lay regarding the men without particular interest, their tongues hanging long and thin and their sides moving in and out with an easy, rhythmic quickness.

Virgil was rocking a little on his heels, his hands shoved deep into his pockets. "Well," he said. Then he said "Well," again. He bent over and peered at the dogs, but he did not move forward; it was almost as though he were afraid of getting too close to them. He straightened up and looked at Samuel and then back at the dogs and finally down to the ground.

"Figurin' on swappin' the store fur them there hounds, Virgil?" one of the men asked.

"Ha!" Virgil said, but it was merely sound, not laughter. He looked at Samuel again, almost angrily. "All right, goddam it. What's wrong with 'em?"

"Why Virgil, I'm surprised at you," Samuel said gently.

"Let's don't talk nothin' but figures," Virgil said. "What'll you take for the two?"

Samuel looked around at the other men and moved his hands in a helpless gesture of surprise.

Then Virgil pulled one of his hands from his pocket and held a check out toward Samuel. He was staring at the dogs; he did not look at the check, and the hand that held it was trembling. "Take it," he said. "Take it, by God, and then let the damned dogs drop dead in the road as soon as you're out o' sight. But get the hell on out o' here so's I won't have to look at that face o' yours when they do."

Samuel bent over and studied the check and finally he shook his head, slowly and sadly. "I'd rather give 'em to you, Virgil," he said, "than take a beating like that. They might call me crazy, but leastways they couldn't laugh."

Then Virgil was carefully tearing the check into pieces. And still he had not taken his eyes from the dogs, which lay silently looking away from him down the road. "Sam," he said in a high voice, and then he was silent for a moment. "Sam, go on and move that junk out of here. It's bad for business." Then he moved jerkily across the road and up onto the sidewalk and into the store. They heard him yell "Chester!" just as he hit the door.

"Hit looks plumb like Virge wants him a coupla dogs," drawled the man who had been sitting on the curb. "Or maybe he's aimin' to make a trail hound outa Chester."

Jeff watched Samuel lower the back of the trunk and pull the sack of tobacco from his pocket. The old man took his time pouring the tobacco and wetting the paper and when he had the cigarette rolled and lit, he drew the large round watch from his overalls and looked at it. "Maybe Virge's figurin' on doin' a little trailin' hisself," he said, putting the watch back into his pocket. "He's shore as hell workin' up the voice for it." Then he looked over at Jeff, his face long and lined and somewhat melancholy, his eyes pale blue in the sunlight. "I reckon we better git goin', boy. I got another call to make before noon."

The men were still standing there in the road as they drove off. Samuel waved and one of the men waved back, and Jeff watched them start moving slowly back toward the store. Then almost before he was aware of its passing, they had left Four Corners behind them. Its one street flowed evenly from prairie into prairie, and the town, like a single tree on the horizon, served mainly to make one suddenly and acutely aware of the boundlessness of the grasslands.

"I'm beginnin' to think that maybe Virge really does want them dogs," Samuel said. He drove with both hands gripping the wheel and with his arms held out almost to full length, his head erect and thrown back a little as though he were enjoying to the fullest his mastery over the machine. Occasionally he leaned to the window to spit, but even that motion was accomplished with a kind of carefree dignity. "Didn't you think so, from the way he acted?"

Jeff smiled. "There's no doubt about his wanting the dogs. Wasn't his offer high enough?"

"Oh, it ain't so much the money," Samuel said. "I'd just like to make him pay enough so's he wouldn't turn right around and sell 'em to somebody."

"What difference would it make?" Jeff shrugged. "So long as he gives you what you think they're worth."

"I don't rightly know what they are worth, Jeff boy," Samuel said. "But I'd like to make him think that he knows what they're worth, and I'd like to make it high, when I can judge what high is for him. Then maybe he'd hang onto 'em, on account of the investment if for no better reason. Groceries is one thing, but hounds is another; bein' in business like he is, Virge has kinda got the grocery habit."

Jeff nodded, but he was no longer really listening. Rather he was thinking of how Samuel had been here all these years, fooling with his hounds and peddling a cheap line of merchandise while other men, hard and determined, had taken the land and had built the fences, men who would leave behind them their names and their children and the stories of what they had done. And this was denied to Samuel, for he had drifted along between the fences like a tumbleweed, rootless, without possessions, without the rightful belongings of age. The realization of it made Jeff suddenly wonder if he had done the wrong thing in coming. Somehow it was as though the sun shone too brightly, exposing things which he had not wished to see.

CHAPTER IV

☐ Sometimes Jeff felt that everything might have gone better if he had only come at a different time of year. The September heat, lingering on into October, had been a steady and withering blast which had left land and people brown and enervated. The days were like perfectly round beads on an immense necklace, threaded through by the fiery blaze of noons, and he found that the simple act of moving from one room to another in a futile effort to avoid the heat took all the energy he could summon. He had counted on doing some reading, but even that seemed too great an effort when the sweat dripped from his elbows and stung his eyes. Samuel had an old phonograph and a dozen or so ancient records, and in the afternoon he would play the machine and write letters to his fox-hunting friends or laboriously fill out endless forms for the Higgins Company. But for Jeff the slow hours stretched hot and empty and barren, and as time wore on he grew more restless.

The evenings became somewhat cooler with the approach of fall and often he and Samuel would load up the hounds and go hunting. It had been a dry summer and the ground was hard and cracked, and Samuel had said in advance that their luck would probably not be good. But even with warning, Jeff had been disappointed in this part of the old man's life which Samuel set such store by. They would sit by a small fire in the darkness and the barking of the dogs would be sporadic and aimless and finally Samuel would call them in with his horn and they would go home. It all seemed strangely pointless to Jeff now, meager, even dull when there was not the least desire to catch the fox. And he could not help feeling that the bright hopes which had brought him here were fading with the passing of each day.

For in some ways his journey to Grey Horse had been in the nature of a pilgrimage. He had wanted to ask about his father, to discover if he might the meaning of the suicide which his mother had so unexpectedly disclosed before her death. But thus far he had found himself unable to speak of it, for there was an old and vital bond with Samuel which he felt that he must first somehow renew. It was the farm in Tennessee which lay furthest back in his memory. He had gone there the summer that he was five and then again the next summer and the next until it had become for him no more than the natural order of things. His home, suburban Connecticut from which his father had commuted daily to New York, became associated in his mind with school and winter and loneliness, although it was much later before he realized it was loneliness and not just something that went along with the little academy which he attended and the short, dark days of winter. And the farm came to mean summer and freedom and loneliness, too, but different somehow because this was a loneliness which he enjoyed, like a silence filled with the cries of birds. So finally he came to take it all as a matter of course, the advent of spring and the steadily mounting anticipation until the day would come when he and his mother would board the train and start the long journey south. There was a regularity about it all which suited him, the same kind of regularity that he felt about birthdays or Christmas, for his grandfather was always waiting there at the station when they arrived. There would be a taxi in attendance out of deference to his mother who would not endure the wagon and who could not see why Samuel would not buy a car, and then Samuel would load them

in and they would drive the twelve miles to the farm,
Samuel seeming tall and cramped and awkward in the
front seat beside the driver and turning now and then to
ask something about the trip or about things at home, but
not much because his mother would be looking in her
purse to make sure that she had her return ticket or simply sitting there in a posture of discomfort, flicking at
her skirt with one long, white, bright-nailed hand. Always as soon as they got to the farm he and his mother
would retire to take naps, and neither of them would
sleep although no words would pass between them. Later
they would have dinner, served in silence by his grandmother who never ate until everyone else had finished,
and his grandfather would ask him about school and
whether he had played on any of the teams and the talk
would be slow and broken and quiet, the silences filled
only by the sputter of the kerosene lamp that lit the
table. The following morning his mother would leave,
alone since she always insisted that it be that way. He
would stand at the gate, watching the taxi drive away,
and with her going there was always a gentle kind of sadness as though he should perhaps have kissed her once
more before she left or told her again how much he
would miss her until the fall. But she would be gone
then, and he would turn and go back to the house and lie
down for a while on the porch swing or go out to the
kitchen and watch his grandmother as she rolled dough
or churned the butter and maybe she would let him
knead a little dough and he would feel better. By supper
time he would be teasing the hounds or wrestling with
Pap and it would be summer again.

The next day he would wake with dawn and slip into
the overalls which he wore all summer and then, his feet
still tender, he would leave the house and walk carefully
out to the shed where Pap would be milking, breaking in
spite of himself into a kind of exultant skip as the morning breeze made goose pimples rise along his arms. It was
his job to carry the full pails back to the house and he

was always glad when once in a while the morning would be sharp and the milk would steam a little. And every morning when he got to the kitchen door, he would stand for a moment in the chill hush and watch the sky blooming vast and pink in the east.

There was nothing he had to do when breakfast was over; the day was his. He would fill the woodbox by the stove and help Pap feed the hounds and then he might go out to the cornfield to get some silk for drying or he might take the cane pole and go down to the creek to fish. There was usually somebody there, checking trotlines or maybe just lying on the bank with a cane pole arching long and slender out over the water. It might be some of the Indians who lived in the hills behind the farm or it might be one of the neighbor boys who lived along the creek, but whoever it was, the gathering would be for the most part silent, dedicated to the mysterious ways of the few sun perch and occasional gars that took the bait, to the smoking of corn silk or dried peach leaves rolled in newspaper and to the sleepy pleasure of lying flat on one's back, looking up through the heavy foliage at the sky. In the afternoon he might go to a special place that he had found in the cornfield where he could sleep in the shade, a place between the rows where he could listen to the rustle of the stalks. Later, after he got the BB gun, he would take pot shots at the hogs which were always rooting their way into the field through the fence, and finally, after he had the pony, it was pretty much just the pony, morning and afternoon and sometimes after supper until dusk. But usually after supper he would pitch horseshoes in front of the house with Pap until it got too dark to see. And that was it, a regular, ordered procession of days unless the creek flooded or lightning started a fire somewhere close by or Pap decided to go out with the hounds on a night that was clear and cool. One day followed close upon another and the nights seemed impossibly short and things went along in the same pattern, fishing and horseshoes and weather and

porch sitting with Pap in the evening while his grandmother read her Bible in the kitchen by the light of the
kerosene lamp. So the summer would stretch full and
round through July and August and finally about Labor
Day he would suddenly feel unhappy and then forget
about it for another week until the time had actually
come and he would be getting on the train. His grandmother would be along this time, sitting silently in the
seat of the wagon beside his grandfather, wearing the
sunbonnet and the black silk dress she always wore to
town. He would be sitting back in the wagon bed, hot
and uncomfortable in the suit and shoes that he had put
away at the beginning of summer, watching the familiar
land fading slow and small behind him, and it would
begin to get him a little when they had rounded the first
bend in the road and the farm was gone. At the station he
would sit with his grandmother, not saying much, while
Pap disappeared and then returned with a sack of jawbreakers or some licorice sticks. And this would be when
he would have said it if he could, but he could only look
first at his grandmother and then at Pap and finally down
at the dusty, splintered floor of the station. There was
something that needed saying; he realized that. But he
could do no better than a mumbled thanks to his grandmother when she bent to kiss him good-by. For it was to
her in particular that he needed to say what he felt. Pap
knew, he was sure, and sometimes he thought that his
grandmother knew, but somehow the summer always
passed and was gone before he ever got around to talking
with her. And it was not that he was uncomfortable with
her in the way that he was with his mother. It was just
that she had always seemed apart from the rest of the life
at the farm. He wondered sometimes if Pap felt the same
way towards her that he himself did, for she seemed to
treat them both in much the same manner. He would
think of this on the train as he rode home, and he would
go over and over in his mind the few pictures of her
which he had—the way she looked from the porch as she

sat reading at the oil-cloth-covered table in the kitchen, her finger moving slowly back and forth across the page, or the way she would stand by the stove, looking out the window, waiting for them, the men, to finish eating. He would not understand until later, but that was the way he recalled her when the time for remembering came. That was the way she remained in his mind forever.

And it was not merely her presence, shadowy and severe; all the old memories were forever just around a corner in his mind, waiting fresh and pristine as always. During his years at Harvard he had had a favorite spot along the river where he often went on afternoons in spring. Beyond the college houses he would cross the bridge, pausing perhaps for a moment to lean out over the water and watch his features gently rippling up at him. Usually he could find something in his pockets to drop down to the shifting surface of the wind-ruffled river, and he would watch it bobble for a moment before he went on across the bridge and down along the bank to lay his blanket in the green, sharp-edged grass beside the water. He would always have a book along and he would rarely read it because the sun would get ensnared in the wool of the blanket and the grass would be new and sweetish in his nostrils and he would be aware of the ground's uneven surface and suddenly he would be thinking of the cornfield, of the spot where he had lain so often listening to the stir of the corn in the wind. He would be remembering the same discomforts of the earth along his shoulders and his ribs and his buttocks and then he would put a piece of grass into his mouth, feeling the little saw blade of its edge with his tongue, and when he closed his eyes with his face upturned to the sun he would feel memory coming over him like water, warm as the sun itself, sharp as the thin blade which lay fragrant as April in his mouth.

But after college, when he had returned to his home and a job on the town newspaper, the memories of those early years had almost faded from his mind. Their going was not unmarked for they left behind an emptiness, a desire for something natural and complete which his life with his mother could not satisfy. He had settled into the busy tedium of his work, into a routine whose only real pleasures were sailing on the week ends and the training of two horses which he had bought. His job he enjoyed moderately while knowing that were it not for his mother he would not have been there at all. Being a small-town newspaper, its requirements were various and seldom regular and yet Jeff had had the sense of forever plodding in a circle. It was a life which never, as he often put it to himself, seemed to come to much. He had little time of his own because his mother had come to depend on him almost entirely. He drank with her, nursed her, drove her to see her former friends and endured their scarcely concealed coolness and satisfaction. As much as he was able he gave her that love for which she had hungered behind her brittleness. And when she died and he was suddenly free and without immediate obligation, he had known instinctively and at once what he must do. Along with the anxiety about his father he felt that he needed clearer air and a more distant horizon, that elsewhere there were deeper waters than those he had sounded. Somehow the thought of the way Samuel might be living or what he, Jeff, might think of the old man after all these years had never crossed his mind with any force until he found himself in this lonely farmhouse on the edge of the vast, parched prairies of Oklahoma. Now he wondered with wry disillusion what it was he had actually hoped to find by coming here, what impossible dream he had created from the fragments of a long-distant boyhood.

One morning as Samuel was playing the usual records and scraching his lead pencil across the tablet paper that he used for stationery, Jeff came in from the porch and stood in front of Samuel until the old man looked up questioningly.

"I thought I'd go for a little ride. Mind if I saddle Carl and take him out for awhile?"

"Help yourself," Samuel answered. "He ain't much for ridin'—feels more comfortable with a plow behind him. Sometimes he'll rare a little at a car—damn near jumps through his ass at a train. Outside of that, he'll fair rock you to sleep."

"Don't wait lunch on me."

"I'll expect you when I see you," the old man said, getting up to wind the machine.

The dust was soft underfoot as Jeff walked out to the back lot. He found the bridle hanging from a gate post and the coarse blanket and saddle beside it on the rail. It took him awhile to catch the black horse and after he settled the bit in Carl's rough mouth and pulled the cinch tight, he swung into the saddle and turned toward the gate. The horse was reluctant at first and skittered sideways, scraping against the fence while Jeff pulled sharply at his head and kicked his sides. Clear of the gate, Carl gave one final buck and then settled resignedly into a kind of cantering compromise. But Jeff was not satisfied until he had urged him into a gallop, until he could feel the powerful legs driving pistonlike beneath him and the wind beating against his face. Carl's black mane streamed flat against his neck and his head was thrust far forward beyond the surging of his shoulders. When the foam began to lather along the edges of the bit, Jeff sat up and Carl slowed easily to a walk. They went on this way for a while, Jeff swaying in the saddle and looking pensively out at the land while the horse blew noisily and shook the reins with his head. Finally Jeff saw the glint of water through the curling leaves of the blackjacks. The pressure of his knee was enough to turn Carl in at the cattle guard, for the horse had already quickened his pace, smelling the water of the stock pond. Standing knee deep in the pond, Carl snorted and flicked his tail quickly against his sides as Jeff lit a cigarette and eased back in the saddle. Down to the south he could see a curving line of trees which probably followed a creek. Before him the land rose gradually to a crest and when after a few moments they left the pond and reached the top of the ridge, he could see a similar ridge thrusting into the prairie beyond a dun-colored sweep of high grass. Around him lay perfect silence; earth and sky were empty of all motion. Leather creaked faintly as he rose in the stirrups to see what lay beyond the far ridge and as he settled back in the saddle, the reins loose in his hands, Carl turned up through the trees, walking steadily with lowered head as though he knew where he was going.

It was not long before they reached a road and Carl's feet were muffled now in yellow sand. Enclosed in the easy, swaying rhythm of the saddle, Jeff stared down at the ground and tried to think about how he would bring the question up with Samuel. He had hoped that with the return of their old familiarity, the matter would somehow take care of itself. But the ease and the rough intimacy of former years seemed gone, at least for Jeff. There was something strained between them, something compounded of Jeff's vague disappointment and Samuel's quiet recognition of how he felt. And yet the question was still there, must still be asked, and as each day passed the silence grew more impenetrable between them.

He did not raise his troubled eyes from the ground until the horse stopped before the gate. Still frowning abstractedly, he slid to the ground and unhooked the gate post, swinging back up into the saddle as the horse came on through the fence. It seemed to Jeff that Carl was moving a little faster, a little more certainly, and now as he looked ahead through the drowsy dappling of sunlight and shade, he saw against the trees' soft vagueness the angular outline of a roof. He checked the horse for a moment and listened. The noon air was murmurous with the drone of insects and bird song and the rattle of dry leaves. The flooding sun held the ridge transfixed as though in amber and in this sleepy stillness time seemed reduced to the dimensions of a terrapin fumbling its way along a dusty road of infinite length. Then the raucous cursing of a bluejay broke the hush and after a moment Jeff heard the barking of a dog. He sat for a moment in indecision and then Carl settled the matter by resuming his easy pace on up the road toward the house.

There was a cyclone fence around the yard and on it the trumpet vines curled in green luxuriance. Ivy was matted darkly upon the chimney of the small house and as Jeff drew closer he could see that the house had been built of fieldstone, not markedly different in color from the dominant yellow and brown of the prairie. Two great oaks cast shade widely across the yard and upon the slanting roof, and in the dust at the base of these ancient trees a red Irish setter ran quickly back and forth, barking and leaping into the air. For a moment the road curved in behind some trees which masked Jeff's view and when he emerged again into full sunlight a man was standing at the gate of the fence, his hands hooked into his belt and his face grave and watchful. He wore the narrow boots of a cowman and trousers the color of sand and a short-sleeved blue shirt; in his mouth was a curve-stemmed pipe, and the walnut coloring of his face contrasted sharply with the silvering hair that was coarse and thick and cut rather close to his head. He looked briefly at the horse and then he took the pipe from his mouth and glanced quickly at Jeff.

"You must be Sam's boy," he said as a smile spread easily across his wide features. When he smiled the flatness at the bridge of his nose was more prominent and his mouth went a little crooked on one side. "Or you've stolen his horse, one. My name's Buck—Hardin Buck. Come on in and sit down for awhile."

Jeff got down and looped the reins through the fence. "Jeff Beecher," he said, putting out his hand to Buck. "I'm glad to know you. If you've got some water I'd certainly appreciate a drink. That sun's warm."

"Get the bucket over at the pump and draw some

66

water for your horse," Buck said, gesturing toward the pump behind the kitchen. "I'll get you some cold out of the box."

Jeff pumped the bucket full and set it by the gate for Carl and then went on around to the side of the house where Buck was sitting beside a round metal table. There was an easel before him holding a partially finished painting and on the table was a scattering of brushes and tubes and paint-smeared rags. A large pair of field glasses dangled from his chair and alongside him on the ground lay two beer cans.

"Hot weather for painting," Jeff said as he sat down at the table.

"I'm not enough of a painter for it to make much difference. I'm trying to get that blackjack—right down there at the end of the point."

"You're not a professional then?"

"Me? No. Just for fun. I've been working on a museum for the Indians here. Hired me a fellow from Chicago to do some paintings of the full bloods and just didn't have enough left over to get him to do this one. I guess maybe I wanted to do it anyway."

"They're peculiar-looking trees—the way the lower branches point down toward the ground."

"Protection. They keep the cattle off and they're mean as hell to ride through. Where's the old man?"

"Samuel?" Jeff said, glancing over at Buck. "He was at the house when I left."

"We're old friends," Buck replied, as though answering the question in Jeff's voice. "He told me you were coming. I kind of wondered when you'd be over."

"We've stuck pretty close to the house. I think the heat bothers him some."

Buck tamped his pipe and said nothing. Jeff cleared his throat and looked down the silent ridge toward the dead blackjack that pierced the sky. After a moment he looked up at the sun.

67

"Getting close to noon," he said, tapping his hands against the arms of the chair. "I suspect I'd better be getting on. Thanks for the water."

"Nonsense," Buck replied as he got up. "You sit right there while I get you a beer and then I'm going to fry some chicken for lunch."

"No, really," Jeff countered, smiling in spite of himself at Buck's easy cheerfulness.

"Not at all. It's not often I get visitors for lunch, and when I do I make the most of it."

"At least let me watch you, then," Jeff said, getting up to follow Buck to the kitchen. "I can't just sit out here drinking while you work."

"It's a hell of a lot easier than you think. But if you want to build up an appetite watching, come ahead."

He cooked the chicken slowly, rolling the pieces in flour and dropping them into the sputtering grease of the black Dutch oven. Occasionally he put his beer aside and raised the cover, drawing a long breath and frowning or nodding his head. Then he picked up his beer again and leaned against the stone wall and the smile would move crookedly across his face as he told of meals that he had cooked on the little kerosene stove. His voice, slow and rich and reflective, had a fine edge of humor in it and as he talked he laughed a little with recollection. "I've had men here six and eight at a time. Quail hunters, hound men—eaters, all of them. A chicken per man and plenty to drink. Or sometimes steaks. I always had a locker in town loaded with beef and venison and once in a while even bear—used to hunt a lot out in New Mexico." He stood for a moment in silence, his arms crossed against his chest, his face bemused with the memory of what had gone. Then he lifted the cover of the deep skillet and poked at the chicken with a fork. "This place has seen lots of good eating—good talk. Sam's been here plenty; he could tell you."

Before they had finished lunch Jeff found himself

laughing and talking as though he had known Buck for many years. There was a vein of warm and sympathetic interest in the older man which gave to his character a glow and a density that Jeff somehow seemed to share as they talked. Buck's attention fell upon him like soft rain and Jeff felt refreshed and newly alive; for the first time in weeks he was free of having to watch what he said, free of what seemed to him Samuel's limitations. He felt that something like this was what he had come here hoping to find, this sort of talk, this sort of deeply rooted living. They spoke of many things, touching experiences here and there that were common to them, and by the time they had finished the last pieces of chicken it was well into afternoon.

"No use leaving now," Buck said as he lit his pipe. "Besides, I want to send a couple of doves home with you. They'll be flying over the saddle down there before long. Not much trouble to shoot and good eating. Oh, to hell with the dishes. I want to work some while I can still see that tree. I guess if I weren't so comfortable here I'd go down there by it, but I know it pretty well by heart and the field glasses do the rest."

The afternoon slipped away as they talked there beneath the trees. Jeff said little, content to sit in the wind that faintly stirred the leaves, looking out toward the prairie and listening to Buck's rambling conversation about his part of the country, as he called it. "I've lived here just about all my life, with a few years out for looking the rest of the world over. I traveled around—went to school in England for awhile and worked at geology, what we used to call natural history. No, I never really wanted to live any place else. It may seem a little slow at first, but the damned country grows on you when you've lived here awhile." He put down his brush and looked around for a cigarette and then stood there with his hands on his hips, looking toward the creek. "You can't get inside these people all at once. You've got to live

69

with them—listen to them—let them soak in on you for awhile. I know, they either sit like stumps or else talk your arm off, but after a little you start to get what they're saying. You'll see," he said, smiling down at Jeff. Then he turned back to the painting and studied it for some time in silence. "Space takes the edge off things a little," he said slowly as he squinted against the smoke of the cigarette. "I've never been able to decide whether life seems less important in this country, or more so. But whatever it is, I like it."

"I like it myself, what I've seen of it. But you pay a high price to live here. It seems cut off in a way, and this heat is deadening. I've hardly been able to move since I got here."

"Oh, it's hot enough. But you get used to it."

"I wonder if I ever would."

"That would depend on something other than the heat, I suspect. But tell me, did you find your granddad pretty much as you expected?"

Jeff looked at the back of Buck's head and wondered what he was thinking. "He hasn't changed much. Of course it's been a long time. We had some business to take care of." It irritated him that he could find nothing more direct to say; yet even within himself his feelings about Samuel were not clear. It was as though Buck had tossed a pebble into the calm pool of this October afternoon and now the ripples of discontent moved vaguely around Jeff and made him feel suddenly that he could not breathe as easily as before.

They spoke no more of Samuel and when the shadows had begun to gather around the front of the house Buck put his paints aside and finished what was left of his beer. He went into the house and when he returned he was carrying a shotgun.

"Look at her," he said, nodding his head at the setter, which leaped against his side excitedly. "She must think it's bird season. You'll have to stay behind this time," and he knelt and held the setter's head in his hand. "You'll get your chance before much longer. . . .

"These doves feed in the wheat fields south of here," Buck explained when they had reached the saddle. He squatted on his heels and put a piece of grass between his teeth. "They fly across here about this time every night."

The sun glowed in the west, sending off great streaming shafts of light that slanted to earth like the columns of some broken temple. The clouds beneath were dark as wine and in the northwest strange light blue clouds were massing, white around the fringes as though with ice.

"We might get some weather tonight," Buck said, and then abruptly he rose and wheeled the gun across the sky and fired. "Too much talk," and he squatted again. "You'll hear a kind of whistling sound if you listen close."

He killed the next bird and two more that followed shortly after. They came slanting very fast above the trees into the opening and then seemed suddenly to collapse as the shot struck them.

"Take a crack at them," he said, holding out the gun to Jeff.

"Oh, I haven't shot in years."

"No, go ahead. Look here," and he showed him how they would come and how he must lead them just a fraction. "Get a little bit ahead of them and let fly. You won't have time to think anyway."

When Jeff heard the whistling again it took him too long to find the bird, and when he shot at the next one, he knew even as he fired that the dove had veered out of his sights.

"Here," he said, smiling awkwardly as he handed Buck the gun. "I can't hit the damned things."

And for a moment Buck stood there without moving, looking at him so keenly that Jeff felt his eyes waver before Buck's steady gaze.

71

"You just need a little practice," Buck said at last as he took the gun, and when he smiled the strange intensity passed from his face.

In half an hour they had seven birds and Buck got a game sack from the house to carry them in. "Tell the old man they're an invitation to come over, and you come again, too. Any time."

"Carl knows the way without any directions from me," Jeff laughed as he waved good-by. And as the road curved past the trees he looked back and waved again, for Buck was still standing where he had left him. Riding along through the late afternoon he thought happily of what a pleasant day it had been. Although he realized now how little Buck had actually told him about himself, still he could not help feeling that Buck was a remarkable man, a man whose life flowed far beneath the surface of things. There was something almost misleading about his easiness, for in that moment of silence when they had looked at one another Jeff had sensed a tension that was curiously at variance with Buck's free and gracious manner. It had been as though Buck had wanted to say something and had then thought better of it. But at least now there was someone to talk with and he decided that he would come to see Buck again as soon as he could get away.

The day was still hot and as he followed the dusty road home he wondered if there would be time for a swim. About a mile from the house the creek widened into a swimming hole, protected from the sun by a veil of boughs that arched above the water. And the water, even though sluggish and brown, would be cooler than the air. He looked at his watch and then spurred Carl into a fast trot until they left the road for a path that led down to the creek. Halfway down the path he dismounted and tied the reins loosely to a small tree and then went on toward the creek, taking off his shirt as he went. When he had stripped off the rest of his clothes, he dove from the bank and let himself drift for a few moments against the cool weight of the water until his need for air brought him to the surface. He blew noisily and shook the water from his hair and then surface dived, descending through layers of coolness until his outstretched hands touched rock. This time when his head broke water he heard a voice.

"I guess you know you plumb played hell with my fishin'."

Jeff wiped the water from his eyes and looked around him until he saw the boy seated on the bank. He was small and barefooted, wearing nothing but faded overalls and a large straw hat. He was down the creek a little way and his cane pole was suspended over a cork that floated quietly in the water.

"Sorry," Jeff said. "I didn't see you."

"I figured you hadn't," the boy said. "Or else you was awful dumb, one."

"Mind if I go on swimming for awhile?" Jeff asked, grinning at him.

"Long as you're in, may's well go ahead. What few fish there is in here is long gone by now."

Jeff, looking at the boy, decided that he must be about the same age that he himself had been when he had quit going to Tennessee. But this boy was thinner and his eyes seemed dull.

"What's your name?" Jeff asked him after a while.

"Peter Paul Fincannon. People call me Bud." The boy gave his pole a tentative jerk and then lowered the cork into the water again. "You don't come from around here, do you, mister."

"No, I don't," Jeff said.

"Didn't think you did," said the boy. "Never saw nobody else swim in that there mud hole before."

"It's not so bad."

"Wouldn't catch me in it." His voice had a petulant quality which Jeff did not like and he was sorry now that

73

he had not seen him before he dove in. He did not like the idea of getting out of the water and dressing with the boy watching him.

"You visitin' around here someplace?"

Jeff turned away from him. "Up the road," he said shortly.

"With old man Beecher I'll bet. He's the one with all them hounds, ain't he. How come he's got all them dogs on his place, anyway? Does he sell 'em or somethin'?"

"He hunts with them." Jeff lay on his back and kicked vigorously to drown the sound of the boy's voice. The sky above him was gray, softened now by the tentative approach of evening. He kicked harder so that the water splashed into his face, and then as he turned slowly in the current of the creek, he caught sight of the boy standing on the bank, waving and shouting something at him. He straightened up quickly and shook the water from his ears.

"It's a moccasin," the boy was shouting, pointing his finger up the creek from Jeff.

Jeff looked quickly in that direction and then he saw the slick and glistening head cutting smoothly through the water. It was no more than five yards away and coming downstream with the current. Jeff felt his stomach knot like a fist and then he was fighting his way through the water toward the shore. When he felt ground beneath him he struggled up onto the bank and stood there trembling and panting with the sweat cold on his forehead.

The boy held his hand to his mouth, giggling foolishly. "You shoulda seen that old cotton mouth take off when you started that splashin'. He wasn't waitin' for nobody." When Jeff did not answer, the boy spoke again. "What the matter, mister. He's gone. He slid up the other side."

But Jeff hardly understood what he was saying. The blood hammered heavily in his ears and he stared dully back at the water where the waves from his frightened course broke on the opposite bank. After a moment he was aware that he was standing naked in the shadows and that the boy was staring at him in rapt silence. With fumbling hands he pulled his clothes on, keeping his eyes averted from the boy's slack-jawed gaze. Then he walked quickly back up the path, wanting to hurry out into the open, into the sun again, to leave behind the hushed gloom of the creek and the revulsion which had uncoiled so violently within him. But Carl was gone. Jeff leaned against the tree where he had tied the horse and swore angrily, cursing himself for his carelessness. The day seemed spoiled now, its fresh pleasures suddenly withered and dead. Finally he pushed his shirt tails into his pants and walked back to the road, and as he went along toward home the dust gradually coated his shoes and a cold perspiration seemed to burst from all his pores.

It had not been much trouble for Carl to rub the bridle loose from the scrub oak. He was hungry and close to home and as soon as he freed himself he followed the familiar road to the lot where supper waited. Samuel, sitting on the porch with his feet propped against the railing, caught sight of him as he plodded up the hill. He lowered his chair with a thud and got to his feet. "Why, that's Carl," he said with surprise to the man who sat beside him.

The man lifted a round, bald, ponderous head and stared at Samuel as though from a distance. "I didn't quite catch it," he said calmly. He was walleyed and the glance he turned on Samuel took in a disconcerting amount of latitude.

"My horse, Dewey," Samuel shouted, leaning to the man's ear and pointing down the road. "That's my horse yonder."

"Purty fair lookin' horse," Dewey replied after a moment, nodding his head judiciously. "A mite hammer headed and rump heavy, but—"

"My grandson took him out this morning and—" Samuel all of a sudden straightened up and took a deep breath. "Dewey, sometimes you're just too goddam much trouble."

Dewey nodded again as though in agreement and rose from his chair to follow Samuel down to the road. He was short and potbellied and he padded along duck-fashion in a pair of creased brown slippers that came up around his ankles. The loose grayish trousers that he wore ballooned across his stomach and were supported by broad yellow braces that cut into his fat shoulders. He took the porch steps slowly, sighing deeply when he reached the bottom, and his large, divergent eyes blinked with difficulty so that he appeared to be just on the verge of emerging from a state of profound meditation. "The mark of the spirit" was the way his scattered congregations defined this expression although a less interested observer might rather have seen a considerable indication of the flesh in his swollen red nose and pudgy lips, in the way he stroked his hand across his mouth, in his sudden throaty laughter that sounded on occasions as though Dewey Fink had seen and touched too much.

"Yeah," he said gravely. "Purty fair horse. But where at's the one who's a-ridin' him?"

Samuel led Carl through the gate and took down the game bag that hung from the saddle horn. "This belongs to Hardin," he said quietly as though talking to himself. He opened the bag and when he saw the doves he frowned and slowly scratched his head.

"Yonder he comes. Had himself a little walk," and Dewey's mouth widened around the cigar as he chuckled. He took the black stub from his teeth, spat, and wiped his mouth with the back of his hand. "Yessir. Had himself a little old country stroll. Reckon he wishes he'd taken that machine of his now."

Samuel looked down the road and smiled. "That's him all right. Carl got loose from him somewhere."

They stood there watching as Jeff came up the road,

76

and when he was close enough to hear Samuel called and waved to him. "We was just gettin' ready to go look for you."

Jeff did not reply until he got to the gate. "I was swimming down at the creek," he said dryly. "He pulled the reins loose, I guess."

"We was a-wonderin' how that horse had been able to shoot them there doves all by hisself," Dewey drawled.

Jeff looked at him without expression and said nothing.

"Thisyere's Dewey Fink, Jeff. My grandson," he said to Dewey, gesturing at Jeff with a turn of his head.

"I never caught the name," Dewey said, slowly, blinking his eyes.

"Jeff Beecher," Samuel shouted. "Dewey's a spot deaf," he said matter-of-factly to Jeff. "So you brought me some doves. Let's go on up to the kitchen and git 'em cleaned. Everything all right at Buck's? Did he know who you was?"

"Yeah. Just fine. I think I'll wash up a little."

They watched him go quickly up the porch steps and then Dewey turned to Samuel. "Mighty fine lookin' boy there."

"What?" Samuel said as though he had not heard him. Then he nodded his head vigorously. "Oh, you bet. He's a good boy, all right. Well, come on. We got work to do."

But when they got to the porch Dewey sank into his chair and sighed, bending over a little to loosen his slippers. Samuel looked at him for a moment, laughed, and went on into the kitchen by himself.

If there had been any doubts about Dewey's willingness to talk, he dispelled them once and forever during dinner. It was almost as though he had been winding himself up as he had sat rocking on the porch, for as they ate he talked almost steadily, hearing no one else, interrupting without hesitation, going on interminably about his baseball days with Samuel.

77

"Yore grand daddy had this team, see. He was what you might call the manager, and I was the catcher on this outfit. I was a little porer flesh-wise than how you see me now, the good Lord willing, and I could squat behind that there plate with the best of 'em. Well, there was an ole boy lived in a town down the road had him a team likewise. We always had our big game with them boys—people'd come from all over."

"This fellow was a doctor," Samuel interjected, "and he just loved—"

"Like I say, it was big doin's. Annual affair and all that. People would bet money and such. Well, Sam made him a big bet with this bird and told us boys on the team about it and said we wouldn't have to worry none about his losin' money and not payin' us 'cause he had located us a pretty fair country ball player. Somebody who all by hisself could make the difference. Didn't tell us who it was, and made us promise we'd keep our mouths shut good. A little more of that sweet milk, please sir, Sam."

"Dewey Fink," Samuel said to Jeff as he poured the milk from the pitcher, "grew up in the same town with me. Just like he's tellin' you, he played on this team for me and then when his knees gave out on him he took to preachin' and finally got on up to where he was faith healin'. Made a real success out of himself. He preaches all over this—"

"Day of the game," Dewey continued after he had majestically set his glass back on the table, "we was all lookin' around for this fella that Sam had promised us. Purty soon a tall skinny guy with a country way of talkin' came up to where we boys was settin' and said, 'Which one o' you does the catchin'?' I said I figured that would be me and he said, 'Well, now maybe you better git somethin' for your glove.' I kinda scratched my head and said, 'Mister, I don't know you and I been catchin' this team for a good many years. Let's just warm up a little first.' He threw me five pitches and I walked away

78

from the plate. 'Son boy,' I says to the kid that kept our bats for us, 'run on down town and don't you come back till you find me a real good thick piece o' steak.' He was that fast. He throwed like he was mad at somebody. That's how I come to catch Walter Johnson. I'll never forget it. Sam had just plain hired him for the day, and Walter had them Flat Rock boys six feet back from the plate and choppin' wood on every pitch. It wasn't what a man'd call a contest a-tall."

"I won the bet, too," Samuel laughed. "It cost me a hundred dollars to get him there but—"

"How was that?" Dewey said, raising his eyebrows.

"I won the bet," Samuel roared, leaning around the table toward him.

"You won the bet, for a fact," Dewey gravely replied.

The preacher lapsed into drowsiness when the meal was done. Samuel started clearing the dishes and the sudden activity seemed to rouse Dewey just enough to enable him to get up from his chair.

"It's been a long day," he said solemnly, his walleye staring whitely through the kitchen's gloom. " 'Spect I'd better turn in."

"You're tired," Samuel said. "Go ahead."

"I'll be up for breakfast," he announced, and disappeared down the hall.

Jeff had scarcely touched his food during dinner. He helped with the dishes in silence and then he went out to the porch while Samuel fed the hounds. After a while the old man came around to the front and they sat in the dusk together, watching through the spreading darkness the thunderheads pile up in the northwest. The air had turned cool and the wind stirred the dust into fitful whorls. Above them the thunder rolled heavily and the sky shone with the serpentine flickerings of lightning. The hound at Samuel's feet was restless, getting up and then lying down again, whining and thumping its tail. A night hawk veered across the road down toward the creek bottom as the night came on in silence, and all at once there was the flat spatter of raindrops against hard ground. And even now in the darkness, Jeff could not forget what had happened at the creek. The long moment of terror followed by a sudden sense of shame as he had stood naked before the dull eyes of the boy had been painfully reminiscent of long-buried sensations from his childhood, sensations which were always somehow connected with the fact that his father was dead. He remembered with what agony he had always waited for the inevitable questions, and how his answers, mumbled and awkward, would leave him trembling with emotions he could not fathom. *He's dead. . . . He's dead*—the words dry as ashes in his mouth.

"I don't like it when it cools off that quick," Samuel was saying, standing at the corner of the porch to look at the clouds. "Too much like tornado weather, even if it is fall. I guess summer is gonna give up—feels like October ought to feel."

"I suppose we'll have rain, now," Jeff said quietly.

"Yeah. Rain. Maybe not much tonight, but it'll come. Got to git in some wood."

"I guess so."

"Yeah."

Jeff lit a cigarette and listened to the solid splatting of the rain on the roof. He could see it slanting down through the lamplight that reached feebly into the darkness.

"I'm just as glad winter's comin' on. Summer lasts too long around here to suit me." Samuel walked back across the porch and sat down, putting his foot lightly on the hound's neck. "We'll have some huntin' now for sure."

They listened to the rain for a while, saying nothing. When Jeff spoke, his voice was restrained and quite deliberate. "I wonder if you would mind telling me what you know about Dad's death."

Samuel looked over at him and rubbed his hands

80

slowly against his legs. "I kinda figured you might have that on your mind."

"I never did really know just how it happened."

"He didn't want you to."

"Mother said that, too. She told me about it just before she died."

"Why it was that way, you mean?" Samuel asked after a moment.

Jeff could see part of his face in the lamplight, and suddenly it seemed sad and old and worn. "Why it happened that way. She thought you might know."

"And that's why you came."

"That was one reason," Jeff said.

"Well, I don't know how much you remember about him, son. He was awful quick about everything. Whatever he wanted he wanted it right now and no waitin' around. Little things bothered him—I couldn't tease him when he was little like I could the other boys. He was kinda sober-like—I always thought he mighta made a good preacher if he coulda got behind it just right. But he was hard to please. I always thought that there was somethin' about your mother that got to workin' on him —no disrespect meant to the departed but she did have a pretty sharp edge on her—somethin' about her people and that part o' the country and all. George never was nothin' but a overgrowed country boy, no matter how hard he tried. I guess he just never could fit all the things he wanted together."

"What was it he wanted that he didn't have or couldn't get?"

"I always kinda felt like he wanted it all or would have to git it all to pry your mother loose from off his back. Them people had a eye for the old scratch, no matter how high they talked or carried on. I think he looked good to 'em, looked like a winner, and they ran him 'til he dropped. He couldn't complain because they had done him a favor, see, lettin' him marry this girl. I always

81

believed he just never belonged back there, that's all. I think sometimes he felt like he wanted to come on back home. There wasn't anybody could say for absolute positive what really happened. The gun was there and patches and a cleaning rod. Whether he actually forgot it was loaded or not nobody will ever know."

"Do you think he forgot?" Jeff asked quietly.

Samuel said nothing for a while and then he leaned forward and spat into the rain. "It's all behind us now, boy," he said a little sharply. "Don't do no good to bring it all back. They's lots of things we'd all do different if we could do 'em again. But it's over and done with. Whatever happened that day is between him and his Maker. I'm sorry. If there was more I could tell you I would."

"He didn't forget, did he." Jeff's voice was tense and insistent. "There's no use pretending about it—"

"Who said anything about pretending? He's gone and it was your mother—"

"Hit feels like hit's commencin' to blow." Dewey pushed open the screen and padded out to the edge of the porch, peering widely at the rain. "Man can kindly feel it in the air." He sat down in the rocker and folded his hands across his stomach. "I seen one o' them cy-whizzes when I was a kid. Cain't say as I care for 'em, neither."

They sat for a long time on the porch as the rain beat gustily against the roof. Jeff smoked, listening with growing irritation to the droning voice of the preacher, while Samuel rubbed his foot along the hound's back. Finally Dewey sighed and lifted himself heavily from the chair. "Amen," he said reverently as though he had just finished a prayer, and they heard the fading flap of his feet as he went down the hall to his room.

"So you was over at Hardin's today," Samuel said when he heard the door close behind Dewey.

"Yeah," Jeff said shortly. "How long's Fink planning to stay?"

82

Samuel turned his head quickly and looked at him through the half light. "Dewey Fink's been a friend o' mine longer than you've been on this earth, boy. He comes every fall for a vacation—has for years. He's a hound man and a bell-tongued preacher. I couldn't say off hand how long he'll stay."

Jeff sat for a moment longer before rising abruptly and going to his room. As the screen door slammed the hound raised its head and looked at Samuel, and its depthless eyes glowed dark red in the lamplight. But Samuel did not look down; he seemed lost in the contemplation of darkness. And it was many hours later before he went to bed.

CHAPTER V

☐ Buck stood for a while on the saddle when Jeff had gone, wondering at the loneliness which had come upon him as softly and as suddenly as the late shadows which now lay upon the earth. About him the silence clung like a shroud and the air seemed to grow chill beneath the darkening clouds. The flavor of the afternoon had turned like a too long opened wine and now he stood there alone against the great sky, listening in vain for the faint clash of a hoof upon stone, looking without success for a last glimpse of the boy. He was frowning at the strangeness of what he felt, for it resembled more than anything else the helpless sense of loss that comes with the departure of someone very dear. It was as though he had forgotten himself in the golden flow of this day, and then when the boy had gone and he had returned to himself again he had found a change, leaves cast across the land by a winter wind, last flowers curled and withered before their term. It seemed almost that he had watched some precious part of his own life ride away that afternoon, some last remaining vestige of youth or hope.

Finally he cradled the gun in his arm and went somewhat slowly up the road to the yard where the setter lay waiting for him in the shade. When he had cleaned the doves and packed them in the refrigerator, he took a bottle of Scotch and some ice and went out to the table. He looked at the painting for a little and shook his head and turned his eyes down toward the point, needing to look hard again at trees and rocks and land familiar to him as his own house, as though he must fix them indelibly in his mind before it was too late. There was something about the boy that had cast this twilight upon his spirit, something which had leaped between them as they had stood together in the clearing. There seemed a flame smoldering in Jeff, a flame overlaid with ashes of the past or shut away from the quickening air, which Buck had felt a sudden desire to fan into life. Yet now as he stared intently across the land he smiled wryly as though at his own folly, for there were no fires in danger of going gray more quickly than those within himself, nor was there a way for him to place these things that he had loved beyond the reach of death. His body would return to the ground from which it had risen, to mingle and grow and live again in sun heat and drip of rain and the dark, fertile bloomings of life and of death. But the harvest of his mind and of his senses could only rest secure in a human heart, and he was alone.

As he sat drinking his Scotch beside the table in the fading afternoon, he could not help thinking of the far different loneliness of his boyhood. He had grown up on the prairie with a dog and a horse for companions, his mind filled with rabbits and quail and red-tailed hawks and the silences of the plains. He had hunted in all seasons, in all weathers, and almost always by himself since he had no brothers and the nearest neighbors had lived some fifteen miles away. And it was the place itself that was the loom on which his life had been woven, its rocks and shadowed ravines and coppery grasses, the creek, the blackjack trees, and the far spread of sky. If people might have added something more, he had not been aware of it and he had not missed them, for in those years the fences at the limits of the ranch had seemed to contain more than he could ever hope to know.

But the time came when he had had to move into town. His father had decided to open a bank in Grey Horse and he recalled leaving the ranch with apprehension, notwithstanding the knowledge that he could return whenever he wished and in spite of the promising name which the town bore. Yet life in town had had some advantages; there were livery stables, blacksmith shops, more horses than he could count and a barn in back of the house that he could ride into at top speed if he ducked his head at just the right time. And there were boys who could ride almost as well as he could and who had chased rabbits for just about as long as he had and who were ready for anything provided it was outdoors and fun. So he had found some friends. But still he was a country boy, and quiet like a country boy, and he was part Chetopa and that made him quieter yet, and a lot of the time he would want to go his own way, by himself.

Whenever he was able he had gone back to the ranch where he could ride through the wind-slanted grasses down to the creek, and from the bluffs there he could look away toward the far-off horizon or watch the glittering kingfishers swooping along the water below him. Now and then a woodpecker would knock at a tree somewhere upstream and the noise would be hollow and loud, and occasionally through the ringing of the locusts would come the rasp of a jay or the busy chattering of a squirrel. But these were sounds that had made him more aware than ever of the silence, the silence that was like a sea in which these heard stirrings briefly lived and died. And yet powerful as this had been, it was something else which had drawn him here. It was something which he could hardly even wonder at and something he couldn't think about at all, but it had been there and he could feel it and it was good. It was a rightness, a fitting together, a harmony that seemed somehow to include even himself. And on the way back from the creek he would always stop on the ridge just south of the ranch house and he would get down and stand there at the point for a few moments while the pony lowered its head into the wind and he would look out for thirty miles and more to the west where the sun would be going down, and he would think then that this would be the place to build a house, to live, to be buried.

And fifty years later he still believed these things; his house and his life were here and here his bones would settle into dust. There had been many years between the day he first left Grey Horse and the day he returned, and more years still before he had come back to the point. Many things had happened and he had known the distant places of the world, and yet through moments clustered dense as stars had shown the single light by which his life was brightened, and he had followed it home. And now, after all the turnings of the years, the bloomings and the snows, the plantings and the harvests, he was alone and he must die.

He had not really noticed the darkness until rain began to spatter the table. The trees swayed noisily in the wind as he covered the painting and carried it quickly into the house. Then he returned for the bottle and his paints and by the time the rain was loud on the roof he had lit the lamps and settled into his leather chair by the fireplace. He sat for a long time that night, his pipe dead in his hand, his shadowed face graven with lines of weariness and thought. The room was tranquil and the rain fell soft and fragrant as balm and yet in this October there was already the chill of winter in Buck's heart.

The rain still fell next morning when he rose from a troubled sleep, rain that hung in gossamer nets among the shining boughs of the blackjacks, that like the feet of running squirrels pattered suddenly on the roof when the wind rode through the trees. The damp gray light against the window seemed to dissolve into drops that oozed without order down the pane, and in the fireplace the flame stirred fitfully, sending occasional puffs of smoke into the room. It was the best sort of morning for a pot full of fragrant coffee, an old pipe, a long-familiar book and a small fire, even if it should smoke as this one did. Sitting in the leather chair, Buck stretched his feet toward the snapping wood, the coarse blanket pulled in tight around his body, and as he read he drank the steaming coffee which seemed to drive the mingled chill and loneliness from his bones. He sat this way for most of the morning until a pounding at the back door made him raise his head in wonder. When the noise was repeated he threw off the blanket and went back to the kitchen to find Samuel peering in through the glass of the door, his face screened by a fringe of water that poured from his hat and by the hand that he held to his eyes to shade the window. Buck opened the door and the old man stepped quickly inside, shaking himself like a dog.

"I'll be damned if it ain't a reg'lar chip floater," he said, gingerly removing his hat and wiping his streaming face with a towel which Buck had handed him. "Mighty good thing that horse can swim. He was up to his butt best part of the way. Why I felt like I had a saddle on a alligator."

"Slow down," Buck laughed. "We've had bigger rains than this before."

"I wouldn't argue it." Samuel grinned. "But I've just about forgot what the stuff looks like. Where's my cup?"

"Come on in by the fire. I told your boy yesterday to bring you over but I can't say as I expected to see you so soon."

Samuel steamed a little as he stood before the fire and he held the coffee close to his nose to smell it. "What would a man do without it," he said. He blew across the top of the cup and took a sip.

"Jeff stayed back at the house, I guess."

"Yeah?" He set the cup on the mantel and wiped his hands again on the towel before rolling a cigarette. "He had him a swim yesterday—reckon he figured oncet was enough."

"He was over here until pretty late."

"This was on the way home. He stopped at the creek and Carl got loose on him and came on up to the house. Boy was kinda sore about it."

"I guess he would be," Buck said. "Seems to handle a horse pretty well, though."

"I figured maybe you hit it off, him bein' over here all day like he was." Samuel reached slowly for his cup and kept his eyes on Buck as though he were waiting for an answer.

"Yes, I liked him fine," Buck said quickly. "Good boy."

Samuel nodded and finished his coffee. When he sat down he poked at the fire for a while before he spoke. "I might as well tell you right off, Hardin, I got me a little problem there." He was silent for a moment and then he sat back and looked directly at Buck, his eyes narrow and puzzled in his lean face. "Things just ain't been what you might call the best."

"Is that right?" Buck said quietly. He had wondered about it the day before talking to Jeff, but the boy had said nothing to indicate how things stood.

"Well, it's hard to pin down. We git along fine and all that but the edges just don't seem to fit flush. He say anything to you yesterday?"

Buck shifted in his chair. "No, not about that. I guess I did most of the talking. He was a little quiet but I thought that was probably just his way."

"Somethin' eatin' on him, Hardin. He's too quiet. I'll be damned if I know what he figured to find out here," he said aggressively, "but it's gittin' plain as hell that he ain't found it." He threw the cigarette into the fire and sat there with his hands on his knees, looking hard at Buck as though he could not see him clearly enough. "There's nothin' about me that a man cain't tell in five minutes and what's more—"

"Getting mad won't do any good."

Samuel sighed and then collapsed against the back of the chair, resting his chin in his hand. "Hell, I know it. It just works on me that I cain't seem to git at him."

Buck filled their cups again and lit his pipe. "These things take time. You know that yourself. You can't just pick up overnight where you left off fifteen years ago."

"That's just what I'm gittin' at. I think the boy's fixin' to leave. Things was bad enough like they was and then who come walkin' down the road yesterday but Dewey Fink." He leaned forward as he said this and then he settled back again with the air of having made a final point.

"You mean the preacher."

"That's exactly who I'm talkin' about."

"Not the best company in the world at a time like this."

"Dewey Fink," Samuel said matter-of-factly, "could wear a hog down to a frazzle without even puttin' his mind to it. But he's as good a friend as I've got."

Buck looked at the fire for a while without speaking. "Dewey's got to go," he said at last.

"I was gittin' around to that. But he's about as easy to move as a jackass on a mad."

Buck pulled at his ear and listened for a long time to the rain. After a bit he got up and walked slowly to the far end of the room where he could look down the point. Then he paced back and forth a few times, his hands in his pockets, his face quiet and his eyes turned to the floor. Samuel watched him without moving until the silence became too much for him.

"I've just got to have a chew," he muttered apologetically, but Buck gave no indication of having heard him.

When Buck at last sat down he looked up at the ceiling and brought the tips of his fingers together just below his chin.

"Man's a preacher," he said. "What else does he do?"

"Used to play some ball."

"Too late in the year. What else?"

"Mighty strong at faith healin', layin' on the hand of the spirit, even talkin' in tongues in a pinch."

"Faith healing, you say?" Buck mused.

"Man, beast, or woman."

"What about fox hounds—he's a hunter, isn't he?"

"That's the funny thing about Dewey. He can hear

hounds a whole lot better than he can people. They ain't hardly a fox hunter in this part of the country don't know Dewey Fink."

Buck got his pipe going and then looked sharply at Samuel. "Now. What's coming up in the way of fox-hunting meets? Those get-togethers you're always driving five hundred miles to."

Samuel pulled a wallet from his back pocket and extracted a creased and faded piece of tablet paper. "The schedule," he announced. He studied it for a moment, leaned toward the fireplace and spat, and studied it some more. "Ash Flats," he said finally. "North Arkansas Fox Hunters Association. Two weeks from today."

"Know who's running it?"

"Ed Silver has run it ever since I can remember."

"See what I'm getting at?" Buck was beginning to smile just a little.

"Seems like I can hear somethin' way off in the distance. Keep talkin'."

" 'Friends—fox hunters—brothers! Some folks call Him the first Rotarian; some speak of the power of His word; some recall the hell He raised in the temple and some remember Him that He was a carpenter, that He had the touch to heal, that He could talk loaves and fishes right out of thin air. But brothers, to tell you the plain truth of the matter, I've always liked to think of Him as a man that got a little restless when fall came on, a man who knowed that there wasn't enough money in all the temples in the world to buy what He could get out of a good pack of hounds and the ground just damp enough to hold the scent. I'm talkin' about a man who had the faith, who didn't have to see or touch to know that there was something holy out there in the dark—' "

"A chaplain—ain't that what they call 'em?" Samuel said excitedly.

"This Ed Silver can honor him with an official invitation to preside over the meet in a spiritual way."

"Not to mention the fact that some o' them sorry

92

hounds down there could use more than a little of the hand that heals. Ed'll do it—git out the damned paper—we'll have Dewey on the bus in a week, the good Lord willing."

The letter was somewhat prolonged by Samuel's insistence on informing Ed Silver what he thought about Arkansas foxes, Arkansas hounds, Arkansas hunters in general and especially Ash Flat hunters. "I've known Ed for twenty years. Why he'd even send a crate to ship Dewey in if I was to ask him." They finished at last, having made it plain that Dewey Fink was to be asked to come immediately, that Ed was to enclose expense money in his letter and that Samuel would repay him. "So that's it." Samuel laughed with relief. "Ed writes him a letter right away tellin' Dewey that they have decided on him as grand master of the hunt, spiritually speakin', that is. Full scale preachin' at the start and at the finish and spot prayers as required in between. Expenses, all he can eat, bench show, trials, and hound music for three nights runnin'. If that don't move him, dynamite won't."

"He'll move," Buck said from the kitchen as he got the skillet for lunch. "Over at your place he's only got two, and one not listening very closely. Down there he'll have a congregation."

"If you can help me as good with the rest of it as you did on that," Samuel answered, pasting a stamp on the envelope, "I'll begin to feel like there's a chance for beatin' this thing."

Over a lunch of fried doves and sliced tomatoes and onions in oil and vinegar and rice soaked brown with skillet drippings, Samuel described for Buck how Jeff had been acting. At least he tried to describe it, for he found that the words eluded him as his hands searched awkwardly through the empty air. "Seems like he's almost a little mad, sort of disappointed. I'll admit it's been ungodly hot and the huntin' poor and then that farm ain't just exactly what a man would drive two thousand miles to see. But you'd expect him to at least relax after awhile, even if he didn't like the place. It started right out the day after he got here." Samuel was in the act of helping himself from the skillet and now he held the bird before him on the fork, moving it up and down as though for emphasis. "I had a call to make at Four Corners, took him along, and by God that first day I could tell he was thinkin', 'Now these are a sorry bunch of people for old Pap to be tied up with.' I tell you he come out here lookin' for the real thing and ain't found nothin' but fool's gold—that's the way he acts."

"What do you think I can do?" Buck asked, raising his eyebrows a little.

"You can help me keep him here." Samuel paused in his chewing with his mouth half full and pointed his fork at Buck. "Show him the museum, take him to Indian dances, talk with him, anything. Just give me time to try and find out where he's at. Get him to stay till quail season. He's all I've got anymore, Hardin." These last words were uttered in a low, intense, appealing voice, and the grimness in the old man's face, seemingly just at the edge of despair, made Buck realize how deeply he must feel his estrangement from Jeff.

"But why do you ask me to do this? I've had no experience in these things. You know I've been alone most of my life." Buck felt a sudden desire to resist as though he sensed somehow that there were grave risks in his becoming involved with the boy.

"Because you can talk to him, that's why. He might listen to you, and there's damn sure nobody else around here he's gonna listen to. I just want to keep him here a little longer—long enough to where we've had a fair chance to git back together. Then if he wants to leave, well," and he moved his hands in a gesture of resignation.

They ate for a while without saying anything. Presently Buck pushed his plate away and sat back in his chair, his eyes narrow and meditative and his face set. "All right," he said, "I'll do what I can. But there's this much about it; I want you to remember that you asked me. If anything should go wrong, I want it straight between us that I only got into this because you wanted it that way."

"Things can't go much worse than they are right now," Samuel replied. "I'm askin' you because I need help."

Buck nodded quickly, almost impatiently. "Good enough. The Chetopa are dancing outside of Rock Springs a week from Friday. If we have any luck Dewey will be long gone by then."

"I've got to be over there that morning. Why don't we meet at the drugstore and then you two can go on to the dance." Samuel was speaking carefully now, for he had sensed a kind of strained reluctance in Buck which he had not been prepared for. It seemed strange that Hardin should have any hesitation about a thing like this, and yet his face had all at once grown hard and wary. "I don't aim to put you to any trouble about—"

"It's not that." Buck frowned, and then when he had looked intently at Samuel for a moment he smiled crookedly and rubbed his hand along his jaw. "There won't be any trouble. Why I'm going to take care of him so good that he's liable to be around here the rest of his life."

"I'll tell you for sure," Samuel said, his eyes wide and candid, "there could be just a whole lot of things worse than that. I might not live to see it but I reckon I'd rest a damn sight easier, wherever I was at."

The day was well gone and the rain had stopped when Samuel sloshed back through the mud to get on the horse again. "Anybody with sense woulda drove his car," he said, "but this thing's been turnin' me ever' way but loose. I kinda feel like I might sleep right tonight for a change." He leaned down from the saddle and took Buck's hand. "I appreciate it, Hardin. You know that."

"A week from Friday, then," Buck said, and Samuel turned the horse toward the gate.

On his way back to the house Buck picked up some wood and he soon had the fire leaping far up the back wall of the chimney. The house seemed more cheerful when the fire was bright and noisy and right now he felt that he needed all the cheer he could find. He poured a Scotch and settled himself at the typewriter to catch up on his correspondence concerning the museum. An hour went slowly by, then another, and finally he gave it up. He had done five letters, none of them really satisfactory, for he could not clear his mind of the echoes of his talk with Samuel. He heated some soup and ate it by the fireside, wondering what he had let himself in for. Any other time, perhaps, it would not have mattered so much, but now he needed what little time and strength were left to him for the museum. For it was all he had, his life had come to ripeness in it, and he would live by it or not at all. Then too, the long heat of summer and the news he had received in Kansas City had so blunted the edges of his will, so loosened the tension of his being, that he was not sure he could spare the effort, no matter how important this might be to Samuel. It was after all not a question of judging dogs or repairing a gun or hitting a deer squarely when the shadows lay dark or even assessing the value of a ranch. He had done these things before and done them well but this had to do with a man and his grandson, and Buck felt beyond his depth walking into the life of a boy young enough to be his son. Perhaps it was the pain that he feared most, the inevitable thrust of loneliness that must come no matter how he fought it. It seemed grimly ironic to engage himself in bringing Samuel and Jeff together when the contrast with his own life was so plain.

And yet as these thoughts flowed in confusion through his mind, one recollection stood solid as an island in the flood. For he owed a debt to Samuel, a debt that he would be paying on as long as he might live. It had all started while he still owned the bank and Samuel's boys were making arrangements through him to buy the farm for the old man. He had been struck with Samuel the first time he met him and then he began to hear stories

96

about him, how Samuel had gone bankrupt at least three times and how he had left his family strung out behind him from here to Tennessee as he had sought whatever country might remain where a man might hunt foxes to his heart's content without having to bother too much about his daily bread. The bankruptcy itself would not have signified much in a place like this where it just seemed the sporting thing to do every three or four years; it was the reason for it that made the difference, because it was not on account of women or drink or cards or horses but hounds, long-eared, lean-bellied hounds voiced like first-class revivalist preachers. And foxes, too; it was known that he brought them in from Tennessee at some considerable expense and stocked the hills with them and wouldn't mind at all sighting in on anyone who harmed them in the least way. And then preachers; any man of the Gospel could have a meal or lodging on him at any time with a little donation to boot, and the privilege was freely employed. Every tent show in the area made Grey Horse and Samuel was usually in one of the front chairs, singing off key in his powerful voice and watching with approval as the sinners came forward to lay down their burden of sin. It was hounds, foxes, and preachers in something like that order which did him in, and because of this unreasonable combination many people in Grey Horse thought and said that the old man was a little off. Yet for the fox hunters, whether farmers or merchants or glad-handing politicians or even domino players enjoying squatters' rights in the back room of the pool hall, he was the flesh-and-blood embodiment of the freedom, the independence, the devotion to the cause which they had always yearned for and would never have. And amidst the jibes and the adulation walked this tall, strangely saintly, long-faced man whose idea of heaven must have been mainly a good hickory-wood fire which never went out and wooded country with plenty of running room and ground that was always fresh and a little moist and foxes with the hearts of stallions and the craft of Satan and then beyond all the hounds with voices like the trumpets of judgment day.

But Buck had seen him in a somewhat different light. In those years he lived in Grey Horse, running the bank which he had inherited at his father's death. He had been glad to return to the town, and along with the bank he had been bequeathed as vice president a spare, immaculate, righteous Scotch Presbyterian named MacGregor who had known more about finance at the age of ten than Buck would know on his deathbed and who had effected Buck's absorption into the bank without so much as a change in his habitual dour expression. It did not take long to discover that MacGregor had been directing the bank for years and fully intended to continue in this capacity. So Buck talked amiably with the customers, in whom the Scotchman took little interest, and spent the days pleasantly enough at his desk in the quiet, cool, marble-floored building which housed the Citizens Bank of Grey Horse. He had what seemed to him a good post of observation and he soon had reached a frank and easy footing of familiarity with ranchers and Indians and business people whose names he remembered from far back or who in some cases had been the friends of his youth. Being alone as he was he had the time to work in various ways for the projects of the town and particularly for the tribe, and by middle age he was known as a useful, accepted member of the community, living much the same life as that of his associates except for the long hunting trips which he had never given up and the library in the family house in town to which he had retired every evening. It had been a great change from the wandering years of his early manhood, but there were other changes yet to come.

One night he had found in an unused room of the house some dusty, moth-ravaged, stuffed birds which brought with sudden nostaligia to his mind the memory of the taxidermy course which he had taken by correspondence from Denver when he was still a boy. The next day he left the bank early and drove out to the site of the old ranch house. Leaving the car on the county road he walked through the blackjacks and bluestem grass until he came to the clearing where the house had stood. It was prairie again; the only trace of the house where he had been born was a low, broken, stone foundation almost hidden from sight in the weeds. He found a wagon tongue and an old wheel and a corroded iron crowbar; not far from the crumbling stone rectangle the bleached skull of a steer lay partially buried in the ground. He stood there in the sunlight listening as though he might hear the old familiar voices, and then the past came back to him so sharply that his legs felt unsteady beneath him. He closed his eyes and held the back of his hand to his forehead as the day dissolved into shimmering scenes of all that had gone, and as he trembled there in the wind of his remembering he realized how swiftly the years had passed him by.

His journey that afternoon had been in some ways a beginning, and an end as well. For he found himself now no longer content with the simple round of obligations and pleasures through which his life had moved. An urgent voice had called to him from the shadowed regions of his past, a voice that had seemed to speak for the generations of men which lay behind him. He had the strange sense of a duty to perform and yet he had been at a loss to know what he must do. It was just at this time that he first met Samuel and the old fox hunter had struck him at once as a man who had found what he wanted and had taken it without hesitation, a man who could die with some measure of peace because he had lived to the sound of his own particular music. And because of this Buck began to spend time with him, calling him over to his desk whenever Samuel came into the bank and finally joining him in the nightly ritual of the hunt, the two of them sitting beside a small fire with a bottle passing back and forth while the baying of the hounds was interspaced with slow talk that crossed and recrossed the years which lay behind. Their conversations were not unlike the questing of the dogs in that they too pursued a quarry which they never caught. Often the trails of their thought grew cold or faded in the empty hush of night but their talk went on, whether bemused or laughing or simply the sound of a mind backtracking along the paths of the past.

Then one night Samuel told Buck that he thought it was time to try a new location. "I picked it out yesterday morning—walked some with the dogs just to get the feel of the place. It looks likely and we've plumb wore out those foxes south of town."

"I've got an idea I know where we're going," Buck said after they had driven along the county road for a while. "There's only one real good rise in the ground in this part of the country—at least where there's trees and water."

"I thought I'd surprise you," Samuel said. "You knew about it all the time."

"I'm kind of hard to surprise out this way. I told you I grew up here."

"Yeah. Well, let's hope there's some fox. It's a mighty nice piece of land; I can say that for it."

When they were settled by the fire Buck told him where the ranch house had been and how many head of cattle they had run, turning through the firelight all the facets of his old life here where the two ridges rose in crests above the prairie and the blackjacks stood grotesque against the sky. Samuel listened, occasionally nodding and spitting into the fire, and presently he looked over at Buck, his eyes squinting through the shadows and his lips curved in a half smile.

"Seems like whenever we git squatted down by a fire you always end up talkin' about this place."

"I suppose I do." Buck smiled. "It's been on my mind some."

"I kinda figured you was turnin' somethin' over."

"Oh, I don't know. I've had a crazy idea that I'd like to move back here."

"Build, you mean?"

"Yeah," Buck said eagerly. "I know just where I'd put it. There's a point right over there on that other ridge— I'd put the place just a couple of hundred yards up the ridge from it. Wouldn't have to be much—one big room, a kitchen, maybe a screened porch on front. Big fireplace, of course—I'd have to dig for water—and built out of fieldstone, heavy walls and a thick floor. Tornado proof."

"Sounds like you been doin' some close thinkin'."

Buck looked out through the darkness toward the ridge and then stirred the fire with his boot. "Thinking's cheap. I've got the time to do a lot of it."

"Why think about it so much?" Samuel said, shrugging his shoulders. "Grab the bear by the ass is what I say."

"I can't pull out of the bank that way. I've got commitments—"

"You've got a big desk and a soft chair and a good shady place to talk. That dried-up Scotchman runs the damned show. Make the poor bastard happy—sell out to him for ten bucks less than it's worth and he'll live on the kick of it the rest of his life."

"I wish it was that easy," Buck answered, leaning against the tree and putting his hands together behind his head.

"Now look," Samuel said, taking the cowhorn from his belt and pointing it at Buck. "You and I aren't too far apart in this deal. I don't have nothin' much in the way of people—neither do you. Nobody's gonna look out for what I want but me; same goes for you. Either you do it, or you think about it. And you'll go right on thinkin' about it till you die, feelin' sorrier for yourself every day. There's plenty o' birds in town takin' care o' that part o' the Maker's plan, Hardin; you're too good a man to waste. Come on out here where the wind can git to you

101

before it's crossed somebody else's back yard. But there's no use of me preachin' at you. If you want it enough, you'll come, and if you don't, what the hell difference does it make."

He had wanted it all right and as Samuel had said, he had come. He had never forgotten what those nights by the fire had meant to him, and he knew that much of what he now had he owed to the sympathy and the wisdom of the old man. The time had come for repayment, unexpectedly as he should have known it would, and he thought suddenly of how much had become involved with the dancing at Rock Springs. White Eagle had asked him to be there, and now Samuel, both for strangely similar reasons. A remnant of forgotten Indians in dyed long underwear and gaudy feathers and a tinkling of cheap ornaments, dancing to the drums of their extinction beneath a pitiless sky. It was a poor instrument at best on which to sound a song of affirmation.

CHAPTER VI

☐ "Dewey's so proud he's near 'bout to bust," Samuel said as he and Jeff drove along the road to Rock Springs. "Why he'll be so swelled up, time he gits to Little Rock they'll have to poke a hole in him before he can make it off that bus."

They had brought Dewey Fink to the bus station that morning, where with his letter from Ed Silver in one hand and a shiny black tin suitcase in the other he had padded importantly up to the cage of the ticket seller.

"One way to Ash Flats, Arkansas, please sir," he had announced with the solemn and rumbling tone that he employed to make announcements from the pulpit. One of two men sleeping in the back of the room pushed the hat from his eyes and stretched a little on the bench.

"To where?" the ticket seller asked, thrusting his sallow face at Dewey with an expression of pained disbelief.

Samuel leaned over Dewey's shoulder. "Man wants to go to Ash—" he began confidentially but Dewey's majestic voice drowned him out.

"You don't appear to hear any too good, friend. Ash Flats, Arkansas."

After a few minutes of confused roaring during which both men in the back sat up hurriedly and straightened their hats on their heads, Samuel succeeded in convincing the man in the cage that Dewey's destination was in fact the town which he had mentioned.

103

"Can I help it if the goddamn place ain't even on the map?" the man said with weary scorn.

"One of the biggest little cities in Arkansas," Dewey declared to the room in general and then stood staring with his oblique, owllike expression at the two men as though he expected them to chorus "Amen." He had time for a Coke and a sack of peanuts before the Little Rock bus came in, and just as he got aboard he turned and put his hand on Samuel's shoulder.

"Samuel," he had said gravely, "there wouldn't have no less reason been able to pull me away from your place before quail season, anyway. The way I figure, it was a call. The Lord He works in mysterious ways and when He talks, this man's got to listen. Don't get worried now if the wind starts blowin' up in a day or two—that'll be me over in Ash Flats. I'm gonna preach them hounds to a standstill."

"Yeah," Samuel said again now, raising his voice above the car engine after he had whistled a few bars of a hymn. "He's puffed up like a toad. But I reckon it's quite a honor at that. Only thing that bothers me in the deal is that he might put the spirit in them Ash Flat hounds to the point where they can just leave them there heathen dogs o' mine in the dust. Dewey's tricky that way—any man who can talk in tongues can do about anything he puts his mind to. Dewey claims it's all mind power, anyway—just gittin' his mind over the top of the other fella's, more or less like a lid."

"Well, he ought to be a pretty even match for a fox hound." Jeff yawned. "I'm afraid I didn't understand Mr. Dewey Fink very well. His mental powers escaped me for some reason." He still felt numb, still seemed to hear the sonorous droning of Fink's interminable monologues. Of the last week and a half he could remember nothing clearly except the sound of the man's voice, rolling on inexorably as the sea. By the middle of Fink's stay, Jeff had passed beyond mere boredom into a state of mental and physical lethargy wherein he slept the days away open-eyed, motionless, transfixed by the weight of the preacher's presence. Life had moved with painful slowness from kitchen to porch to bed to kitchen again, and all night long the house had seemed to echo softly with the rolling of Fink's talk that ground on steadily as a mill wheel. Twice Jeff had risen from his chair with the desperation of a swimmer lunging up toward the air. He had saddled Carl with fumbling and eager hands and had ridden hopefully over to Buck's but the yard had been empty the first time and on the next visit a faded red pickup truck was parked before the gate. Jeff had sat his horse anxiously for a while, looking for some sign of movement in the little stone house, and then he had turned and followed the dusty road back to the farm. And submerged as he had been in the heat and isolation he had suddenly realized that the hopes which had brought him all this way had gradually withered and that he was staying on not out of belief or desire or even obligation but simply because he lacked the courage to tell Samuel that he must go. He had decided finally that he would have the satisfaction of outlasting Fink and that then he would tell the old man as gently as he was able. But as he rode along this morning on what he imagined would be almost his last day with Samuel, he wondered if there were any way to say it without pain. Then it occurred to him that he should ask Buck about it at the dance that afternoon, for if anyone could foretell how Samuel might react, Buck would be the man.

Rock Springs had all the finality of a dust-swept, wind-scored skeleton bleaching beneath a desert sun. At the edge of town stood the gutted remains of a building that must once have been a garage. Weeds grew tall around it, stretching up toward window frames long emptied of glass, and at the front a sign, anonymous with rust, creaked in the wind. It was empty except for the weeds which had broken up through the concrete floor. Beyond this ruin was the crossroads where the dirt highway intersected the one street of the town. Here the buildings still stood, their windows shattered or boarded over, their sandstone sides covered with the faded remains of advertisements for movies or snuff or feed or politicians. Halfway down the street was the drugstore, a building little different from the square two-storied structures that flanked it save that a freshly painted sign hung in front, advertising Coca-Cola. One car was parked against the curbing; the only other sign of life was a thin plume of dust that the wind had picked up from the street.

"There she is," Samuel said. He stopped for a moment at the crossroads, his hand resting on the gearshift, moving it slowly back and forth in neutral. "Rock Springs. That's the doc's car there in front of the drugstore. Town looks kinda slow, don't it."

Jeff smiled wryly. "Slow? I think dead's more the word for it."

"Aw, it picks up a little on Saturdays. Farmers come to town, those that ain't got the money or the car to make it to Grey Horse. I understand they get up some pretty fair domino games in back of the drugstore."

"I imagine. How in the world would a town ever get started in a god-forsaken place like this?"

Samuel shifted into low and turned onto the main street, driving past the buildings of the old business district toward a scattering of houses that had taken a tentative step into the prairie. "Well," he said, "I reckon most towns got started for the same reason. Somebody figured he could make some money. A wildcat well came in north of here, and the word got around like it always does that this was a big field. The smart boys come in to pick up the money, and when the oil didn't just pop up outa the ground like they figgered it would, then they had to get busy and do somethin' to make other people come on so's they, the first ones, the smart boys who've always got the deal figgered cold, could get out from under. So they build some buildings and lay out the lots nice and even and sell the deeds reg'lar and legal and when they're clear, they just pack up the extry shirt they always carry and clean out. And then there ain't nothin' for the others to do save to try and make a go of it, seein' that they've gone so far as to build houses and elect mayors and the rest of it. I don't guess Rock Springs came to be on account of anyone much wantin' it to be; it just sorta started rollin' and they wasn't nobody knew how to stop her. Wonder where that eat house is at, anyway? Why don't we go there for lunch after we see Missus Parmalee, that is if the danged fool who runs it hasn't already come to his senses and got the hell out."

"Sure," Jeff said. "Maybe this fellow's starting the whole thing over again; maybe he's figuring on catching it the second time around."

"Jeff," Samuel said, "I think you'd fit real well around here. You got a mind for this country. That may be just exactly what the poor sonofabitch is thinkin' o' doin'." Then he leaned to the window and spat his cud into the street. "That's Missus Parmalee on the porch," he said, motioning toward the house with his head.

Samuel stopped the car before a dwelling that at first glance might have been any of the houses that Jeff had seen in Four Corners. A narrow concrete walk ran from the curbing to the porch, and then three concrete steps led up to the door. But there was something different about this house, something which removed it from the others even though in appearance it seemed to have been cast in the same simple mold. Jeff sensed this at once, but it was difficult to tell just where the difference lay. There was a trellis on one side of the porch to which a vine clung, somewhat withered and brown but a vine, nonetheless. He noticed also that there were two umbrella trees in the yard, evenly spaced on either side of the walk. They were trimmed, and the ground at their roots had been turned. The grass, like all the other grass that he had seen here, was pale and yellowish, but it did not straggle. It had been recently cut, and there was a kind of defiance in its very neatness. The lawn, if one could call it that, ended precisely at a tiny trough which bordered the walk; it was apparent that the grass there had been trimmed by hand. Throughout the yard there was a grim kind of order, seemingly exaggerated and incredible because of the chaos that surrounded it.

Jeff could see Mrs. Parmalee through the vines. She was seated in a porch swing, motionless, leaning forward a little as though she were peering at them through the network of leaves and trellis and twisted stalk. When they got out of the car she leaned back and the swing began to move and Jeff could hear the faint creak of the chains as he and Samuel walked up to the porch. Midway up the walk, the old man had removed his hat and he held it before him now in both hands, bending forward a little from the waist, his hair gray and thin and shining in the sun above the shadowed hollows in his face. There was something almost courtly in his manner.

"Missus Parmalee?" he said.

"Good morning, Mr. Beecher."

"I'd like to present my grandson, Missus Parmalee. This is Jeff Beecher."

Jeff saw her get up from the swing and he knew that she was coming to offer her hand. He went up the steps and took it. "I'm happy to know you, Mrs. Parmalee," he said.

She nodded, looking at him with eyes that watered in the severe light. Then she turned to Samuel. "You should have let me know that you were planning to bring company, Mr. Beecher."

"I guess I should've at that," Samuel said apologetically. "I never thought."

Jeff looked at her as she talked, noticing how her gently wrinkled face was covered with a fine, almost invisible down. In her aged features, and particularly in the long and sensitive and slightly clefted nose, there was ebbing strength, feeling worn a little threadbare, and a dignity that seemed the residuum of long endurance. There was weariness in the slow movements of her body,

108

in the tightness of her smile. Jeff wondered how long she had lived here alone.

"I've got my list in the house," she was saying to Samuel. "You men make yourself comfortable here on the porch and I'll go in and get it."

As she opened the door, Jeff noticed how the skin hung loose at her elbow beneath the short sleeve of her dress. It was a silk dress, full-skirted, in which her body seemed large and soft and shapeless. She was still carrying a fan in one hand.

"How long has she been here?" he asked, turning to look at Samuel.

"I couldn't rightly say, boy. But it's been a good many years." His voice was quiet, remote, suddenly lonely.

And somehow it seemed fitting that Samuel could assign her no definite place in time. For she was of an older way, an older tradition, isolate now beyond the reach of years. When she had returned with the list and Samuel had procured for her the few articles which she desired, the three of them sat on the porch for a while and talked. Jeff felt her remoteness in the very manner of her speech. It was not in anything that she said or in any failing of graciousness; her attention did not waver nor did she show the least sign of indifference. But there was a faint smile which remained on her face throughout the conversation, and as she talked she had a way of looking to one side across the prairie while her old hands smoothed imagined wrinkles in her dress. It was as though she were savoring the moment through her memory, as though Jeff and Samuel were simply players, unimportant in themselves but useful in bringing back scenes of other porches, other conversations, other days.

Nothing much was said. It was a simple, slow-moving exchange of words, somewhat formal and highly localized. They spoke of the weather, of previous summers, of Mrs. Parmalee's last journey to Grey Horse, of the activities of the District Seven farm women. Then after a time they grew silent. Mrs. Parmalee gazed out across the prairie, bemused, her hands working gently across her dress. Finally she turned to Jeff. "You've come a long way, haven't you, son. Mr. Beecher says you've come visiting. Will you be staying long?" Her faded eyes were faintly quizzical, and the smile still rested on her lips. To Jeff it semed that she was smiling tolerantly upon him, almost as though he were a small boy. He hardly knew how to answer her, partly because her expression still seemed detached and far away, and partly because her question aroused a peculiar anxiety within him.

"A while longer," he said hesitantly. "I haven't really made any plans." He glanced quickly at Samuel but the old man's face was without expression.

Mrs. Parmalee smiled and nodded and then she began to pick up the articles which Samuel had brought from the car. "I guess you'll be wanting to get on toward home now, won't you," she said quietly. "You've quite a piece to go for lunch."

"We thought we might eat here in town," Samuel said, getting up. "I heard that there was a lunch counter opened up; know anything about it?"

"I've seen it," she said. "It's just north of town. I always eat here at home, so I couldn't tell you about the food. Doc Aiken tells me that it's a young man that's opened it." Then she turned to Jeff and took his hand, holding it firmly while she looked with the same questioning expression into his eyes, searching his face as though she knew all the time that she would not find there what she sought. "Good-by, son. Come again when you can. We don't get many visitors here any more."

And suddenly, holding her wrinkled hand and looking into her pale eyes, Jeff was aware of the same feeling that always came over him at Christmas as he walked past the cold, gray figure of someone ringing a bell before a donation box. "Your yard," he said awkwardly, "you've done an awfully good job with it. I hope you get some rain."

110

For a moment her face bloomed. She smiled, even laughing a little, soundlessly. "There'll be rain," she said. "There always has been before. Most people never notice."

As they got into the car, she was standing on the porch watching them. They turned around at the end of the street, using the weed-choked driveway of an abandoned house, and she was still standing on the porch, waving, shading her eyes against the sun when they drove past again. Jeff looked back at her through the rear window and watched the dust roll up from the road to mingle with the colorless grass. Then he saw her drop her hand and disappear into the house.

"She's gone to get the broom," Samuel said.

"What?"

"The broom. She's gone inside to get it so's she can sweep the porch."

"Because of the dust?"

"Yeah."

"God," Jeff said softly. He turned in the seat now, hoping to see her once again sitting in the swing, fanning herself, looking out across the prairie. He wanted anything but the image of her working against the inexorable drifting of the dust. But the house was out of sight; barren sandstone buildings cut off his view. "If there were only something she could look forward to—just grass or a few flowers—anything." He stared at the dust-palled town, at the gaunt emptiness, at a silence so final and complete that it seemed visible, tangible. The street was bone clean, devoid of life so that there was not even paper to lift limply in the wind and scud along the borders of the road. They passed the one car, which seemed now to Jeff like a hulk left stranded by a receding sea, and then they were once again at the crossroads.

"She said that bird was on the road north of town, didn't she?" Samuel said, turning onto the highway.

"I think she did," Jeff answered listlessly. He could no

longer feel any sense of anticipation, even about meeting Buck that afternoon; his only desire at the moment was to leave the town as far behind as possible.

"Well, let's look in on him. I still cain't hardly believe it, and I wouldn't feel right comin' all the way over here without seein' it with my own eyes."

They found the place almost at once. In the high hard light of noon it glittered like burnished steel, a small, precise square box of a building which had the appearance of having been ejected from some metallic womb. It sat starkly alone on the edge of the sandstone waste, but it had none of the despair of the rest of the town. Rather it appeared brash, cocksure, almost pitilessly invulnerable. It seemed impossible that its large glass exposures could ever be shattered, that its spotless gleam could in any way be sullied.

Samuel stopped the car in front of it and sat for a moment staring. "I'll be goddamned," he said finally, with a grudging note of respect in his voice. Then he shook his head and looked over at Jeff. "Well," he said, "I cain't rightly say I believe it, but there the sonofabitch is. I just got to go in now."

The jukebox was playing when they pushed open the swinging door, and immediately Jeff was reminded of the music that he had heard that first day in the lobby of the State Hotel. There was the same heavy beat, the same bent, metallic guitar notes, the same high twanging voice. But now the sound seemed to enclose him like liquid, especially after the silence of the street. A gray-faced man was seated behind the counter. He had on a white shirt with the sleeves rolled up to the elbows, and on his head was a stiffly starched white cap. As they sat down on the stools before the counter, Jeff saw him grind his cigarette and lay aside the western that he was reading. Then he adjusted his rimless glasses and walked over to where they sat, picking up two menus as he came. He smiled rapidly at them, nodded, and began wiping the spotless counter with a rag which he held clenched in his hand.

"Howdy, gents. What can I do you for?"

The glasses distorted his eyes so that they seemed large and vague, and his thin lips narrowed to a line around his teeth.

"Got any water?" Samuel asked.

"Water? You betcha."

Jeff watched him fill the glasses from a gleaming faucet at the far end of the room, and looking at his face as he returned with the water, he wondered how old the fellow was. His expression was one of almost calculated blankness, notwithstanding the smile that remained fixed on his face; he seemed the kind of person that age would not mark until it came upon him all at once with terrible and irrevocable finality.

"Hamburgers, chili, hot beef, barbecued pork? Anything you want, gents."

"Hamburger," Jeff said. "And coffee."

"You make it kinda hard on a man with all them choices," Samuel said. "That chili fresh?"

"Yessir."

"Gimme the chili."

Samuel rolled a cigarette and the counter man tossed a patty of meat on the griddle and began flattening it with his spatula. Jeff watched him absently, unable to erase from his mind the image of the lonely street and of the old woman, probably seated again now in the porch swing, moving slowly back and forth, gently fanning herself. He lit a cigarette and sat staring before him at his glass, turning it little by little with his fingers. Something seemed to be pressing in against him, and at last he realized that it was silence. The jukebox had stopped. Then he began to hear the faint sputter of grease.

"Been open long?" Samuel was leaning forward, his elbows on the counter and his face cupped in his hands.

"Ten days is all."

"You mean to tell me it's taken you ten whole days?"

"Ten whole days for what?" The man turned around and looked at Samuel, still holding the spatula so that the grease began to drip unnoticed to the floor.

"Ten days to find out they ain't no people in this town."

"Oh, that," the man said. Then he turned back to the griddle.

"Don't tell me somebody's talkin' up oil round here again," Samuel said. "If it's gold, or diamonds maybe, all right, but not oil."

"Who said anybody was talkin' about oil?"

"Well, maybe I'm the one that's off. I just kinda figgered that when a man opened hisself a eat house that he might be countin' on somebody stoppin' in ever so often. Just to keep things from gittin' slow, you might say."

The man put the dishes in front of them and leaned back against the counter. He was still smiling, and now he began picking his teeth with satisfaction. Behind the blur of the glasses it was difficult to tell whether or not his eyes were amused. "Mister," he said, "you people up here sure are slow on gettin' the idea. Didn't you ever hear of Kansas?"

Samuel looked over at Jeff. "Man here wants to know did I ever hear of Kansas."

"That's right. They had an election up in Kansas. State went wet. That mean anything?"

"You mean that a man can buy whiskey from the politicians now instead of from his friends."

"I mean right here I'm twelve miles from Kansas—that road out there will take everybody in this part of the state up to the border. This is the only real eating place for fifty miles either way, so—" and he spread his hands in simple illustration.

"So that's it." Samuel was silent until he had finished his chili and then he pushed the bowl across the counter. "Happen to have an extra toothpick on you? Much obliged." He sat there picking his teeth, watching Jeff finish the last of his coffee. After a while he turned back to the counter man. "How much do we owe you?"

"Sixty cents."

Samuel put the change on the counter and got up. "All set, boy?"

"All ready."

Samuel settled his hat carefully on his head. "Say, mister," he said. "You wouldn't happen to come from down around Oklahoma City, would you?"

"That's right," the man said. "Why?"

"Oh, I just wondered. Capital's about the only place I know of where folks git worked up about such things. And you know somethin'? You could go Kansas one better. You could start sellin' the stuff yourself. You'd do a helluva lot more business, I'll guarantee you. Well, see you next week if you're still around."

Back outside again Jeff shaded his eyes and looked at the shattered skeleton of the town. Upon it the sun fell in all its bright fury and through the gaping buildings the wind roamed like a ghost.

"Ain't he a damned fool, though," Samuel said.

Jeff was silent for a moment. "Well, who knows— maybe he'll make some money. That's what he wants, and perhaps he's right about the road. Probably there are people who'll be going up to wherever it is in Kansas." He felt the need to contradict the old man on something, even on this when he knew that Samuel was right. For he had had his fill of Samuel's easy assurance, of being shown to and explained to and guided about like a child. "The place can't stay the same forever."

"Aw hell, boy. He ain't got sense enough to come in outa the rain. Well, let's see." Samuel pulled out his watch and looked at it. "Close on to one. We oughta be gittin' over to the drugstore. I told Hardin we'd meet him there."

"There's no need for you to wait around. He'll be along pretty soon; you go ahead."

115

Samuel stood in the road and looked at him for a moment as though he were not sure what he should do. "All right," he said at last. "You know where the store's at. Just wait for him there." He nodded his head and yet he seemed to hesitate. Finally he got into the car and backed slowly into the street. "You wait for him at the store, now," he repeated, leaning out the window. "I reckon I'll see you tonight. Take care of yourself."

"Sure." Jeff waved to him and watched the car until it was out of sight. The dust settled back into the road, and now the only movement was the glance of sunlight from the drugstore sign, which creaked a little in the wind. He started for the store, and the noise of his shoes against the broken board walk was startling. He stepped off into the street and went on through the yellow dust. High above him he could see a buzzard circling the sky.

When he got to the drugstore he sat down on a bench just outside the door. He lit a cigarette, and the smoke was dry and hot against his tongue.

"Anything I can do for you, bud?"

Jeff looked up quickly; the man's face was dim against the screen door. "I'm just waiting for someone."

"Yeah. This is the kind of place a man can wait a mighty long time in. Come inside if it gets too hot for you; fall never did amount to a helluva lot around here."

"Thanks," Jeff said. "I may take you up on it."

"Stays awful hot for awful long; I never saw the place that could tie it for sun. I put in some time in east Texas, some in Louisiana. This place beats 'em all, when it comes to just plain hot."

Jeff nodded and looked at his watch. Buck should have been here by now; he wondered what was keeping him.

"Fella gets around a lot followin' the fields comin' in. It's a lot like throwin' dice, and I just kinda crapped out when my turn came along. You ain't from around here, are you, bud?"

"No, I'm not," Jeff said. "Have you got the right time in there anywhere?"

116

"Let's guess," the man said. "Go ahead."

"I was supposed to meet somebody here—"

"You go ahead and be first."

"O.K.," Jeff laughed dryly. "Quarter of two."

"Nope. Almost exactly one-thirty."

Jeff turned around and looked at him.

"I kinda have it down to a science, you might say. I've practiced at it for pretty close onto fifteen years."

It was hard to see him through the screen, but his voice was plaintive and lonely.

"I can tell by them shadows in the road—you really didn't have much of a chance."

"Guessing never was a strong point of mine," Jeff answered, turning back again toward the light. He rubbed his hand against the back of his neck and stared at the empty road.

It was as though time had suddenly ceased, as though there would be no more movement or change. He had never felt more utterly alone, and somehow now he was not even particularly concerned.

"Have you got anything cold to drink in there?"

"Got some good, cold three-point-two beer, made in the state."

"I think I'll have some," Jeff said, getting up. He no longer cared whether Buck came or not, and he was sorry that the engagement had ever been made. But in a way, this fittingly completed the fiasco which his stay here had been—it would not take him long now to pack his bags.

"Good and cold," the man said, putting the bottle in front of Jeff. "Mind if I sit down?"

"Go ahead." His cigarette tasted better with the beer. He held out the pack.

"Thank you, no. Tell you how I come to give it up." His face was narrow and pointed and his cheeks were hollow where the teeth were gone. He leaned forward when he spoke, and his voice was low-pitched and confidential and a little incredulous, as though he were won-

117

dering at the mystery of what he was saying. "Smoked, chewed, dipped snuff, all of it; two, three, four packs of cigarettes a day, cigars one after another—never used a pipe only because it was too slow. I did it all. One day I went to church for a joke; had a big revival goin' and a preacher they said really made God move under that tent. I was known to be a man that no preacher could touch, so they kidded me into goin'. When he come up to the pulpit, he looked at us all for awhile before he said anything. Then he rared back and let 'er go. 'Come let us reason together.' I'll never forget it. He hollered it three times, and the third time around I jumped a foot in the air and ran for the altar. I felt like there was tobacco smoke blowin' out of every pore in my body. He got me plumb good, and there wasn't any two ways about it. I knowed I was had."

"So you gave it up," Jeff said.

"I gave it up. Let me bring you another. And by the way, around here they call me Doc."

Before it was over Jeff had learned the life story of Mrs. Parmalee, the history of Oklahoma, the best way to find oil, the inside story of the First World War as well as of the World Series of '19, and hymns without number. He remembered that much, plus a discussion of the after-life which he didn't remember too well. Somewhere along the line Doc had brought out some white lightning which he proudly assured Jeff was guaranteed to be not over thirty days old, and when Jeff went outside to the privy for the third time he knew that it was late, that he was drunk, and that he had been going to an Indian dance that afternoon. And as he told Doc, if there was one thing he knew about himself, it was that he was dependable.

"It's a fair walk," Doc said. "You're sure you want to go?"

"Yessir."

So Doc put him on the road and pointed out the direc-

118

tion he was to take. Jeff didn't remember just how he got there, except that cars kept passing him going the other way, making him choke with their dust. It was almost dark when he found the place, a big, round building in the center of a field. Some people were watching him as he came across the uneven ground toward them, and he tried his best to walk straight and upright. He was blinking his eyes rapidly and breathing hard and when he tried to talk the words seemed to knot in his mouth. He recognized the people as Indians and one of them, an old man with his hair in braids to his shoulders and a hat that was very tall on his head, seemed to understand what he was saying. At least he nodded when Jeff repeated Buck's name and Jeff felt the painful clutch of fingers on his arm. Through the blur before him he strove to see the old man's eyes when suddenly the earth tilted violently beneath him and he knew that he was falling a long, long way.

Buck had just finished dressing that morning and was standing at the stove in the kitchen when he heard the frightened squawking of the chickens out beyond the fence. From the way they sounded he figured that it was a hawk and that maybe he would still have time. He seized the twelve-gauge from the rack and ran out the door into the still, clear light of morning and was almost to the gate when the pain ripped through his chest. He staggered and fell into the fence and leaned there, gasping laboriously for air, hearing in his ears the choked and laboring pump of his heart while the day seemed to go dark around him. He was distantly aware of the frenzied movements of the setter and then gradually he sank to the ground until he lay twisted with pain in the cool and shadowy dust. It was not until the sun was high overhead and warm that he crawled brokenly back to the house while the dog half-whined, half-howled in fear. Somehow he managed to get into bed, and when he awoke again he was trembling in the late-afternoon chill. He sat up very carefully, gently rubbing his chest and arm; after a while he rose and made his way gradually to the kitchen. The hot beef broth seemed to strengthen him and presently he was able to light the fire which he had laid in the fireplace that morning. The attack had been a bad one; worse, he thought, than the others. So now it was simply a matter of waiting while they closed in on him until finally he would be in bed for good. In the shifting light of the fire he could see his guns standing against the wall, and he reflected with grim satisfaction that as long as they were in reach, he was still a free man. But how much longer would it be before he could not reach them, and how much longer would he have the strength to squeeze the trigger?

That evening he heard the pickup as it came along the road from the pasture and he knew that it was White Eagle by the way the loose fender was banging. He heard the car door slam and the creak of the gate and after a moment White Eagle was standing inside the door. He had his blanket around his shoulders and Buck knew that he had come straight from the dance. In White Eagle's face as he stood there was a dark and questioning silence.

"There was a boy at the dance asking for you," he said finally. "He's outside. You want to help me bring him in?"

Buck closed his eyes and gripped his hands along his legs. "That's Sam's boy. What's happened to him?"

"Nothing much," John replied. The firelight moved along his body and made him seem taller than he was. "He's just drunk and passed out."

"Drunk!" Buck stared at him for a moment as though he had not heard him, and then he tightened his jaw. "I can't help you, John. You'll have to bring him in by yourself."

White Eagle came up to the fire, bending over to look

120

into Buck's face. "What's the matter with you?" he asked softly. "You said you were coming to the dance. I watched for you all afternoon."

"I haven't felt right today, that's all," Buck answered brusquely. "Why don't you bring him in and put him to bed."

"You look bad in the face. Why don't you let me help you."

"To hell with that, John," Buck said savagely. "Get the boy in here where he can get some rest."

When Jeff was at last in bed, White Eagle sat down across from Buck by the fire. "It was good I was still there; he was pretty drunk. He came up the road from Rock Springs."

"I was supposed to meet him there," Buck said. "Where do you suppose he got the whiskey?"

"Man in the drugstore there—Doc Aiken—he makes the stuff. Sells it mostly to my people. This boy ain't the first one gone out on it." White Eagle reached up and touched his hat and turned his blunt face toward the fire. "Is there anything I can do for you?" he asked.

"You could drop by Sam's and tell him you came home with us—that Jeff is spending the night here with me. I wouldn't say anything more than that."

"No." Then he pointed to the twelve-gauge that he had leaned against the wall. "I found it out by the gate." When he stood up he reached into his pocket and put some shells on the mantel. "I better get on over to Sam's," he said.

Buck nodded. "I'll be coming in soon about the museum."

White Eagle stood for a while without speaking, looking down at the fire. "You can take care of yourself, I guess." His voice was deep and troubled.

"Certainly. And thanks for looking after the boy, John."

He sat for a long time after White Eagle left, thinking

how strangely complicated his life had become. And as he stared at the fire, he wondered suddenly what had made John decide to remove the shells from the shotgun, and just how much the old Indian had guessed of what was in his mind.

An expression of sleepy discomfort crossed Jeff's face as he raised himself slowly to his elbows and sat up. He fumbled alongside the bed for his shoes, found them, and as he began to pull them on he realized that he had no idea at all where he was. He recalled that he had sat for a long time in the drugstore and he winced now, thinking of how much he had drunk; after that he had walked on and on for what had seemed like hours; there had been the Indian standing in the doorway of the peculiar round building, and now this. He pressed his fingers against his aching forehead and looking around him he saw that he was sleeping on a screened-in porch that contained another bed beside his own, made and apparently unslept in, a saddle mounted on a sawhorse, a rusted scythe and a very worn and weathered steamer trunk. The concrete porch showed gray through the thin coat of green paint which had once covered it and the wall against which his bed stood was of fieldstone, rough and brown and massive. Then as he stood up to put on his crumpled shirt and pants he stopped for a moment, gazing out before him toward a valley filled and trembling with the flaming sun of dawning. Through the twisted silence of the blackjacks stood immense pillars of light and on the surface of the air the cry of a bluejay scraped like sandpaper. Jeff frowned at the familiarity of what he saw, and as his gaze swept down the valley he recognized the dark line of trees along the creek and then the lone blackjack stark as a many-armed divinity against the severe blue of the sky. He knew at once where he was and when he had finished dressing he lit a cigarette and pushed open the door to the main room of the house. The darkness blinded him momentarily and he started as the voice came to him from the far end of the room.

"I'm sorry I failed you."

The inflection was drawled and casual and Jeff knew the voice belonged to Hardin Buck. "I'm afraid that I'm the one," he began confusedly. "I hardly know what to say except that I'm awfully sorry about the whole thing."

"I think I was probably just suffering a bad case of indigestion; can't eat the way I used to. Well, yesterday we missed connections and today you're here. Why don't we leave it at that. And you're probably hungry." There was something direct and simple in his tone and Jeff was swept by a sudden sense of gratitude. Now that his eyes were more accustomed to the darkness of the room he could see Buck sitting in the chair by the fireplace, and he could tell that Buck was looking at him even though he could not see his face at all clearly. "I'm going to have to ask you to do the cooking this morning because I don't think I can make it—I'm a little weak in the legs yet and I'd just as soon let you do the honors."

"Fine." He welcomed the prospect of cooking breakfast as though by doing so he might make up for his lapse of the previous day. "If you'll tell me where things are—" he said eagerly.

"Call for whatever you need; I don't think you'll have trouble."

The kitchen was just as it had been on the day when he had sat here listening to Buck, watching him fry chicken. The memory of that afternoon came back to him with pleasure now as he lit the kerosene stove and heated the grease in the heavy black skillet.

"Do whatever's the easiest," Buck called.

"You name it," Jeff laughed. "I can take a crack at it any way you want."

"Scrambled, then, with just a touch of Worcestershire sauce. And not too dry."

"Coming up." He did it all slowly and carefully and as

123

well as he was able. It was a foolish thing to take pride in, perhaps, but just at this moment it seemed important. The toast might be a little cold and the coffee he could only pray about but the eggs—they were steaming and moist and filled with sunlight. Quickly then he carried the breakfast in on a tray, and set it on the table which Buck pointed out to him.

"It's right here by my chair. Just put it down—that's right—fine. Now for some light; there's a Venetian blind on that east window—if you'll just pull the rope out to the side and stop and then let go, she'll hold." Light seemed to flood into the room as though a dam had broken before it. Jeff turned with anticipation, smiling, and then for one terrible moment it was as though he had looked upon the face of death itself. Buck's eyes were stony and unblinking, the lines of his face were like wounds, and his head was the head of some ancient and proud and weathered man, graven in stone.

"There is no way that I can keep you here against your will," Buck said quietly, deliberately. "If your heart is set on going, I can't stop you. But if you go away now, feeling the way I think you feel, I will always remember you as a fool and worse. Because your grandfather is an old man and you are a very young one—both you and I owe him many things, but you more than I because you have his blood. If you leave now you'll be sorry for it the rest of your life. Stay. Stay until quail season, anyway. Give yourself a chance."

Jeff's eyes were on the floor and the tears that blurred his sight were hot and painful. "I don't know what to do about it. There's something standing in the way, something I just don't know how to handle. I can't see any—"

"I can help you. There are things I can tell you, things I can show you. I want you to promise you'll stay."

It seemed to Jeff that for the first time in as long as he could remember, someone was speaking words which winged their way straight to his heart. He nodded, and

124

when his voice came it was low and trembling. He pressed his hand against his eyes and then his face hardened. "All right. I'll stay until quail season. But I can't promise you any more than that."

"That's all I want." Buck smiled, holding out his hand. "What do you say to some breakfast."

PART TWO

So nous avons sçeu vivre constamment et tranquillement, nous sçaurons mourir de mesme.

Montaigne

CHAPTER VII

☐ Summer went out hard, lingering long into autumn so that the leaves dried and clattered in the wind and the grass stood stiff and sere across the plains. The mornings would be deceptively chill and then by noon the heat would be shimmering along the roads and the people would stand on their porches or in their front yards, watching for the sluggish coils of smoke on the horizon, smoke that meant somebody's grass was on fire. During this time there was always the feeling that the whole country might go up in one big burst of flame for it was bone dry and the angry clash of the leaves in the wind was ominous.

So the days bloomed and faded, ephemeral, weightless, unremembered. For there was no desire to hold fast to the arid present; rather, the mind leaped forward in anticipation to that bright morning when the frost would cling white and glittering to the grass and the sky would be more purely blue and the sun would gently rub the skin as though through depths of cool water. Then the blood raced and the trees rioted in crimson and yellow and through the quick dusk the moon moved with new majesty, burnt red and unbelievably fecund. And when the first frost finally came and the new wind made the air sharp and clean, Buck felt as though his life had somehow been renewed. Perhaps, as with the trees which stood resplendent now along the ridge, he was feeling no more than his own last shake of the fist against the approaching winter. Whatever it was he was glad for there were many things he had to do; yet at the same time he could not help feeling a certain regret as though he had seen the passing of summer for the last time.

So there were still things to take care of, details to set in order, before the current of his life might like some gradually slowing desert stream sink quietly back into the earth. There was the museum—almost finished now. It had been successively a vague idea, a dream, a piece of land high on a hill overlooking the town, then fieldstone and cement and oak beams and finally now almost a reality. It was built, and almost all of the paintings he wanted were finished and in it, and its cases held the clothing and the weapons and the art and in reality the history of a people and of a way of life, as much as such things could ever contain and reproduce the substance of life itself. It was a banner in the wind, a memorial to the heart's bootless and eternal yearning, a cry into the void saying we were here, too; we walked this earth and watched these skies and made the prairies thunder with our horses; we knew the tides of the blood, the seasons of the heart; and we wandered the ways of the earth. It was all these things and then beyond them something personal, for it had been his triumph, too, one fall at least in the match which each man had to wage, however blindly and instinctively, a triumph because this stone was beyond the clutch of death. And it was personal because it had been mortared with his own sweat and driven into being by his will.

Years earlier when he had owned the bank and had been a member of the tribal council, he had seen the signs of death in the faces of the Chetopa. Luckily or unluckily they had become rich, suddenly and overwhelmingly rich, they who had been driven off to the most unwanted land the government could locate only to have the land turn out to be, ironically enough, soaked in oil. There had been a flash flood of dollars then, and Grey Horse, a sleepy, sandstone, dirt-road-and-hitching-post kind of town, had been washed out. What they built in its place bore the same name, but it was another town. The lawyers flocked to it like buzzards to a fresh carcass, oil-field drifters made the streets loud with their brawling, and the tall, strong grace of the Chetopa rotted in the alcohol so that now they were grotesques, the hawk faces gone soft and fat and the muscled bellies bloated and not seldom the whole body a syphilitic wreckage. Many of the old men had remained aloof, remote from the rooting among the coin. But the young had been swept along on the whiskied tide of rotgut and easy women and the money that came effortlessly and without end.

From his office in the bank, Buck had had a ringside seat and what he had to watch had not been pleasant to look on. A group of people to whom he happened to belong by blood was passing from the earth, and whether it was from vanity or sympathy or love or perhaps all three, he could not help feeling that there must be some provision made for preserving whatever was left of the old life, for creating some memorial to what had once been. Finally one hot August afternoon in the agency building he had presented the idea to the council. Even as he talked, he knew that they did not understand what he was saying. They moved the eagle-feather fans before their faces and sat impassive, staring at the table. The sweat stood on Buck's face as he spoke against their silence and then finally he sat down. No one spoke for a while. Strikeaxe lifted his massive head and stared at Buck through the heat. "You askin' us to buy a cemetery, Hardin. We don't want no cemetery. Cemetery's for Poncas or Creeks; we Chetopa—we got th' oil."

He should have known that they would resent it. But the idea stayed with him, and gradually he began to collect things, clothing, early paintings, ceremonial objects, all that pertained to the traditions of the tribe. Many of these things were in the possession of people scattered all over the county, having been given in payment to bill collectors, taxi drivers, bootleggers, lawyers, anyone in short who had despaired of getting his hands on actual money. For his contact man Buck used a fellow who was a born entrepreneur on a stunted scale, a gargoylelike miracle of effrontery who always appeared at the Legion fights sporting an English derby and riding boots and selling cushions with a voice that conveyed not so much words as merely the primitive essentials of trafficking. He hawked canes and balloons at the fair, beribboned badges at the high-school football games, and his slightly bowlegged gait and outthrust tortoise-featured face were familiar to every person in town. For some reason he was known as Spot, and though his dealings were exceptionally public, he kept his own life private. If he slipped off to Tulsa now and then it was with silence and discretion, and Buck had found him ideal for his purposes. There was never any indication that an old piece of turquoise or a particularly beautiful headdress ever meant any more to him than the gimcracks he usually handled; apparently it was not so much the materials that he valued as merely the ritual as he stood there squinting behind the smoke, the cigarette wet in his lips, and his voice growling figures with all the articulation of a cement mixer. But he was efficient and he found a lot, and finally Buck had realized that he would have to decide soon what to do with all these things which he and Spot had brought together.

This was the period in which he had come to know Samuel Beecher well, just past middle life when he had suddenly found himself confused, drifting without direction, knowing that deep hungers had not been satisfied by the way he had lived. It was almost as though he were listening to the two voices of his blood, one white, one Chetopa, listening to a dialogue which had been going on within him for as long as he could remember. But now he had begun to understand it; he was old enough and seasoned enough to know what the voices said and what they meant. So he had sat through the nights beside the hickory fires, watching the vast cast of stars or the thin veil of rain against the flames and listening to the hounds and to hunting talk and to the murmur of the voices within him. And then that night on the ridge south of the old ranch house one voice had suddenly stopped and the other voice had spoken on alone.

So he had sold the bank and the old family house in town and had built the stone house on the ridge. It took a spring and a summer to build and that fall he went deer hunting. It was something which he had done for years, even while he had had the bank, but this time there was no hurry about getting back. And by the time he returned, the dream had come full circle in his mind. He would build a museum, dedicated to the preservation of a past that was forever gone but which might live at least in the time-rippled pages of some traveler's diary, in an arrowhead fashioned to its severe beauty by someone long forgotten, in a trailing feather headdress or a frayed thong which had contained the strength of a half-wild mustang. And while it would be principally Chetopa, it would be a shrine for all those Indians who had known this part of the earth, whether they had tasted its air in freedom with the fierce delights of hunting and of war, or whether they had come here along some bitter trail of tears. It would be for all of them, so that the generations to come might have something to remember.

He was not long in finding a piece of land that suited him. It occupied the top of a hill just north of Grey Horse, and from its crest one could look down into the valley of the town and then across to the hills beyond. There were many trees and a great deal of space and a view serene and uncomplicated. He had first come to the place in the beginnings of an autumnal twilight, and when the lights had suddenly blossomed in silence below him, he had known in his heart that this was the place.

The ground was cleared that fall and the room was made not only for the museum but for a dancing ground and a campsite. On the off days between quail shooting

he would come early in the morning and help the labor-
ers with the clearing and the leveling, and the uprooted
trees he chopped and hauled for firewood until he had
logs piled shoulder high all across the back of the house.
It was heavy work, and yet when he felt the weariness
weighting his muscles he drove himself even more; it was
almost as if he were hurrying to make up for so many
lost years. So they cleared the land and staked the building and got the foundations dug and by that time it was
late summer of 1941. They poured the footings early in
the fall, and Buck could not help smiling a little with relief as he watched the cement settle into the wooden
forms. More than once he had wondered if they would
ever get this far, for seldom had the same men shown up
for two weeks running. They were paid after work on
Saturday, and it was their custom then simply to disappear until the money was gone. But just as these men
went in the bar the others would be crawling out, so by
following a system of two and sometimes three shifts
they had made it after a fashion.

Most of the townspeople had decided long before that
Buck had taken leave of his senses. It was plain crazy—
selling a perfectly sound bank and putting up a rock
house back in the hills and then sinking what money he
had left into a pile of sandstone for a bunch of beer-
bellied Indians. And worse—working side by side with a
gang of rag pickers who busted his rock for a week and
then spent the next week busting that other pile of rock
down at the city jail. Not to mention hunting fox with
old man Beecher that everybody knew was touched. But
then Buck was half Chetopa; it was bound to come out.
And Buck had laughed at them, knowing exactly what
he wanted to do. He wondered only that it had taken
him so long to make up his mind.

Six months later he was back in the Air Corps, where
he had spent some years during and following the first
war. He had been given command of a flight training
school in Texas, and again he drove himself until his

134

heart began to balk. It was the post doctor who had told him that first time. "You'll have to ease up, Hardin. More sleep, not so many drinks, and stay away from flying. You'll be all right if you'll just take it easy." He took a rest leave then, but before it was over he had found a couple of overage stone masons and the three of them began shaping the sandstone blocks and raising the walls. He made a contract with them before he left, arranged credit for them at the grocery store and at the smoke house where they drank their beer, and told them how he wanted the job done. Whatever they did on Saturday night, during the week they played it straight. Buck came home whenever he could and he always found them on the job, whether it was a trowel or a beer that they had in hand. He would squat down and talk things over with them for a while and then one of them would bring him a beer from the back of the car and pretty soon the three of them would be cutting and laying the stone as though they were still in their twenties.

So it had gone like that right along—slow sometimes and halting, making him think in his worse moments that it would probably never get done. Now it was almost finished after years of exasperation and anger and worry interspersed with the inevitable moments of laughter. If people were suddenly interested in it now that the work was done, that was all right, too. Because it was a stone-and-timber reality now; it was born and he knew that it would live and that it was something of his own which would cast his shadow down the endless revolution of the years. He supposed that it was his heart which had made him start thinking like that, his heart old and cracking like dried-out earth and the sure knowledge now, murmuring through his veins, that he must die. But even though he would die, he told himself that the things he believed in would live because he had carved wood and shaped stone and lifted an edifice for their shelter, and he believed it; at least he wanted to believe it. And then unaccountably a strange loneliness would settle in his heart and he would curse the futility of his hoping. "The old ways cannot live in that museum," was the way White Eagle had put it, his fingers resting above his heart. "They live here or they do not live at all."

Now the museum was almost finished, but there was still his obligation to Samuel. He had made Jeff promise to stay until quail season; that had been a beginning. And he had spent as much time with him as possible even though it was a strange and unaccustomed experience to be giving of himself this way, he who more than anyone else he knew had lived in isolation. Yet he did it willingly, for Samuel was his friend and more. And what the outcome of his effort might be he had not bothered to ask himself until the time came when he realized that there was much more at stake.

It was a day in mid-November, cold, clear, gun-metal blue. He had risen early, scrubbed himself hard in the icy sting of the shower, and dried himself before the fire. By the time he finished his coffee Jeff had appeared.

"I just felt like walking over. Wonderful morning." His face was red and shining from the cold.

"Isn't it fine. Let's have some coffee and get outside. Bird season's only a few days off—the dog needs hardening."

Their walk was leisurely and their conversation casual and wandering. The red setter worked nervously along the road, stopping suddenly at a scent and then bursting irrepressibly through the coppery grass. They would lose sight of her for a while and suddenly she would be racing up behind them, her tongue out and her eyes laughing as though she knew that nothing was serious yet.

"I don't think there's any better hunting in the world," Buck said, stopping to light his pipe again. "I hunted a good deal in England and Scotland years ago, and it was good hunting, no doubt of it. But it never seemed as quick, as instinctive as this. You only have a split second before they're in the trees and gone—you have to get on them right away."

"I'll be lucky to hit anything."

"Well, that doesn't matter so much," Buck said, and then he knew that he was lying. "Yes, it matters—hell. But there's so much more; just the weather and watching the dogs and how hungry you get and then the first Scotch when you get back to the house." He turned to Jeff and smiled. "You'll see."

It was almost noon when they saw the car. They were standing on the ridge to the east of the house, letting the dog cool herself in the pond, when they heard the rattle and saw the sun glancing off the metal.

"Looks like John White Eagle," Buck said, frowning against the light. He watched the pickup bounce along the road until it disappeared in the trees on the far ridge. Then he whistled for the dog. "We'd better start back," he said.

White Eagle was waiting for them in the yard when they got there. Buck could not see his eyes behind the dark glasses, but there was trouble in the way he stood there by the gate, watching them come up the road.

"You're in time for lunch," Buck said as they got to the yard.

"That dog of yours is soft." White Eagle sounded almost angry, as though it were a personal offense.

"She needs work, all right," Buck agreed quickly. "Come on in—I've got some beer in the ice box."

But White Eagle stood there by the gate until the dog came up to him. He leaned over and rubbed his hand against the base of her skull. "I need some money, Hardin," he said.

"Whatever you want."

"Paul took my billfold last night—today's Saturday and the bank is closed—" He was still looking at the dog and his voice was heavy and abrupt.

Buck shrugged his shoulders. "I can write you a check. Just tell me—"

White Eagle stood up then and looked at him. His mouth moved a little before he spoke, as though his

137

thoughts were traveling ahead of his words. "He's in jail. He was at the Pig Stand last night, drunk—got mixed up in a fight. His wife told me this morning that he was locked up."

"My keys are in the house," Buck said, starting for the door. "We'll follow you in." He had seen too much of it to be surprised, even to think about it particularly. For just a moment he felt tired and hungry and then he put it out of his mind.

"What's the story?" Jeff asked him as he got into the car.

"It's his boy, Paul. I'm going to bail him out. I don't like to think of John doing it alone."

In silence they followed the whirling dust of the pickup into town. When they stopped in back of the courthouse, John was standing on the curb, waiting.

"Why don't you stay out here," Buck said. "We'll be back in a minute."

Sparrows flew noisily up before them and then they went through the screen door and down the dark hall to the office. The jailer had his feet on the desk and his hat lay slanted on his forehead and he was reading a dog-eared western pulp. When he saw Buck in the doorway he sat up quickly and pushed his hat back.

"What can I do for you, Mr. Buck?"

"I want Paul White Eagle."

"I just come on," he said. "Let's see—"

"He was picked up last night at the Pig Stand—drunk and fighting. What's the bail?"

"Well—"

Buck saw the greed in his eyes and it sickened him. "All right," he said.

"Judge ain't come in yet," the jailer drawled, reaching for his watch. He studied it for a minute and then returned it to his pants pocket. "Bail ain't set." He spat into the mottled cuspidor and raised a questioning face toward Buck.

"You know what I'm talking about," Buck said.

"I guess since it's you," the jailer said, running his hand across his mouth, "that maybe twenty-five bucks'd buy enough eraser to rub it off the books."

When his warty fingers had closed around the money, the jailer rattled his keys and walked on back toward the cells.

Paul was following him when he came back into the room. He was tall and soft and a little unsteady on his feet, and his eyes blinked at the light that shone along his glasses. In the corner of his mouth there was a thin crust of blood and his hands rubbed nervously along his legs. He opened his mouth once as though to speak and then he lowered his face and was silent.

"You can go home, Paul," Buck said, his voice strangely gentle in the shadowless chill of fluorescent light. "John's outside, waiting for you." The jailer stood there slack-jawed, watching them, and the sound of Paul's breathing filled the room. For a long moment Paul looked up at Buck until his eyes faulted and began to water. He shook his head ponderously, bewildered, and then they heard his footsteps fading along the hall.

"I guess he musta jest got homesick," the jailer said, twisting his mouth into a smile. "Prob'ly missed the free meals and the sack time." His tone was broad and inclusive and then suddenly the smirk withered on his face because Buck was simply looking at him, staring down at him with scorn and pity in his face. After a moment Buck flipped a quarter onto the desk. "Thank you for your trouble," he said quietly.

When they were in the car he sat for a moment, smiling. "You know," he said, "sometimes I believe that that museum is the craziest damned fool thing anybody ever did around this town. We've had some quixotic gestures that would stand with the best but I'm damned if I don't think I've got the crown."

"How do you mean?"

"Do you really think that Paul will ever get within a country mile of the place?" Buck shook his head. "He or any of the rest of the young ones?"

"What does he do?" Jeff asked.

"Do? Drinks, mostly; spends what money he can get his hands on; marries tramp women and then pays them alimony—he stays pretty busy."

"What about the old man?"

Buck shook his head briefly. "I think he's given up on it—Paul broke his heart a long time ago." Then he frowned and rubbed his chin. "No, I don't suppose he'll ever give up, actually. He could have let him stay there today easy enough."

"It's a strange thing," Jeff said. "White Eagle seems so strong, so solid—what ever went wrong between them?"

"Oh, it's an old story." They were on the road home now and there were doves along the telephone wires and he could hear the red-winged blackbirds as they passed the reservoir. His anger was gone and the breeze was cool on his face. He could feel the day settling again, the ripples of disturbance gradually flowing back into calm. "What goes wrong so often from one generation to the next? I mean anyone, no matter who it is, not just John and Paul. I've seen it so many times. And then look at how the old people and the grandchildren get along; at the dances there are mainly old men and boys—no in betweens. There's something wrong between father and son, it seems to me, and they both dispute for the grandson. How much do you remember of your father?"

Jeff frowned and leaned back a little in the seat. "Not much. He died a long time ago. I have scattered memories, feelings, but nothing whole."

"How did he feel about Samuel?"

Jeff turned and looked at him, his eyes perplexed and wondering. "From what I remember, things I saw and heard, I'd say he had turned against him. Not completely, perhaps, but just enough so that they couldn't get along.

140

I think Dad was mixed up—he wanted things that wouldn't fit together."

Buck nodded and said nothing. In a peculiar way he seemed suddenly aware of Jeff for the first time, aware of him as an entity in himself and not merely as an extension of Samuel. "Jeff," he said softly, "what did you really come here for? What was it you were hoping to find?"

Jeff turned away and looked out of the window toward the barren simplicity of the prairie. There was nothing there to correspond to the arabesque of his thoughts, nothing by which to objectify the flux of his feelings. "If you're thinking that it was because Dad was dead," he said slowly, his voice tentative, groping, less articulation than simply the sound of his mind leafing back through the past, "and that Pap was all I had, that's part of it. But there's more." He turned again to Buck, his face grave and his eyes detached so that he seemed to be looking beyond him to the horizon. "It's more complicated than that. It's all mixed up with the fact that I grew up without my father and that somewhere along the line I lost something—" he stopped and shook his head. "I can't really explain it," and then his hands moved like swallows hunting through the dusk. "It was something I had hold of and then it just slipped away." He lit a cigarette and then his voice was quieter, more matter-of-fact. "I don't know how much you know about this or whether it would make any sense to you, but I used to see Pap every summer when I was a kid. There was a quality about those summers—well, you've probably seen a glass filled with water right up to the top and then a little more so that the water is actually over the edge—it was a little like that."

Buck listened to him in silence, all the way home and then longer as they sat by the fire. The words were different, but he had known their meaning for a long time. And through the searching eyes of the young man sitting across from him he saw himself as he had been in those

141

rife years. He knew this road; he had traveled it before. And as they sat there among the shadows of the fire, their words uncertain as the flames in the darkness, Buck felt his loneliness flowing out of him toward Jeff. For Jeff was alone, too, this tall, lean, wondering boy who had followed his dream to its source; wondering because he had chosen the high road of intuition where the winds of uncertainty blew strong, alone because he had known no answer to his heart's yearning. Our blood sings the same song, Buck thought to himself. He might almost have been my son.

And in Buck's eyes then there was something hot of hope and pride and desire, for he remembered that he had said, "quail season—wait until quail season." He had without thinking set the terms of Jeff's stay at that time when the lists of life would be crowded with death's bright pennants. And in his mind's eye, as clear and vivid and absolute as though it had been there always, was the image of Jeff kneeling, the gun jolting his shoulder, a puff of feathers drifting serenely across a ragged sky. It was a scene that spoke of old hungers, for blood and the heart's initiation, for the miraculous touch of the gods that once in a great while walked upon the earth. And now unaccountably, almost beyond his believing, through the dry soil of his heart a seed had pushed its way to the light, a seed tender and alive that he had long ago given up for dead.

CHAPTER VIII

☐ Like yellowing leaves the days turned and drifted and died, wheeling through dawn and dusk and starlight and dawn again, vanishing down the winds and leaving no trace save for scattered memories recollected as though through rain or golden pall of dust, memories of a blackjack etched in rigid violence against a setting sun, of geese crying southward through a gusty night, of quick swallows at early twilight, of autumn, its gold and its blood. It was a time of suspension, of rest, when the earth was lulled into a kind of infinite calm, forgetting now the battering shock of summer and unmindful of winter's iron shroud. Soft winds dallied in the sun-burned grasses and colors modulated into shades, as though there had been added to this stark chessboard the beneficent dimensions of shadow. In place of pain now there was nostalgia, for even the sharpest of memories blurred in the smoky haze of Indian summer. Yet more than anything else it was a time of remembering, in some ways simply an extended moment of reflection upon old moods, old emotions that would suddenly stir again like drifted leaves in a wind.

Often Jeff recalled—it seemed so long ago now—how the house had looked that first morning, how compact and solid in appearance, a small keep of stone beneath spreading trees, commanding a view of the sun-swept valley. It was the house of a man who lived alone, and entering it Jeff had had the impression of walking into

143

the man's very life as though the house, its stones and its earth and the trees which formed its garland, were all of a piece with the spirit which it sheltered and the land on which it stood. The books had surprised him, old books dusty and without order and faintly redolent of hickory smoke and yet obviously marked and read. And he had turned to Buck with curiosity, to this man in whose seasoned face there was something wild and free that would beat unexpectedly behind the veil of his eyes. And as Buck had talked, shaping the movements of his words with long, thin fingers, Jeff had felt that this was a man whom civilization had graced without crippling, a man who somehow had never really surrendered.

He remembered, too, the promise he had made to Buck that morning when the light had burst into the room and Buck's face had glowed like agate in the fires of dawn. He kept the promise, and the days which followed were days of companionship, of work and of idleness, of meals shared off the tail gate of the station wagon on back country roads, of drinks at dusk while the fire caught and sputtered in the chimney, of talk and of silence, even of love. And yet through these days there ran a trace of guilt and uncertainty, for when Buck spoke of Samuel, of his ways and of his life, it was Buck about whom Jeff thought, Buck to whom he listened, to words that in some mysterious way called forth answering echoes from his soul. It was Buck's tanned face that he saw and it was to Buck that he finally told some of what was in his heart. Yet there were things he could not say even to him, emotions which he did not understand, feelings which, like fledgling birds, could not yet be trusted on their own.

As for Samuel, it seemed to Jeff that he lived in a world of his own, an old man's world shadowed by the memories of all the years, a countryman's world sounding with the cries of the hunt and with the music of the seasons, the world of a solitary giant living on out of an earlier time. For there was in the old man a devotion, a

144

love, almost a nobility, in the presence of which lesser men were somehow transfigured, privileged for a moment all too brief to share the rare joy and the simple happiness of this curiously saintly man. Perhaps it had been the dim recollection of this which had brought Jeff back to him, and yet to find the innocent pleasures of childhood translated into the flinty and chiseled tongues of hawk and rattlesnake, into the hard dimensions of wind-haunted prairie, had shaken him far beyond mere disappointment. Little by little he had begun to sense meanings, watching the old man through the days, listening by night to the talk around the fires. But somehow Samuel remained beyond his reach so that their eyes groped vaguely toward one another and their words trailed off into unquiet silence. Perhaps they had been apart too long, and maybe there were no words for what they felt; whatever it was, Jeff could find no way to shatter the silence which separated them.

Yet there was no trace of this on Samuel's leathery face. He had been busy during the early days of November, preparing for the bench show and field trials of the Southwestern Fox Hunters Association. This year it was being held at the state park ten miles east of Grey Horse, and to Samuel had fallen the job of making sure that everything was ready. For him, of course, it was not really a job but a pleasure and his days were filled with the mailing of handbills accompanied by laboriously penciled letters, with the solving of problems of housing for dogs and men, with the gathering of provisions and the appointing of field judges and all the hundred other details that attended the gathering of the clan. For this was a special occasion in any man's language; this was the time waited for and thought about and talked over by devotees who had no equal in passionate dedication. This was the time when dog was matched against dog, when pride and even glory, disappointment and sometimes shame hovered in the balance. It was the ultimate test in the company of one's peers, and over it all presided Samuel, whose years and vast knowledge and Olympian detachment wove the mantle of his authority. This was his domain; here he was the sceptered king, and in him the others found their dreams made flesh.

For two weeks Jeff did not see much of Samuel until at last one night the old man announced proudly that everything was ready.

"They're comin' in from all over," he said, as they sat over their coffee in the kitchen. "There isn't a hound man for five hundred miles who can walk, crawl, or stand who won't be here. A ring-tailed sonofabitch, that's what it is; more dogs than a man could shake a stick at. Sing? Christamighty!" He shook his head and blew on his coffee to cool it.

"What about the foxes?" Jeff asked, smiling. "You sent out letters to everybody but them. You better hope they get the word or you'll have an awful lot of mad hunters on your back. Maybe you could get some rabbits—"

"Listen." Samuel was leaning across the table, grinning a little, pointing his finger at Jeff. "You musta forgot who you're talkin' to. I brought those foxes in here myself, grew 'em by hand, trained 'em, taught 'em everything they know. That's the best bunch o' pet foxes from the Smokies west. They'll be there, don't worry. They haven't made the hound yet that them foxes won't run his ass off."

"So long as the hounds don't catch them, you're all right."

"They won't catch 'em."

"And when it's all over the men are worn out, some of the dogs are lost, all of them footsore, somebody's broken a leg chasing around the woods at night, and not a thing to show for it." Jeff got up and brought the coffee pot back to the table. "No heads to nail on the wall, no rugs for the fireplace, no pictures—just the pleasure of knowing you didn't catch the fox. You got to lose to win."

"Yeah," Samuel snorted. "The only thing good about what you just said was that it didn't take you long to say

146

it. Now look—you probably know somethin' about how them Mexicans fight them bulls. Sure. Hell, anybody can kill the big bastard but that isn't the idea of it. And if it was killin' the fox that was the point of it all, why waste time runnin' him down with a bunch o' hounds? No, that isn't it. If I thought you was doin' anything but jokin' I'd run you off the place."

"But in bullfighting you can at least see it—there's something right in front of you—"

"So you see it. Well, we listen. I don't know how the hell to tell you any other way." Then he smiled and rubbed the back of his hand along his chin. "You know somethin'? You kind of put me in mind of those old boys who got to have somebody prove to 'em that there's a God before they can believe it. They want it all worked out in numbers like, and the more God puts the spirit on 'em, the harder they work those pencils to prove that it just cain't be. Of course, if they really wanted to find out, all they'd have to do would be to come on down to the tent and lay theirselves on the line and let that preacher stomp at 'em a coupla times—they'd know. But I figured it out a long time ago that they just don't want to know, they're afraid to know, so they keep those pencils hot workin' up reasons. What I mean is that all you got to do is just come on out there and listen if you really want to know."

"Maybe."

"Maybe, hell! If there's anything in this world I know, it's the devil and hounds. I'm tellin' you."

It was two nights later when they picked up Buck and drove out to the Chetopa Hills Park where the meet was being held. The night was chill and rent with stars and far down the western sky a pale edge of moon shone through a lacework of cloud. There had been soaking rains the previous week so that the ground was still moist, and it was a hunter's night—earth that would hold a scent sweet and demanding and air that would ring like a silver bell.

"You got your weather," Buck said from the back seat of the car. "I never did quite get the pitch before on this fox-hunting, revival-meeting combination of yours, but now it's beginning to make a little sense."

"Course it makes sense," Samuel said. "I always knowed you was smart, Hardin, but it's taken you a good while to prove it."

Jeff could tell that the old man was elated from the way that he drove the car, arms straight out before him holding the wheel, head thrown back so that he could turn and talk to Buck out of the corner of his mouth. In between comments he whistled snatches of a hymn, and from time to time he would lower the window and lean out to spit.

They drove through Grey Horse and beyond and it was eight o'clock by the time they reached the park. From the entrance it was a little more than three miles into the area where they were holding the show, three miles of scrub oak and sandstone and hills that bounced sound and a creek that lazied along in various stages of dryness. Almost as soon as they were inside the park they began to pass cars parked on the side of the road, cars that were sometimes alone but more often than not in groups of twos and threes with the occupants clustered along the bumpers, talking or listening or just feeling the night.

"Looks like there's going to be a crowd," Buck said. "Wonder if there'll be room for the fox."

"We figured on better than four hundred hounds," Samuel said. "I didn't count the people. Hounds are the ones need the room—fox just needs a seat where he can set down and watch."

The cars became thicker and then they could see the lights and the buildings and the dust and the people moving back and forth across the road. The cars were everywhere, crowded together in the open fields beside the road, and they ranged from Model A's to Cadillacs. Some had kennels in the back end, some pulled trailers, some were cars where the hounds rode in the front seat with the driver. They bore the license plates of a dozen states and the dust of two hundred counties, but these were unimportant differences. The paths to it might be many, but the heaven for all of them was the same.

Samuel wedged the car into the crowded field and even before he had opened the door, his friends had begun to gather. While he was shaking hands and recalling names, Buck took Jeff by the elbow.

"Why don't we go on over to the ring," he said. "He's got a lot of people to see and lots of things to talk about. We'd just be in his way."

The ring was a large, roped-off enclosure filled with some twenty benches and lighted by a network of electric bulbs which were fastened to the surrounding trees. Around this circle were from a hundred to two hundred people, sitting in chairs, standing, kneeling or squatting on the ground. Some held dogs and others held children while everywhere the talk flowed without cease.

"This used to be a CCC camp," Buck was saying, and then he caught sight of someone waving to him from the crowd. "There's somebody over there I know," he said. "Go ahead and walk around. I'll find you in a little bit."

Jeff watched him move away through the crowd, his head held high, his body tautly erect as always. Then after a moment he lost sight of Buck among the shifting, shadowed mass of coats and faces and hats and gesturing hands. He walked aimlessly around for a while, looking at the people and at their dogs, listening to the words that came to him like sudden ripples of light along the surface of the sound. It was hound talk, of money spent shrewdly or foolishly, of immortal dogs, of storied foxes and famous runs, and all of this heard by bits and pieces which put together formed the mythology of a belief, of a faith, almost of a way of life.

"Well, the damned fox musta been twenty years old if he was a day—my dad hunted him before I was ever borned and I got good mileage outa the rascal myself.

Hell, he was just like one of the family; I reckon we woulda had a reg'lar funeral for him if we'd knowed when it was he died. But it was his sense that you had to respect, and what he could do with them dogs. Damned if sometimes I didn't think he was one of them there wolf boys that you read in the paper about ever' now and then. I ain't kiddin' you—he could make them hounds rare straight up on their hind legs, fife, drum, and bandage for all the world like the spirit o' seventy-six, and quick march right down the main street blowin' 'Yankee Doodle' just to beat hell . . ."

". . . and he was a preacher, see, and this bitch of his littered and she was a goin' jessie if ever there was one. When I heard what dog she'd been bred with, I took it in mind to get me one of them pups. Well, preacher lived down in the Ozarks—little bit of a town—claimed he'd had better offers but that it wasn't no kind of a trade to give up the kinda huntin' he had jest for a bigger church. Kinda went against his religion, you might say. Anyhow, I fixed my route so's I could git into that town—it was about six months after I had heard about the pups. Course when I got to the house and he showed me his dogs I told him right off that they were a poor lookin' bunch o' pups for sure and that some dog other'n the one he claimed musta got in behind his bitch. Well, we went out that night—good night, too, I remember—and this one pup of his belled like a fire engine all night. Course I didn't know which dog it was since I didn't know his pack, but he pointed out this kinda skinny little one and said, 'That's the one, right there.' 'Got to admit he's a goer,' I told him, 'but what I'm wonderin' is can the little bastard stay.' 'Stay!' he said, and he fair shouted. 'Like a Baptist preacher on Sunday.' So we went out again the next night. And I mean to tell you he just run all night, hollerin' to beat the band. It fair got to the point where I couldn't hardly stand it. But I was scared of that preacher because there wasn't no grass ever growed under his feet, so we went one more night. And hell, there wasn't no way around it—that pup was just a runnin' sonofabitch. I paid a hundred dollars for him and left town the next day. Well, sir, the first night I took him out I couldn't have heard him if he hadn't stayed so close in to the fire. Just a little squawk now and then like he was layin' or somethin'. I don't believe he ever did get over seventy-five yards from the car. Sometimes I think the poor little bastard hollered himself out on that three night binge, and then sometimes I think that the preacher just managed to get aholt of me where it hurt."

Men in overalls, in business suits, their faces shadowed by straw hats or ball caps or the wide-brimmed cowman's Stetson; men eying the dogs a little tensely, their lips pursed, their faces studious and concentrated, their hands, knowing and sure, moving suddenly along the heads and sleek sides of hounds that trembled a little with nervousness; men who talked, telling the same stories that they had told for years but stories still worth the telling, still worth the hearing. And whether they really listened to each other was a question; it was more as though by the repetition of these words the intangible bonds which bound them together were fastened more firmly. A man could talk about most anything as long as it had to do with hounds.

And as Jeff wandered among them, it seemed to him that many of these men were marked by a kind of swirling of the grain around some inner knot. Some of them were cripples, many were misshapen in tongue or face or body, and yet in their eyes there was a strangely humble, strangely beautiful detachment. Whether cattlemen, farmers, salesmen, or drifters, there was a noticeable gentleness about them, a quiet patience of men long used to listening. And now they stood and talked and studied the hounds, these hounds so strangely similar to the men who owned them in that from their long-eared and lean-bellied and melancholy mien came forth the poetry of

151

earth and of night, of the old virtues of fleetness and cunning and strength, in a strange and grotesque language that yet was music to those who could understand.

Suddenly there began a general movement toward the ring and Jeff worked his way slowly through the crowd until he was in close against the rope. He could see Samuel and another man standing together in the center of the ring and through the faces on the other side he caught a glimpse of Buck. He waved and after a moment Buck joined him.

"They're getting ready for the bench show now."

"What's Pap doing out there?"

"Didn't he tell you?" Buck asked, frowning at him. "He's ringmaster—he'll do the judging."

"He didn't say anything about it," Jeff said.

"He wouldn't."

They were bringing the puppies into the enclosure now for the first show. When the handlers had arranged them around the ring, Samuel walked quickly along the line, silently making gestures to the handlers until the best pups had been put on the benches and the others had left the ring. Then another rapid walk along the line and the order of finish was fixed. The man on the public address system drawled the names of the winners and called for female dogs under a year. Again the handlers entered the ring and Samuel again moved among the dogs, working a little more slowly now with the older dogs, but still quick, still decisive as he gestured in the silence.

There were many different classifications and the judging went on for almost two hours. Samuel strode around the ring with ease and certainty, unhurried and yet swift, his eye sharp and his hand firm while the faces of the crowd followed his movements and murmured at his decisions.

"Old son of a buck knows his hounds," the man next to Jeff commented.

"I guess he does," Jeff said, smiling with pride almost in spite of himself.

"Why he's bought and sold more hounds than most people'll hear or see in a lifetime. He's made a fortune at it, they tell me. Sam Beecher. Got to git up early to whip him on hounds."

Jeff nodded and then looked back out toward the ring. The old man was right at seventy, yet there was still strength in everything he did, and it was plain that his dignity came not so much from age as from his mastery of this thing that he loved so deeply.

"How do you like it?" Buck asked, his voice almost a whisper in the quiet.

"He works awfully fast. I don't see how he can judge them that quickly."

"Well, he's had about fifty years of practice. That helps."

Jeff lit a cigarette and turned up his jacket collar against his neck. "They all know him, don't they."

"Sam?" Buck said, looking at Jeff. "He's known all over this part of the country. I've told you about some of the things he's done."

"Yeah," Jeff said. "I guess I just had to see it."

"I suppose you realize you were selling him a little short," Buck said after a while.

And when Jeff looked at him, he was puzzled by the quiet urgency in Buck's eyes. "I kind of had something else in mind. It takes awhile."

Then the announcer was calling all entries for the best-in-show classifications. This was the final contest of the bench show and all of the winners of the previous classes were returned to the ring. The silence was deep now; handlers knelt beside their dogs, chucking them under the chin, pulling the legs back, running hard fingers along the chest, straightening and stiffening the tail. The benches were in a single straight line and Samuel made a preliminary arrangement of dogs on the benches so that he could see them more easily. Up and down the line he strode, pausing to grip a muzzle, to study the height of a dog that looked a little big, to

153

examine the legs and shoulders. Then he would gesture suddenly for the handler to move the dog up or back, and in each man's face there was anxiety and hope and hard-jawed disappointment. Finally two dogs had worked forward to the first two benches, and now for almost the first time, Samuel hesitated. The dog temporarily occupying the first bench was a lean, brown-spotted female with a shining coat and severe lines. Her position was rigid, head thrust forward and legs back, and in her nervousness she trembled ever so slightly. Samuel put his hand on her chest and looked closely into her face; then he stepped back and looked at her from the side; after a moment he took hold of her muzzle and held her head up again. Her handler, a big man with heavy black hair and blunt, Indian features, knelt on the ground beside the bench, talking low to the dog and watching Samuel's face. And still the dog trembled, taut as a pennant in the wind.

Abruptly then Samuel moved on to the second dog. The crowd could tell from his actions that he had narrowed his choice down to the two, and there was no talking, no sound, as they watched the old man move around the dogs. The second hound was a black and tan, big-shouldered, stolid, motionless, standing squarely on the bench as though he were nailed to it. His handler was a slender man, white-haired and elderly. He wore khakis and a brown windbreaker and the metal rims of his glasses glittered in the light as he looked back and forth between Samuel and the dog. For a good minute and a half Samuel was motionless, looking from the black and tan to the bitch and then back again. Then with a sudden movement of his hands he motioned for the two dogs to change places and lifted his arms in the air to indicate that the bench show was over. The intake of air was audible, a woman laughed nervously, and then the crowd was clapping the tension away.

Buck and Jeff worked through the noisy throng until

they got to the judges' table, where Samuel was drinking a cup of steaming coffee.

"That last pair kind of slowed you down, didn't they?" Buck laughed, reaching out to shake his hand.

"Couldn't hardly pick between 'em. Coupla fine dogs."

"Sam, you had 'em just backwards. They musta fed that black and tan glue to stiffen him out like that. Why, when they carried him outa the ring his legs didn't give a inch. That just ain't human." It was Virgil Sands, slapping Samuel on the back and looking up at him out of his barrel of a body.

"Virge, if I'd knowed you was here I woulda called you out to help. I didn't figure you got so far away from the store on week nights."

There were a number of people around Samuel now, laughing, showing him dogs, congratulating him on his judging. Suddenly the old man straightened up and looked over their heads until he caught Jeff's eye. He winked and smiled at him.

"Listen, boy. I got to go down to the barn with Virge and mark some hounds. You could come with me but we'll prob'ly be at it for a good while yet, and we're gonna cast at five o'clock tomorrow. Why don't you go on up to the car and git some sleep so you can enjoy yourself in the morning. How about you, Hardin?"

"I'll go with him," Buck said. "Tomorrow's what I came along for. We'll get some sleep."

Samuel waved his hand and then he and Virge and the others walked on down toward the barn.

"Well," Buck said, "it's after midnight."

"He had them right in the palm of his hand."

"What?"

"Working on those dogs. He knew just what he was doing."

"Sam always did know what he was doing," Buck said, knocking his pipe against his boot heel. "It took some of the rest of us a little longer to find out. And fair warning

155

—that fox horn they blow at four will lift the hair right off your head. Let's get some sleep."

Jeff slept in the front seat of the car, falling asleep to the comfortable stir of men and cars along the road and awaking in the rustling silence of early morning just before the horn sounded its high and husky blast. The echoes rolled down the valley and almost at once the camp was astir with lights and voices and the distant barking of dogs. Jeff sat up and rubbed his face hard and reached for a cigarette.

"How about some coffee?" It was Buck, unscrewing the top from the Thermos bottle.

"Wonderful," Jeff yawned. "I feel like I just closed my eyes."

"Same here. Well, this'll help. Sam's coffee doesn't leave a man much choice."

They drank the coffee in silence while the night dissolved around them. The stars grew faint and now they could make out the figures of men and animals as they moved across the fields. It was cold and the windshield of the car was moist with dew.

Then the door opened and Samuel put his head in. "You up?"

"Almost finished with breakfast," Jeff said.

"Good. I got to go down where they're gonna cast the dogs. You can either come with me there," he said, looking from Jeff to Buck, "or you can walk on down to a spot I got in mind where you might get a look at the hounds on a scent—maybe even a fox if you're real lucky."

"What do you say?" Buck asked Jeff.

"I'd just as soon see them running."

Buck nodded and turned back to Samuel. "How do we get there?"

"Well, it's on down the road about two and a half, three miles. There's a ford there—you'll see it—you cross the creek right at that spot. Then there's a trail, kind of a

156

cow path, that climbs on up a hill on the other side. You git up to the top of that hill, you'll have a view."

"We'll meet back here at the car," said Buck.

" 'Bout eleven o'clock," Samuel nodded.

"Good enough."

The day was shadowed pearl and then coral and finally a kind of wet and shining silver as the sun poured over the rim of the horizon. As they left the camp behind them, sounds became smaller and yet more intense, more clearly heard—the rapid hammering of a woodpecker, the sudden joyous whistle of a meadow lark. The earth beneath their feet was reddish brown and hard for the previous week's rains had settled the dust, and there was a cold and sparkling clarity in the air which made it a pleasure simply to breathe.

Jeff stooped and picked up a rock and let fly at a dead tree across the road. "Nice morning."

"Beautiful morning," Buck said. He threw at the same tree and missed and they both laughed. "We'll have to do better than that when bird season gets here."

Jeff stopped laughing and put his hands in his pockets. "Yeah, I guess that's right," he said. In the excitement of the night before and the beauty of the morning he had forgotten, and now the thought of how little time was left to him closed upon his heart like a fist.

"It ought to be a good year even though this drouth has made the cover a little thin. And say, I've got a gun for you, so don't be concerned about that."

"Well, I think maybe Pap's got one," Jeff answered quietly, looking down at the road. Somehow he could not respond to Buck's enthusiasm, for the thought of this hunt had stirred a strange fear within him, as though there were more at stake than he could grasp just now.

"I think that's the ford down ahead," Buck said presently, pointing below them where the creek rippled thinly over rock.

And as Jeff looked at the water, he heard the high-

157

pitched cry of a hound three times, then four, and suddenly the cry had multiplied into a myriad of voices, eager and full-throated, charging the air with excitement.

"They're on him," Buck said, seizing Jeff's arm. "Come on."

They ran down the long slope to the ford and then as they hit the water Buck seemed to lose his footing. He splashed wildly for a moment on the slippery rocks and then went down to one knee, bending and gripping his leg as though he had turned his ankle. Jeff stopped and waited for him, feeling the water quick and cool at his ankles and hearing everywhere now the rhythmic singing of the hounds. Suddenly Buck struggled up, his face contorted and hard and his arms held tightly across his chest.

"Go on," he said harshly. "I'll catch you." His eyes were shut tight and the words seemed to force their way through his teeth.

"You all right?"

He waved his hand angrily. "God damn it, hurry up."

Jeff hesitated a moment longer, fixed there by the severity in Buck's face. Then he splashed on through the ford and ran full tilt up the slope until he was at the crest of the knoll. As he stood there, his heart pounding and his breath coming short, the cries of the hounds seemed to beat in his ears like a pulse. The air was vibrant with their eagerness, and their voices were timbred with such hot urgency that Jeff felt a sudden impulse to run again. At last he saw them, briefly but quite distinctly, a scattered pack nose down filtering whitely through the scrub oak of the opposite ridge. As they disappeared and his breath came more easily, Jeff reflected that the sight of them was nothing to their sound, that great wild cry which seemed to float above them like the trumpeting of the hosts of heaven.

"Did you make it?" It was Buck, calling to him, limping slowly up the ridge.

"Just in time," Jeff said. "They were in those trees across the valley."

"They sounded so close I thought that fox might run between your legs. I'm glad you got there."

"You O.K.?" Jeff said anxiously. For there was again in Buck's face what he had seen that morning at the house, the same wounded fierceness, the same wild pride staring into death's darkness.

But Buck did not answer. He sat down slowly against a tree and carefully filled his pipe. There was such deliberation in his movements that it seemed to Jeff that he was holding himself together by some immense and silent effort of the will. Then Buck looked up at him, his face bemused, even strangely, distantly happy. "Well, you saw them, didn't you. You've had your first taste now. Maybe you've got an idea why it doesn't matter whether you can see them or not."

Jeff looked at him for a moment, at those deep eyes clouded with hurt and suffering and yet somehow still proud, still almost defiantly alive. Then he looked down at the ground and struggled against the pain which seared his eyelids. For there was a light in Buck's eyes which had gone out for Jeff when his father had died, a light that he had blindly sought for many years, and now that he had found it again he was afraid to look.

CHAPTER IX

☐ Buck went to the museum on Monday and it was dark before he got back home. As he drove up to the gate his headlights cut through the night and he saw White Eagle's truck parked there beneath the trees. He noticed a tiny orange glow in the blackness over by the chimney when he got into the yard and as he came closer he could see John sitting there on a box, leaning back against the ivy-covered stone.

"Whatever it was, it took you a good long time."

"I didn't have anything to hurry for," Buck laughed. "Why didn't you tell me you were coming?"

"Well," John said, getting up, "I woulda had to come all the way out here just to tell you, and then there wouldn't a been a helluva lot of point. I figured you had to come back sooner or later. How about givin' me a hand with this box."

After he had lit the lamps and stirred up the fire, Buck went over to the table at White Eagle's suggestion and opened the box. Then he looked over to the fireplace where John was standing. "What's this all about?"

"I was out in the car last night," John said. "I was thinkin' that I ought to drive on out here and pay you what I owed you."

"Oh, that." Buck smiled. "You don't owe me anything. All the—"

"Then I thought—what would he do with the money? Anyway, I hadn't been up to Kansas for too long. So the

161

Scotch is for you and the bourbon for me and the beer for both of us and the steaks and that other stuff for dinner. If you'll do the cooking."

He was standing there with his back to the fire, a cigar clenched in his teeth, his hands held out behind him and the hat sitting high and uncreased on his head. Buck looked at him and laughed again. "You sure as hell paid me back with interest and then some."

He rubbed the steaks down with butter and garlic and broiled them on the fire so that they were black and crusted outside and rare in the center. While the eggs sputtered in the steak drippings, he heated the spaghetti and before long everything was ready. They ate slowly, enjoying it, watching the fire crumble and wane. Then when they had finished Buck went out behind the house for another log and threw it on the coals.

"I've been tryin' to think of some of them old songs," John said after his glass had been filled again. "Singers don't use 'em much anymore. I want those old ones for the dances when we open the museum."

"It would take a long memory," Buck said, puffing on his pipe.

"Maybe," John said. After a while he got up and went out to his truck. When he returned he was carrying a drum. "The coyotes was talkin' last night real good. Kind of made my mind go back. Listen." His eyes squinted a little and his fingers began to tap the drum that he held on his knees. Then he began to sing, his high and minor voice driving thinly through the drum throb, and presently Buck too was singing, leaning back with his eyes closed, chanting a strange song that worked jaggedly around the rhythm. Their voices crossed and followed, coming together and wandering apart until finally on a sudden loud pound of the drum they stopped. White Eagle laughed, his face creasing into shadows in the firelight. "Who's got a long memory?" he said. Then his fingers were moving again on the drum, sorting through fragments of rhythms until the beat emerged, deep this

162

time and muffled, heavy as flesh, while above it the frail spirit of the voice quivered through the cracked registers of the coyote, wandering urgently on in pain to the very brink of wildness. Then silence.

"I never heard you sing that before."

"I heard that one while I was drivin' around last night. I can't make up my mind whether I like it or not." He laid the drum aside and lit his cigar. "Talkin' about the museum, that painter finished my picture yesterday. He said to tell you that I was the last one and that everything is done."

Buck smiled at him. "You made him earn his money all right."

"I just put him off a little, that's all. I wanted to wait until it got cool—I'm too old to sit still that long in the heat. He got mad when I wanted to hold a can of beer in my hand. Made him thirsty, I guess."

"So it's all done, then."

"That's what he said."

Buck got up and poked at the fire and filled their glasses again. "I remember once when you said you wouldn't let anybody paint your picture for the museum."

White Eagle grunted. "I guess I was still young then, or thought I was; I guess I was still lookin' up the road. I got to look back now; it all changes."

"Yes," Buck said. He held his glass up and looked at it, turning it in his hand. "I suppose you've noticed," he said slowly, "that I'm not in very good shape."

"I've noticed it some," White Eagle said, watching him.

"It's my heart," he said, rubbing his hand across his chest. "It's not worth much anymore. That night you brought Jeff out—I'd had an attack that morning and I've had another one since, at the field trials the other day. That's what was wrong."

"I thought maybe that was it," John said quietly.

"You knew about it then."

163

John shrugged his shoulders. "People watch what you do, Hardin—there's been talk in town—I had a feeling what it was."

"I wasn't sure. Of course it doesn't matter except for the museum. If anything should happen—oh, I suppose I'm just a little anxious," he said, clenching his fingers into fists and then opening them again. "It's been a long time getting ready—I wouldn't want anything to go wrong."

"There won't anything go wrong."

"I'm counting on you for that, John."

White Eagle looked across at him and nodded. "I'll be looking after things," he said. "It will all be just the way you want it."

Buck was staring at the fire, his pipe dead in his hand and his glass poised before him. "I'm too old to be a cripple, you know." In the silent room his voice was low and still. "When I can't live any more the way I want to, then I'm ready to go." The log cracked in the fireplace and sparks fled into the darkness of the chimney. Buck looked over at White Eagle and smiled and rattled the ice in his glass. "Another quail season—it ought to be a good one."

"You take care of yourself." John's face was dark and shadowed and he was sitting straight and stiff in the chair.

"I will," Buck said. "I will."

When they went outside they stopped for a moment beyond the door to look up at the soft silver of the heavens. Their breath showed before them like mist, and Buck turned his coat collar up against his neck. Just as they reached the gate they heard suddenly the baying of hounds, pealing through the great silence of the night. They listened for a moment and then looked at each other.

"Couldn't be anybody else," John said.

Buck looked across the darkness toward the east ridge. "I hope Jeff's with him," he said.

164

When they reached the pickup, he let John get in and then he stood there with his arms on the window. "What I was talking about in there—this boy, Jeff Beecher—he might ask you about me if anything happened. Maybe you could explain to him—you and I have known each other for a long time—you could talk with him, anyway. Just if something happened—it would mean a lot to me."

"However you want it to be," White Eagle said. He pulled the knob on the panel and light streamed suddenly through the night. "So long, Hardin."

Thanksgiving came and went, the skies thickened into gray, and slow rain dripped from the withered blackjack leaves. Autumn was almost gone and it was quail season again. At least it would be at dawn tomorrow, and Buck was whistling to himself as he drove along the road to Samuel's. The windshield wipers squeaked rhythmically across the wet glass and through the mist the headlights were soft and blurred. When he came to Samuel's cattle guard he turned off the road and jolted across the pipes and then pulled up just behind Jeff's car. The rain drummed across the brim of his hat as he got out and he turned his face up for a moment so that the drops beat upon his skin, and in that moment his flesh seemed mingled with wood smoke and drifted leaves and slanting rain and he laughed to himself for the joy of it. While he stood there the door opened and pale light filtered through the darkness. Then he heard the heavy sound of boots on the porch.

"That you, Hardin?" Samuel called.

"I'm on my way in," he said. He walked quickly across the yard and up the porch steps. "It's a little wet."

"I thought maybe you might be over. Come on in by the fire."

"Who owns all the cars?"

"Some of the boys come out for fox but it's a little on the wet side—they thought they'd sit and warm up for awhile and wait for it to stop."

"They may have quite a wait from the way it's going," Buck said.

Samuel smiled at him, the white stubble on his cheek shining a little in the pale lamplight. "They haven't got anyplace to go to," he said. "There's plenty of wood and coffee and they sound like they're wound up to last the night."

The room was obscured with shadows through whose depths the wan glow of the kerosene lamps shone as though through water. Light glancing from the fireplace illumined for a moment of grace the crown of a straw hat, a hand whose fingers trailed loosely across a knee, the corrugations of a boot, the curving stem and bowl of a pipe, a face modeled in cadences of darkness, the gleam of a gun barrel or of a coffee pot, the depthless glow of a hound's eyes, the precise confusion of chair legs upon the splintered floor. Then as Buck entered faces turned, voices called his name, and he felt the almost physical sense of his reception into their rough midst. Suddenly there was an empty chair by the side of the fire, and when he had sat down and filled his pipe and there was a cup of coffee steaming in his hand the pattern seemed to flow back into place. Once again the light flickered across the faces and tobacco smoke eddied around the lamps and the hound's tail thumped the floor.

"Talkin' about birds—" it was Sim Henry who spoke, leaning back in the rocker, his face narrow and reflective above the pipe that he tamped with his thumb. He stroked a match along the bottom of the chair and moved the flame back and forth across the tobacco while his cheeks hollowed and his eyes shone distant and amused through the smoke. "When I was a kid we had a place down by Rock Springs. It was pretty skinny goin'—Dad always said that when he come out here he didn't have nothin' to his name but his hat and his ass and his hat wasn't any too good. He worked hard enough but there was a lot of us and it was tough. He had a rule for all of us kids—we had to eat in the kitchen till we got to where

166

we were big enough to contribute somethin' to the table —earned some money some way, planted a garden, caught some fish or stole somebody else's corn. After that we could eat in the other room with the grown people." He lit another match and Buck looked over toward the table where Jeff was sitting. His head was bent and the fire lit the yellow of his hair and then as the light shifted Buck could see the cleaning rod in his hand. "My mother had brought some books with her when they moved out here—they was stacked in one of the closets and nobody had touched 'em till I stumbled in there one day. I guess I spent a good part of that particular day in the closet and after that I had to sneak 'em out in the weeds somewhere because it made my dad so mad to see me readin'. Naturally it played hell with my contributin', and none of the others could figure why I didn't mind eatin' out in the kitchen by myself until they caught on to the fact that I was readin' while the rest of them had to listen to my dad sound off about one thing or the other. So he really got in behind me, then—took all my books and said that my readin' days was over until I started puttin' somethin' on the table. Well, a lot of those books seemed to be about Englishmen, how they were all the time jumpin' onto their horses and hollerin' tally ho and takin' off across some poor bastard's fields after some fox or other. And when they wasn't doin' that they was blastin' away at stags or pheasants or what have you. I didn't have a horse and I damn sure didn't have any red coat and I didn't figure that fox would be much good for eatin' anyway, but I couldn't help thinkin' that with stags bein' a little on the scarce side in these parts, I could sure as hell blast a pheasant just about as good as any Englishman could. At least from the way they always looked in the pictures —kinda fat and wearin' funny lookin' hats with feathers stuck in the band. So one morning before the rest of the folks was up I copped the old man's twelve-gauge and went out to get me some pheasant. That way I could get my books back and eat with the grown people and everything would be just fine." Sim's voice was as steady and as natural and as pleasant as the sound of the rain against the roof; it was his own rare and unaccountable gift. He was smart, but so were other men; in a country of big-framed people he was on the small side; he was not hearty or open or generous or even uncommonly friendly, but there was the sound of running water in his voice, the summer sound of locusts in the trees. He was a natural born talker, and on the strength of it he had been county attorney for about as long as any of those gathered there could remember. "I was near-sighted then, except that I didn't know it because nobody had ever told me what it was. By noon I had covered the pastures pretty good clear down to the creek and had searched what few trees there were around the place and I was about ready to call it a day on pheasants. Same time I hated to go back with that gun that I had stole and nothing to show for it. Well, I had come up in back of the barn and then all of a sudden I saw the grass moving a little—it was tall grass and anything working through it would make it wiggle a little. I knew I had my pheasant. I kind of had that picture in my mind, the one of the fat Englishman standin' there and a big pheasant flyin' up in front of him and him blastin' away. So I raised my gun and stood there for awhile, but nothin' happened. Just the grass wavin' a little and kind of a scratching sound. Pretty soon I was gittin' a little hot under that high sun, so I thought to myself, I'll rush the sonofabitch. I couldn't see any too well, like I say, but I was too dumb to know better and thirteen years old to boot. So I kind of held that big shot gun out in front of me like a spear and charged. There was a squawk and somethin' jumped up in front of me and I blasted away for all I was worth. I got it, too, the only real good layin' hen on the place. Dad finally found me that afternoon in a tree down by the creek; he gave me a workin' over so that I didn't feel like goin' back to the house until I could tell by the sounds that it was supper time. I washed up and then slipped into the kitchen. There wasn't any plate there, and I wondered whether they was goin' to let me eat anything. Then I heard my dad. 'Bub, come the hell on in here.' I opened the door and looked in—they was all sittin' there and that big hen on a plate right in the middle. 'You contributed the gol-danged thing,' he said, shaking his head at me, 'so set yore butt down to the table and help us get rid of it.' I always ate with the rest of 'em after that."

Virgil Sands shifted his cigar and blinked rapidly behind his glasses. "I always knowed you was nearsighted," he said. "I just hadn't figured on you bein' so dumb."

Sim knocked his pipe against the heel of his hand. "Then I reckon I've been one jump ahead of you, Virge," he said softly. "I always had you figured for both."

Watching him work on the gun, it seemed to Buck that Jeff was more at ease than he had ever seen him before. Even in his silence he seemed to belong to this fireside and to the talk that went on slowly around it. His face, usually distracted and remote, was alert and interested, and from the way that his eyes moved from one speaker to another and then back to what he was doing he seemed unwontedly content. In the beginning, he had struck Buck as someone curiously incapable of either real happiness or pain, someone whose veins of feeling had been cauterized. More than anything else he had seemed a man, or boy, for the two were curiously commingled in him, who came from no place and who had no place to go. But now, somehow, it was different; there was an instinctive sureness in his hands that had not been there before, and his eyes were newly alive. Maybe at long last the old debt to Samuel was being paid off.

"Hardin, you've probably shot more birds than any of us, lessen it's Sam." Will MacIntosh was a big-boned man, somber except on the occasions when he flared into drunkenness, murderously strong and yet by nature simple and instinctive as an animal. His was a blood that ran at crosscurrents, Scotch-Irish and Chetopa, so that no sooner did he hit upon a shrewd financial scheme than he blighted its chances through laziness and waste and simple neglect. There was more than one monument to his folly in the county, and more than one investor who had been wooed and won by Scotch canniness and then deserted by Chetopa disinterest. At the moment he was pouring some bourbon into a silver cup which he carried in his pocket, and through the shadows his face showed smooth and dark with a grain that glowed in the firelight. "I've walked many a mile with you, and you've been at it a lot longer than I have."

Buck shifted in his seat and stretched his legs out in front of him. "I guess I've had my share," he said. "And maybe more. But there's always at least one, or a few at most, that you never forget." He was looking into the fire now, as though he saw in the flames a host of memories. "It's the first one a lot of times; maybe one that you brought down on a day with the wind so cold that your fingers just couldn't feel or one that you hit with a shot that was so good that you wouldn't dare tell anybody about it who hadn't seen it with his own eyes. But the one I remember most was the last day I went out with my dad. I wasn't much more than a kid—just home from the war and full of being a second lieutenant and a flyer in general just talking too much. The old man got it into his head that he was going to take me down a few notches—it always had been his favorite sport. I suppose he figured that it was long enough since I had worked a shot gun so that he could make me look pretty bad on quail. Anyway, he rode me until I took him up on it, betting him that I could match him bird for bird; he had made me mad and that was just what he had wanted to do. Well, the summer had been dry—there wasn't much cover—birds were scarce. The day we went out together I don't remember that we took a shot all morning. It was that bad. He was all smiles and jokes when we ate lunch, but I was still taking it seriously; I figured that there would be time to joke after I had got me a bird. Finally about the middle of the afternoon we got into a covey. They flew out of range and scattered when we first got them up, but we saw where they landed and figured we could pick up some singles. Dad decided to go along the top of the saddle and I worked the side. I got one up and missed him and the second one I got on real good and brought him down. From the noise of the firing up above me it sounded like the old man was getting his limit, but when I saw him he was mad. He had shot four times and didn't have a thing to show for it. It was my turn to joke then, and I kept it up for what there was left of the afternoon. He was walking hard, not saying anything, and I could see the sweat on his face in spite of the fact that it was cold. Pretty soon I began to feel sorry about the kidding I was giving him. By that time I didn't like it any more; I was hoping he would get a couple of birds and then things would be the way they ought to be. And that meant him riding the hell out of me the way he always had; it just wasn't right the other way around. By late afternoon when the wind started picking up again I knew that he wasn't going to get any bird; I had watched him on his last shot and it was all right there plain as day in the way he jerked the gun up to his shoulder like it had all of a sudden got too heavy for him; just the way he fumbled around with his gloves and cussed himself when he missed. I knew I had to get another bird before dark. Well, about that time the dog started working fast close to the ground and it was easy to tell she was on birds. The only thing about it was that it was a bad spot —it was the north edge of that strip of blackjack just above the old ranch. Remember the place, Will? We made it a couple of times last year. It just seems like the birds locate themselves there so that the minute they get up they can veer into the trees and be gone before you can even begin to get on them. It was close to dark by now, though, and bad spot or good, I had me another bird to get. I would have laid a bet where the dog would freeze and she didn't miss it by five feet. We took our gloves off then. 'Look,' I said to him. 'You go in along the trees. You were the one talking about being a quail shot. I'll give you a place where you can prove it.' I don't know whether he heard me or not; I kind of hope he didn't. Anyway, he was already walking in and the wind was whipping through those trees and it was getting dark fast. Then before I had a chance to think any more about it the birds were in the air and whistling toward those blackjacks just like I knew they would. There was one, flying like a single just a little below and behind the rest; he was the only one there was even a chance on. I got behind him just as he made the trunks at the edge of the woods and I let fly. The noise was too big for my gun alone, and then I thought I could see some feathers. For a minute Dad didn't say anything. He was kneeling on the ground just as I was—you had to to get at anything among those damned trees—and then he looked over at me. 'Where was your bird?' he said. 'Mine went right on down the ridge,' I told him. 'It's too dark to hit anything now.' Then he started shaking his head, looking up toward the trees. 'You should have seen that shot of mine,' he said. 'It was a sonofabitch.' The dog came through the grass with the bird in its mouth and we stood there waiting. 'He must have been in the trees when you hit him,' I said. 'I never made a shot like that in my life,' he answered me. 'I guess it's good enough to quit on, don't you think?' That was his last one—he never went out again, that I know of. He was getting old by that time and his eyes weren't much good anymore."

"I've heard 'em talk about him down at the smoke house," Will said. "Some of the real old ones. They always said he was a good shot. Was it you or him got the bird?"

"He was one of the best," Buck said. "I never bothered to try and figure it out."

"I reckon he was at that," Samuel said, placing his

coffee cup on the floor beside the chair. "Old man Revard remembers him—talks about some of the bob cat hunts they used to have."

"That would be a long time ago," Buck said, taking out his tobacco pouch.

"Puts me in mind of a Thanksgiving—way back," Samuel said. His face was tranquil and meditative as he looked into the fire, and one shoulder dropped a little where the hand went down to fondle the hound's head. The wood cracked in the silence and Samuel was quiet for a moment before he spoke, as though he were trying the words for size. "My pop was pretty sick and I was too little to know what it was all about. All I knew was that it was sad and that there were a lot of people round the house that hadn't been there for a long time or even at all as far as I could tell. The funny part of it was that the more people there was the more lonesome I got—I didn't know half of 'em and none of 'em had any time for me. I hardly even saw my mother except when one of my aunts would take me into the room where my old man was sick and then I would be more lonesome than ever. Finally one day when I went in he asked me wasn't it about time for bird huntin' to start—it scared me a little to talk to him, he was so thin and his eyes were so shiny-like, but I said yes that the huntin' ought to be good now because it was just gittin' that time of year. He told me then how much he would like some quail to eat and would I go out and hunt some up. I guess the reason I was lonesome was that I didn't have nothin' to do because this idea struck me as just fine. I could hardly wait. Well, I was still kinda little for the twelve-gauge and I wouldn'ta had the chance of a snowball in hell with a four-ten so we compromised on the sixteen-gauge even though it was mighty rough to hit anything as fast and as little as a quail with it. I'll never forget the day; it was cold as it could be and windy to boot. My hands was cold before I got my gloves on and the gloves didn't seem to do anything but just keep 'em that way. But I

was glad to be a way from the house and to be doin'
somethin' for a change. And the only thing I had in my
mind was gettin' them birds so that my old man could
have 'em to eat." He paused then for a moment and looked
around the circle of faces, almost as though he were looking for someone who might also remember. Then he
looked back at the fire and smiled a little and went on. "I
didn't have but a handful of shells and I probably didn't
git more than five or six shots all day, but wind, sixteen-
gauge, cold and all, I got me two birds. I reckon I was
pretty close to runnin' on the way back. You know how
the wind will make you cry, and when I come into the
kitchen it was too warm all of a sudden and that made me
cry all the more—not actually cryin' but just my eyes
waterin' to beat hell. Well, it was too quiet in there—I
knew that right off. My pop had died that day while I
was gone. I was so tired and cold that it didn't hit me
right away—I couldn't put my mind on anything except
them birds that was still in my sack, pressin' against my
back. Pretty soon I slipped out of the house and went
back into the woods and buried 'em. I just didn't rightly
know what else to do." He looked at them again, and as
he turned the darkness flowed into the long, vertical hollows of his face. "Funny how those things stick in your
mind. I hadn't thought about it for a long time."

The rain was gusty now on the roof, and as the fire
suddenly caved and glowed more intensely, the hound
lifted its head and looked up at Samuel as though
awaiting the renewal of his voice. Sim stretched his arms
and stood up. "Well, boys," he yawned, "we'd better fish
or cut bait. It's gittin' on the late side."

Will MacIntosh drained off his bourbon and looked up
at the shadowed ceiling. "Sounds like it's let up some. I'm
game."

They all got up and stood for a moment in stiff
awkwardness, silent, as though the passing of the rain had
dried the springs of speech. Each man looked at the fire,
once more alone and isolate.

"Yeah," Virge said, speaking as in answer to some thought of his own.

Sim nodded. "You're sure you won't come along," he said, looking at Samuel.

Samuel seemed to start and then turned toward him, his eyes still distant. "No," he said, "no. You boys go on ahead."

Sim nodded again. "Well," he said. "I guess it's been wet before. Come on before that fox gits himself drowned."

When they were gone the room was more deeply silent than before. The three of them had remained standing, and then Buck went over to the table where Jeff was working. He could see that the gun which Jeff had been cleaning belonged to Samuel. "I've got a gun for you over at the house," he said to Jeff. "So don't worry about—"

"Wait a minute," Jeff said, going into the bedroom. When he returned he had a shotgun in his hands.

"When did you get it?"

"A man cain't very well go bird huntin' for the first time without a gun, can he?" Samuel said.

"It's a nice one," said Buck, holding it down to the fire where he could see the light play along the barrel.

Jeff nodded toward Samuel. "He brought it from town just today."

Buck looked at Samuel and when their eyes met it was almost as though they were shaking hands. "I'll be looking for you in the morning," he said.

"Early."

"Early. I'll be ready. Just hope for a good day."

Outside the moon had cut its way through ragged clouds and it was beginning to clear. And now as he drove home Buck was not sure whether what he felt was happiness or pain. He looked up at the moon as though some omen might pass across its face, a cast of birds perhaps or a cloudy portent of his future, for somehow he sensed that he had reached a fork in the road, that his journey now was leading him into a valley of shadows from which he might never emerge again. Something was happening to him, and happening fast, and he was afraid even to think about what it might be. There was winter in his blood, and his spirit stood stark and exposed as the lone blackjack on the point. In some curious way it was as though he awaited the lightning's jagged and fiery and immeasurably final thrust.

CHAPTER X

☐ The night had been long and dream-broken, and Buck awoke in the dawn feeling tired and stiff and strangely nervous. Shivering a little in the shadowed cool, he pulled on wool socks and thrust his feet hard into the bent and wrinkled hunting boots and then went outside to get some wood. To the west the sky was still a dusky blue, silvered by the fading gleam of stars, while the lip of the eastern horizon seemed filled to overflowing with the sun's fire. The fallen leaves, the weeds, the trumpet vines laced along the fence, all sparkled crisply with frost, and the early cries of birds were needle sharp in the quivering silence. Against his hands the logs were cold as he hoisted them under his arms; bent with the weight of them, he kicked the kitchen door open and walked hurriedly to the fireplace.

As soon as the fire had caught he put the coffee pot on and heated his water for shaving. Then he finished dressing, standing before the fire, enjoying as he always did the pleasant roughness of the wool clothing which he had put away eight months ago. As he took the twelve-gauge from the rack and worked the pump quickly back and forth, he laughed at the eagerly grinning face of the red setter which was peering in at the window, her forepaws resting against the sill.

"All right," Buck said. "Just a little longer." And when he went outside with the steaming wash basin and his razor, he had to hold the basin high above the wildly jumping dog. *Let me get shaved, anyway." He grinned. "We'll get there."

But as he shaved, he was unable to shake off the feeling that this was not going to be a particularly good day. There was no real edge to the coolness, and the clear sky and the fountain of fire in the east meant heat by noon. They would need to find birds early or run the risk of a long day spent in vain. And all at once he realized that he never thought of it that way before. For what had always mattered most had been just the quality of the weather, whether glittering with frozen light or leaden or rain-whipped or that once-in-a-while glorious perfection of November when the trees towered like torches into the gilded slate of the sky. What had counted was the walking, and the dog a frenzy of crimson among the old copper of the dead Johnson grass, and the air and the talk and the silence and maybe then, beyond all, the ancient exultation when the bird in its incredible speed seemed to hang for a long moment in the air, plummeting at last through drifting feathers to the earth. With these things around him there could have been no day spent in vain; yet now there was Jeff, and Samuel, and he himself, and strange things were in the wind.

When he had finished washing up, he returned to the kitchen and now the odor of coffee was warm and pungent through the house. He poured a cup and while it cooled he filled the pockets of his hunting jacket with shells. After breakfast he put together some sandwiches, filled the Thermos with what remained of the coffee, and took a final check of his pockets to make sure that he had an extra pipe and plenty of matches. He had the feeling somehow that he was forgetting something, for across his mind lay something blurred and chill as fog. Then as he stood there in the center of the room, looking around him somewhat abstractedly, he suddenly pulled on his gloves and slapped the side of his leg impatiently.

The setter circled him nervously and danced at his side

until he had opened the gate of the yard. As he walked on down the road toward the pasture gate she ran wildly in vast circles through the tall grass, resembling in her careening flight the gyrations of a suddenly released balloon. And after she had run awhile, Buck called her to him where he sat by the gate, and he rubbed her head and trembling sides and talked to her until she had calmed "Birds," he said finally, speaking low and somewhat insistently. "Birds, birds." And suddenly the setter was poised, intent, concentrated on the work. When Buck released her she began at once to nose her way swiftly through the underbrush.

He heard the car rattling across the ruts before he could see it. After a few moments light ricocheted off metal through the blackjacks and there was Samuel, leaning out of the window a little, watching for high center. When he got to the fence he stopped the car, raced the motor twice, and cut the ignition.

"Gonna be too damned warm," he muttered, opening the door and spitting down into the road.

"We might get a break," Buck said, looking into the car toward Jeff. "Maybe it won't warm up too much."

"Well, there's one thing for sure," Samuel replied, leaning into the back seat to get the guns. "Warm or cold, the birds'll be there—let's get the hell after 'em."

"You feel awake enough?" Buck asked, smiling at Jeff, who was yawning and stretching on the other side of the car.

"You said yourself that that coffee of his doesn't leave much choice." Jeff grinned. "I don't think I'll have any excuse in that direction."

Samuel was stamping his feet on the ground and watching the dog as she moved down toward the corner of the fence line. "For God's sake don't start talkin' about excuses yet. All you got to do is get on 'em and squeeze. You're gonna have me nervous in a minute. Dog looks good."

"She's ready," Buck said. "Why don't we start on the east ridge. There's usually a couple of coveys over there somewhere."

Samuel nodded quickly. He was whistling what sounded to Buck like a hymn, he seemed impatient, and in his own way he appeared more detached and intent than the dog. He loaded his gun, whistling loudly to himself, and then he started on down the road, his corduroy pants flapping around his lean legs and the sheepskin riding up high along his hips and seeming too tight across his shoulders.

"Looks like he means business," Buck said to Jeff.

Jeff smiled as he fed shells into his magazine. "I don't know how early he was up this morning—he just couldn't get started soon enough."

"I'm glad you decided to stay."

Jeff glanced up quickly and their eyes met in silence. Then he was almost upset by the sudden rush of the setter between them.

"She's as impatient as Sam," Buck laughed. "We'd better get started."

It was a glittering day when sights and sounds seemed strangely new and sharp, as though the winds of morning and the light of dawn had somehow miraculously quickened senses filmed with the stains of indiscriminate use. The wind scraped dry limbs of the blackjacks, and from a stand of ancient cottonwoods down the road the leaves drifted slow and yellow. A scattered flight of crows flapped loudly across the sky, and through the frost-stiffened grass the setter followed the intricate trails, searching with feverish and yet controlled intensity.

"I just about didn't bring my gloves," Jeff said, cradling the gun diagonally across his chest. "Probably won't need them by noon, but they sure feel good right now."

Buck nodded. "I think I'd take 'em off if I were you when we get to the ridge. You'll have to stay ready."

"The way Pap tells it, if I blink my eyes at the wrong time the birds will be out of range."

"He always was one for understating the case," Buck said, stopping to light his pipe. "No, it's nothing but instinct—don't worry about it."

"I'm afraid my instincts are a bit rusty," Jeff said, smiling quickly.

Buck nodded and said nothing.

By noon they had hunted the east ridge as far down as the creek on the south. Twice they had found coveys and both times the dog had held, frozen in rigid immobility until the drumming flight of the quail had released her tension. Samuel, walking down the center of the ridge, had hit birds cleanly both times. Buck had put Jeff on the left since by the location of the trees it would be natural for the birds to veer in that direction; yet by the time they stopped for lunch, Jeff had fired only once and that a seeming desperation shot with the birds already out of range. Buck himself had taken the extreme right flank of the ridge and had had no chance for shooting; still he had not particularly minded. For rarely had he known a more pleasant day. The dog was performing beautifully, and he was with friends, and there was someone young along to be watched and taught and hoped for. These were primitive satisfactions, felt in the deeps of the soul, and their purity and simplicity were in perfect accord with the hushed harmony of the day. All about him as he walked were the sudden songs of birds, the slow rain of leaves, the orange and yellow flames of autumn. It was in moments such as these that the gods whom he had worshipped stood shining again before his eyes.

The sun was overhead when they stopped for lunch. They had come to some bluffs that stood high above the creek, and there beneath the oak trees they rested and ate their sandwiches.

"Well," Samuel said, pouring coffee from his Thermos

181

bottle, "I've had better mornings. Two birds won't make a supper. And then I've had worse, too."

"I expected to see more birds," Jeff said, frowning as he rubbed some dirt from the stock of his gun.

"You'll see them. The season's far from over." Buck was sitting with his back against a tree, his hat pulled down a little over his eyes.

"I suppose," Jeff said, uncertainly.

Samuel shook his head sharply. "We'll see birds. They just don't make quail country any better than what we've got here. You got to be patient."

"That was a stupid shot I took this morning."

"Needed to git the feel of the gun. Now you're ready to buckle down to business." In the old man's face there was a strange abstracted concentration and his words were clipped and emphatic, as though he could spare but a moment from the matters that crowded his mind. As he finished his last sandwich he rolled his sheepskin into a pillow, pulled off his heavy shoes, and then stretched out in the shade. "Give me a nudge when the sun gits down a little," he said. And in what seemed to be only a matter of moments he was breathing with heavy regularity, sound asleep.

"A man with a peaceful mind," Buck said, chewing at a piece of grass and looking out at Jeff from under his hatbrim.

Jeff was leaning back on his hands, staring up at the sky. "He could go to sleep standing up. And when he wants to he can sit by a fire somewhere all night without even yawning. Almost like a hound."

"An easy man," Buck said again. Through half-closed eyes he was watching a kingfisher that was perched on a dead limb high above the creek. He did not need to look to know what surrounded him—the creek on his right, and to his left the yellowed prairie grasses thrust up into the trough between the cresting ridges. Down these slopes he had ridden many a day, through the wind-

182

driven grasses to this spot that was as familiar to him as his own flesh. Long ago he had sat here just as Jeff sat now, arms thrust back, eyes probing the sky, except that his own moods had almost always been compounded of wonder and veneration and humility; Jeff seemed to be searching without much hope for something from which he had long ago been torn loose. And now as he lay there in the shifting pattern of the sunlight and shade that played through the slanting drift of leaves, Buck could almost feel the currents of continuity, of change and of renewal, pouring through him. How long ago it had been that he had inched his way down these bluffs to look excitedly into the hole where lay the still warm eggs of the kingfisher.

"When do you think you'll be going?"

Jeff turned and looked at him with questioning eyes. "I said I'd stay until quail season."

"What then?"

"I don't know," he said, almost too carelessly. "Back to New York, probably. I've had enough traveling for awhile—perhaps I could get a job there."

Buck looked at him, his eyes narrowed with surprise. "You seem to have it pretty well settled," he said. It was as though the boy had suddenly withdrawn into himself, and Buck had the strange feeling of not being able to reach him at all.

Jeff smiled nervously. "When you asked me to stay," he said, "what was it you were really thinking about?"

And suddenly Buck saw him as he had been when he had stood there by the window, his hand still clutching the sash cord, his eyes shocked and disbelieving. That morning Jeff had seemed humiliated, stunned, at the end of his tether. Now there was almost mockery in his voice.

"I suppose I had Samuel in mind most, then," he answered. "It was later that I began to see your side of it a little." Buck pushed his hat back and sat up against the tree. "I've told you what Sam did for me. I had an idea what your being here meant to him. I wanted it to work out."

"Did you ever think it would?"

The casual quality of Jeff's voice brought a sudden flush of anger to Buck's face, the kind of anger he might have felt if his own son had scornfully ignored some long-meditated piece of advice.

"I didn't think of it that way, whether it would or wouldn't," he said, his words quick and sharp with emotion. "I wanted it to work because it was right and good. But you had me beat right from the start—you were looking for something that wasn't there at all."

"I don't know what it was," Jeff said with strange calmness. "I told you about my father—how I felt about that. Then when Mom died I was all alone—I felt homesick, lost. I didn't know where the hell I was. I started remembering things from way back, sounds, the way a certain house looked in a certain light, the way somebody talked. They were all things from when I was little, things that I remembered from the farm. And then I got to wanting those things more than anything else in the world. It was almost like wanting to believe in God again."

"And Samuel turned out to be just an ordinary man."

"Not ordinary—but not a god. I wanted too much; I was upset from what Mom had told me. But I'm over it now; it doesn't matter so much any more."

Buck was silent for awhile and then he spit out the grass that he was chewing.

"You're probably tired from getting up so early this morning," he said brusquely. "We all are. Better rest for a little before we go on." He turned over on his side then, and shielded his eyes from the sun with his hat. The oak leaves rustled high above him, but it was the silence that he was listening to.

He was awakened from a fitful nap by the cool muzzle of the setter at his neck. He yawned and then looked at

184

his watch. Just after two; three good hours of hunting yet. When he sat up he saw that Jeff was still sitting in the same place, looking at him with eyes that were strangely hard and deliberate, and suddenly a current of hot and angry feeling seemed to spark between them.

"I guess it's time we got going," Buck said abruptly.

Jeff nodded. Then he reached over and shook Samuel by the shoulder. "Come on, Pap," he said gently. "Time to go."

The old man sat up quickly, looked around blinking, and then got to his feet in silence. When he had reloaded his gun he glanced over at Buck and grinned. "I'm two up on you, Hardin," he said. "When you gonna start shootin'?"

"Better hold your count until dark," Buck answered. "There s a lot of hunting left in this day yet." In his mind there was something cold and hard as ice, as though all of his desires had crystallized into a single aim.

It was an afternoon that even he was proud of, and he had had many a good afternoon through the years. As they worked their way back up the east ridge they picked up the covey which they had scattered in the morning. Walking in behind the dog on the first point he winged a single off to the right and then swung back into the center in time to drop another bird just as it banked toward cover.

In the meantime Samuel had missed a difficult angle shot as his bird swept low to his left and into the protection of the scrub oak. He pumped the shell from his shot gun and looked over at Buck. "Well?" he said.

"We're even."

"A pair?"

Buck nodded.

"Why you son of a gun."

Jeff had been behind Buck and a little to his right. "That was beautiful shooting," he said quietly, coming up to look at the birds which the setter had retrieved. He knelt then, and held one in his hand, and when he handed

185

it on to Buck there was just the faintest trace of blood across his fingers. "That was beautiful work."

Buck looked down at him, his jaw working, his throat strangely tight and dry. "It was lucky," he said roughly. Then he rubbed his hand quickly over the setter's head. "Birds," he said intently, "birds."

A hundred yards further down the ridge he picked off a high-flying, straight-away single which had exploded without warning from almost under his feet. It was a relatively easy shot and yet it afforded the satisfaction that always came with fast and accurate shooting. From up on the ridge Samuel waved in recognition and Buck lifted his gun in reply. Later on, behind the site of the old ranch house, he added two more birds to his bag, the last one of which he hit in the haze of approaching dusk. They were working along the rim of the stock pond and the covey had bloomed suddenly in a fan-wise burst of wings. He went to one knee, following the lightning flight of his bird just to the edge of the woods, and then he fired at what seemed to be no more than a ripple in the waters of evening. It was the best way to end a day.

Now the dog stood up to her belly in the pond, breaking the reflections with her lapping tongue. The day had gone all red and black, and the wind that stirred the grass was chill.

"God damn it if your eyes don't git better the older you git," Samuel said, "or else you're pushin' the hell out of your luck, one. You missed easier shots than that last year."

"Maybe this is the year I've always hoped for," Buck laughed, suddenly relaxed. "Maybe this is my year."

"Do we have to quit?" Jeff asked, frowning at him. "There's still a half hour of light." There was something new in his face now, something harder, more intense.

"You shot up fifty cents' worth of shells in broad daylight without raisin' a feather," Samuel said. "Maybe you figure you cain't do no worse in the dark."

"Give him time, Sam," Buck said. "You scattered some

186

buckshot around today yourself." Then he whistled to the setter. "I'll be watching for you on Thursday. Better get some tin cans, old man," he said, putting his hand on Samuel's shoulder, "and practice a little. I'm two up on both of you."

Samuel pursed his lips and grunted. "Yeah. Well, Thursday, then," he muttered. He stood there for a moment looking at Buck, his face long, melancholy, pondering. "God damn it," he said softly, "I still cain't git past that double you hit back there on the ridge. It damn near takes the fun out of it. Thusday."

Buck laughed. "We'll be waiting for you."

He was tired that night with a weariness that seemed to go deep down into his very bones. There was a dull pain in his chest, and the muscles in his legs were tight and sore. He sat for a long time in the old leather chair, drinking Scotch and watching the fire, listening to the wind in the chimney. The setter dozed at his feet on the worn bear rug, trembling now and again as though in dreams, and all about the house was the clear chill silence of winter starlight. It was late when he had supper, and then just before going to bed he went out into the night where the moon shone thin and bright as zinc. Down to the west he could hear the plaintive questioning of the coyotes, and he could see the long waves of grass faintly silver in the pale wash of light. And then as he lay at last in bed, smoking a final cigarette, he thought that it was probably good that Jeff had been without luck on this first day. Whatever peculiar mood had come over the boy seemed to have been shattered by his own reaction and particularly by his shooting. Now, more than anything else, he wanted Jeff to get his bird.

It rained on Thursday, a chill driving rain that made hunting impossible. Unaccountably, Buck was seized by the urge to straighten things up, to put his affairs in order, and he spent the day cleaning his guns, sorting through papers, and generally arranging things as though he expected to be gone for a while. He brought his journal up to date and repaired the sagging bottom of the leather chair and then he dusted and cleaned the books which stood along the walls. It was early afternoon before he stopped long enough to eat, and he was glad when the job was done. It was almost as though he had needed to do it while he still had the strength. He slept uneasily that night, haunted by dreams, and toward morning he had to get up for another blanket. The cold seemed to grip the house in a mailed fist, and beyond the window the night air sparkled icily.

Deep winter came that night, gray, implacable, steel-booted and with heavy hands. The trees groaned in the wind, and birds huddled in miserable isolation on barren branches, their feathers puffed out against the cold. On Saturday morning the sky was dull blue with a gray tracery of cloud hurrying across the foreground; the earth was dark and frozen, and across the prairie the grass lay broken and flat. The three men did not talk much that morning as they hunted, for the wind seemed to tear the very breath from their mouths. They followed the dog in silence, guns cradled across their chests, eyes narrowed against the glitter and the cold.

Buck and Samuel each got two birds during the morning, and then Buck put Jeff between them after lunch. Jeff's face was strained, and Buck could sense his determination in the impatience of his eating. But it was not until late afternoon that Jeff had his first real chance at a bird. The day was darkening, the afternoon slipping imperceptibly into night, and Buck had led them to the point south of the house. There had been a covey there for as long as he could remember, and out of a strange kind of sentimental veneration he had never hunted them. But he needed them now, and he hoped that they would not fail him. He was not long in finding out. For as they approached the point from the creek side, the setter had suddenly stopped dead and now with her tail extending behind her like a banner she was pointing fixedly toward the deep grass just down from the blackjacks.

When Jeff looked around at him, Buck nodded and motioned for him to go on in. He saw Jeff slip the safety and take one cautious step, then another, toward the dog. The stiff grass crackled thinly under his feet as he stepped carefully along, his eyes straining intently toward the earth, the gun held in readiness before him. Buck, standing still and watching, suddenly became aware that Samuel was doing the same thing; both of them were standing there, watching Jeff go in for what they both prayed would be the kill. And then the air was all sound and motion, a great pulsing of wings as the flower of flight unfolded, and Jeff was down on one knee, the gun moving steadily to his right for what seemed surely too long and then suddenly came the explosion and the drift of feathers in the air and the dog was bounding high through the grass toward the dead bird. Buck heard Samuel repeating "Hot damn, hot damn," over and over again, but he could not hear him distinctly because already he was running, past Jeff now where the boy still knelt and on up toward the point, his cheeks stinging where the scalding tears fell, closer and closer until he had almost reached the bird. Then through him surged a great convulsive pain that for a terrible moment appeared to transfix him; he stood in rigid suspension, grasping the air, laboring without success to breathe. To Jeff and Samuel as they watched, it seemed that the spirit which fired his flesh must certainly have fled. And then as darkness came over him Buck saw as at a great distance the stony earth rising to meet his face.

CHAPTER XI

☐ By the time Jeff reached him Samuel was kneeling on the ground, his hand shoved under the hunting jacket and resting on Buck's heart, while from the sky darkness descended like a pall, obscuring the suppliant blackjacks, and the wind keened down the valley like some lost spirit.

"Just like he'd been shot," Samuel murmured. "Just like somebody hit him with a hammer." His face was turned up to Jeff's but his eyes seemed to look right through him. He frowned in the cold, his mouth half open, his breath forming bodiless clouds of mist in the gloom. "Hush," he said then, "hush," pulling the whimpering setter close in against his side.

"I saw him running past me," Jeff said anxiously as though he were asking a question. "He was running hard and he was almost up to the dog, like he was going to get the bird from her. Then all of a sudden something seemed to stop him—" and he shook his head abruptly against the scene which still burned in his mind. "Is he—" but he could not say the word, could not give sound to his fear.

Samuel scowled and buttoned the jacket close around Buck's throat. "He ain't dead yet. If we can git a doctor we might have a chance. Take the guns and go on up to the house."

Jeff hesitated and then looked stubbornly at his grandfather. "You can't do it alone."

191

The old man's jaw was set so that his mouth seemed to turn down at the corners. His eyes were narrow, almost angry. "Do like I say."

"Pap, you can't make it. I've got to carry him myself."

Samuel's chest heaved with his breathing and his face was white in the dusk. "God damn it to hell," he said hoarsely as he reached down for the guns. "You hang onto him like he was a baby, hear?"

Quick flames of pain flickered along Jeff's arms and back, and his legs trembled beneath the weight of Buck's body as he labored through the deepening twilight toward the house. A woodpecker shied from him round the trunk of a tree and flew on down the ridge with a flashing of white, but elsewhere there was only stillness, the fires of day gone dead, the trees standing in dark and voiceless lamentation. He stopped twice and lowered Buck carefully to the earth so that he might catch his breath and rub his shoulders where they were tight and aching. Then he picked him up again, cradling him in his arms as best he could, and went on among the silent trees, his feet uncertain on the rocks and frozen grass. When he reached the gate his breathing was an audible groan and his face was twisted with pain.

"For God's sake let me help you the rest of the way," Samuel said, standing by the open gate with a flashlight.

Between them they got Buck into the house and laid him down and then Samuel knelt on the stone floor beside the bed, his hand tight across his forehead and pressed against his eyes so that Jeff could not tell whether the old man was praying or merely trying to control the trembling of his body. Suddenly Jeff knelt in silence beside him, putting his arms around the hunched shoulders and holding him roughly against his chest. Samuel turned and looked at him with eyes that were filled with grief and as they knelt there staring wordlessly at one another, the room was suddenly loud with the gasping pump of lungs sucking at the air. Buck's mouth hung loosely agape and his half-opened eyes were blurred with the shadows of death. Jeff felt Samuel's body stiffen against him like steel.

"The fire," he said hoarsely. "Git some fire."

With frightened hands Jeff worked the fire into life while the heaving of Buck's body sounded its agony through the shadows. Then once again he knelt beside Samuel, looking at Buck's face, from which all color had vanished, leaving in its place only a pale frame for the trembling orifice of the mouth.

"What is it," he whispered.

"It's his heart," Samuel said, his rough hand gentle on Buck's straining chest. "It's workin' in there to beat hell."

"Can't we—?"

But Samuel was already pulling on his gloves. "Just the doctor. Pray God I can git him back here in time." The fire moved across his face, revealing the bleak outlines of pain, and as he stood there his body seemed to slump with the weight of his weariness and anxiety. He rubbed the back of his hand against his forehead. "O.K.," he said, his voice grave and subdued, speaking as though he were answering some interior command. He put his hand once more upon Buck's body, and then he was gone.

For a long time Jeff knelt there on the cold floor without moving, desperately watching Buck's face for some sign of conscious life. After a while he went to the mantel for a cigarette and when he returned he noticed that Buck had moved his hand until it rested now upon his heart. Quickly Jeff pulled a chair along side the bed and sat down, placing his hand upon Buck's. "Hardin?" he said softly, hopefully. "Hardin?"

It seemed then that there was just the faintest flutter of life across Buck's eyes. His mouth, still trembling, opening and closing like a bellows, worked silently as though in quest of lost words. And when the words came they were heavy with pain, less words at first than merely the soundings of shocked emotion. Jeff bent his head to

Buck's laboring lips. "What?" he whispered, shaking his head in bewilderment and turning once again to look into Buck's eyes.

Then, although he could not be sure, it seemed to him that he understood. For through the thick and groping welter of speech came the word "bird," then "your bird," indistinct and apparently without conscious recognition on Buck's part and yet to Jeff strangely, miraculously moving. The tears that burned down his cheeks were hot and immediate; he swallowed hard against the ache in his throat and then tensed his muscles against the sobs which shook him. And as he took Buck's hand the voice died away and the eyes became dark walls upon which the light of the fire played fitfully. Once again there was only the suck and ebb of Buck's throbbing body.

It took Samuel almost an hour to get back with the doctor. He was a small man, bald-headed and fat, and in the half light his smile was coldly cheerful. He worked quickly—his head cocked birdlike above the stethoscope and the icy glitter of the needle as he administered the adrenalin. Finally he had Buck settled and asleep. There was a brisk sureness and a lack of concern in all that he did which made Jeff expect him to break out whistling at any time. But then, as he told them by the fireplace over a drink, there was not much to be done.

"Oh, yes. He's had the condition for some time. Never was one for looking after himself, was he. Well, that's it. Simple. Running up the slope to pick up a bird, you say." He pursed his lips and then spread his hands before him. "What would you expect. Sure, I told him. He wouldn't believe it. They told him down at San Antonio during the war. It wasn't important; he couldn't be bothered. But he went to Kansas City this summer, see. There's a clinic up there—they wrote me about him. It gets you sooner or later. Do? Well," and then he had stopped smiling and his eyes were perfectly hard as though steeled against the unbelief and unwillingness that it was his lot to talk against every day. "He's got to stay in bed. How long? Two months, at least. We'll see then. And I mean stay in bed; there'll have to be somebody here to tend him. Why he's lucky he's still with us—it was bad, real bad."

There was not much for Jeff or Samuel to say. They looked at each other and then down at the floor or into the fire while the doctor lectured them. And yet they were glad to have him, glad of his fat and bald-headed assurance in this room that had been so fraught with the shadows of finality.

"Two months," he said again as he put the instruments back into his case. "Maybe three. Complete rest." And when he had put on his coat he stood there looking at Buck, the tips of his fingers resting against his chin. "It don't seem right to see him down, does it. Like a race horse with a broken leg." He stood there for a moment longer and then he slapped his gloves rapidly against his leg. "Good. Have to be going now. He'll be all right until morning and I'll be out again early."

"Certainly appreciate it, Cap," Samuel said, almost apologetically.

"We went to high school together," the doctor said. "He was different even then. It wasn't hard to tell." He tightened his mouth and smiled professionally. "Good night," he said cheerily, and after a moment they saw him stride briskly through the light that fell from the window.

"I guess he's all right, then," Jeff said quietly.

"Must be, from what the doc says. Little more Scotch?"

"Please." Jeff held out his glass and looked down the room to where Buck lay asleep in the shadows. "Two months is a long time."

"You bet it's a long time," Samuel said, sitting down again by the fire. "But what else can he do?"

The snapping of the wood was loud in the silence, and a sudden shower of sparks rushed up the black throat of the chimney. Jeff rattled the ice in his glass and looked at Samuel, knowing that there was something on the old man's mind that he was having a hard time finding words for.

"I guess I know what you're thinking," he said after a while. "Somebody's got to be here with Buck; I'd be glad to stay."

"I didn't want to ask you."

Jeff nodded. "Sure. I hope he won't mind, that's all."

"He thinks a lot of you, boy," Samuel said, looking at Jeff now with eyes that had for a moment become distant and meditative.

Jeff frowned and reached for a cigarette. "Whatever I can do," he said quickly, tossing the match into the fireplace and looking fixedly at the flames. For there was a loneliness in Samuel's face that Jeff could not bear to see.

Later that night Jeff sat finishing the Scotch, watching the last glow and flare of the coals in the ashes. Samuel had helped him move the other bed in from the porch and had promised to bring his clothes over the next morning along with some food from town. And when they had said goodnight to one another, there had been a strange poignancy about it almost as though they were saying a last good-by. More than ever, perhaps, on account of what had happened that day, Jeff was aware of the moat of silence that lay between them, aware of the vague uneasiness that made them pause uncertainly and stare at one another and then look away. It was something which he hated and yet something he knew no way to remedy. And he was afraid that his staying here could only make it worse.

He started a little when he heard the sudden scratching at the door and then he smiled at his nervousness. The setter came in eagerly when he opened the door, her nails sounding a quick patter across the concrete floor. She stood for a moment by Buck's bed and then lay down, her head resting on her forepaws, her eyes glowing in what little remained of the firelight. Jeff knelt and rubbed her head for a moment before going down to the fireplace to cover the coals with gray ash. The room was dark and yet mysteriously suspirant and alive, and the wan moon was far down the western sky before Jeff fell asleep.

The snows came, driving down out of the north before mighty winds that raged across the prairie without hindrance. The grass that poked up through the glittering crust was straw-colored and brittle, and trees caught the white flakes in black and barren arms. There were few birds but they were more apparent, flashing through the silence like bright threads in a somber tapestry. And on the snow's pristine surface could be found all the delicate tracework drawn by the stir of life that must go on even more desperately now. It was a time of quick death for the unwary, a time when the cold and shriveled bellies of the marauders drove them mercilessly on silent wing or searching paw until at last there was the sudden panic in the snow, the lashing, convulsive moment of terror, and death. Then once again the white and motionless silence was disturbed by no more than a feather tilting in the wind or a crater in the snow crust where a spot of blood lay like a rose.

But these were clear days for Jeff; there was a zest in everything he did, as though on the very verge of exhaustion he had found the renewed strength and power of second wind. He awoke rested after hard and dreamless sleeps, dressed shiveringly in the sullen dawn, knelt before the fireplace until the flames licked along the heavy logs, and then hurried to the kitchen to set about fixing breakfast for Buck and himself. After breakfast there was wood to chop and stack as well as occasional trips to town for groceries or for taking care of some matter at the museum. Often in the afternoon he would go out for a walk with the dog, sometimes going as far as Samuel's and then returning through the fading crimson of late afternoon to the house that stood like a small fortress above the sweep of the plains. In the evening he would read aloud, stopping to make more tea or to talk about something that Buck had mentioned. And as the night wore on the fire would wane and Jeff would hear Buck's breathing becoming heavy and regular and he would go on reading until he was sure that Buck was asleep. Finally in the silence he would bank the fire and blow out the lamps and go to bed, falling asleep almost as soon as he had settled himself beneath the blankets.

But there was a mood of withdrawal about Buck, a restlessness that stirred uneasy currents in Jeff's mind. That Buck should chafe under his confinement was natural, but there was a look in his eyes that was more than irritation, more than anger or boredom. Sometimes it seemed as though he were looking beyond the limits of matter, of flesh, into a dimension of purity that made his eyes shine with a hard intensity.

He had asked Jeff to shift his bed so that he would be able to look down the ridge beyond the point to the dark line of trees along the creek. There were days when his face was quick and wild as of old as he watched the birds feeding on the snow or flickering among the trees, days when he would talk of the natural life of the ridge with an eloquence and love that made Jeff marvel. And sometimes as he talked Jeff glimpsed through his words an order which, imperfectly though he saw it, still somehow made him almost catch his breath at its stark and elemental beauty. But there were other days when Buck would lie in unbroken silence for hours, staring down toward the lone blackjack at the point of the ridge. When at last he would speak again, more often than not it would be in reference to the museum, some detail that he had not checked or something that he wanted Jeff to do. It appeared to Jeff that during these days Buck thought almost constantly of the museum, and there was in his voice when he spoke of it a kind of apprehension as though he were afraid that now in the very last stages something might go wrong.

One morning Buck asked Jeff if he were planning to go into town that day. "I thought you might go by John White Eagle's for me—ask him to come out. There're some things about the museum that I want to talk over with him."

"Why don't you stop worrying about that museum," Jeff said. "You're supposed to be resting. John's taking care of things, anyway."

"Yes," Buck said dryly, not looking at him. "Tell him I've got to see him. That is, if you're going in."

"Sure. I'll see him."

Buck looked over at him then and smiled. "John wants to take care of things," he said, "but sometimes he forgets. I've worked on this business for a long time, and I can't take any chances with it now."

The sun was shining weakly through soft gray clouds when White Eagle arrived that afternoon. Jeff built up the fire and got White Eagle a beer from the icebox while the two men talked, and as he opened the bottle in the kitchen he could hear Buck explaining the positioning of the portraits of the full bloods that were to be placed along the walls of the entrance hall. Knowing that they would prefer to talk alone, he went outside and whistled for the setter and walked on across the pasture to the east ridge. An idea had been forming in the back of his mind during the last few days, and he wanted to make sure that the usual covey was still feeding where they had been flushed that first day. Jeff had not been on the ridge more than ten minutes before the dog, racing carelessly out ahead of him, suddenly wheeled and froze, pointing into the high grass along the flank of the ridge. With Jeff so far away the dog could not hold, and after a moment she broke and charged, scattering quail in every direction. Jeff watched them as they swung low through the blackjacks and smiled at the thought of what he was planning to do. There was no doubt that the birds were here; the rest would be up to him and the dog.

He walked long and far that leaden afternoon, and by

the time he reached home the feeble and wintry sun had vanished beyond the horizon. While he fixed the dog's food in the kitchen, he could hear Buck and White Eagle still talking in the other room. He was whistling, thinking of how glad he would be when Buck was well again, and he was not really listening until almost subconsciously he realized that they were no longer talking about the museum.

"Just down below the point, where that lone tree stands—the traditional Chetopa burial." It was Buck who spoke, his words hard and decisive.

"We can talk about it again when you get well—there would be people who wouldn't understand."

"I don't give a damn who understands and who doesn't. That's the way I want it, and you're the only one who can manage it."

"Yeah. All right. We can talk about it again."

Their words were too low to hear now, and Jeff lit the stove to prepare the beef tea for Buck's supper. It was probably no more than a disagreement over some aspect of Chetopa ritual. And yet there had been an urgency in Buck's voice which was strange for him, a cold intensity which Jeff did not like to hear.

With the approach of Christmas the days turned clear and cold. The snow disappeared from the prairie while overhead the sun burned away the clouds, leaving the sky flawless and dazzling, and Jeff's ax rang in the burnished silence as he stacked the wood high for the holidays. Samuel and John White Eagle appeared on Christmas Eve, bringing with them whiskey and a roast of beef. Jeff had bought candles and had decorated a small cedar tree with tinsel and bright ornaments and with the fire leaping noisily along the logs, the room shone with gaiety and cheer. They had carried Buck's bed up to the fire and now they all sat in the blaze of light, drinking and talking and carving slices from the beef.

"Yes, that was a good year, all right," Buck was saying.

200

"Went deer hunting in the fall and then came back and hauled the rock for the house. I bet you remember that," he said to Samuel. "I thought we'd both break our backs before we were through. And then the night we got the fireplace up John brought the beer out and by the time the case was gone we were stomp dancing around that chimney and baying the moon like a pack of coyotes."

"Godamighty, didn't we haul rocks! I shoulda made you buy me a new wagon at the end of that job." Samuel had a half-inch slab of roast beef in one hand and a glass of bourbon and ice in the other, and as he laughed the hollows of his face grew dark with shadow. "But I remember that dance now. By the time we got through we was laughin' to where we couldn't stand up."

"Except that it was two cases," John grunted, relighting his dead cigar. "It sure wasn't no Oklahoma beer the day we'd dance on a case."

Jeff kept their glasses filled and watched them as they laughed and talked, but increasingly as the evening went by he could not help feeling a poignant sense of finality in their conversation. And then he realized that everything that they talked about was in the past, as though for them the future had ceased to exist, as though there would be no more hunting together, no more bottles shared around the fire, no more hound song and hickory flame and vast sweep of prairie stretching to the horizon. It was like hearing a requiem for a way of life that had passed into the dusty and motionless perfection of memory.

"And the next Christmas was the one you got married, wasn't it?" Samuel said to John.

"Hah. I guess that was what made me stop believin' in Santy Claus. That was more like the Fourth of July."

"I think I saw more of you that year than I ever did before or since," Buck laughed. "You even went to New Mexico with us."

"Yeah. Well, if it hadn't been for her I wouldn't have Paul. I guess it was worth the price."

It was difficult to tell whether or not there was bitterness in his voice. His face was as stolid as ever as he blinked slowly behind the cigar smoke.

"He'll come around one of these days, John," Buck said after a while.

"Maybe so," John said. "There's not much time left."

Jeff watched them in the silence as they stared at the dying fire, each face weathered, lined, meditative. Then he turned to Buck. "How about going deer hunting next fall? You're the one who got me interested in all this—you owe me at least one good deer hunt before—"

Buck turned toward him, smiling a little and laying his hand on Jeff's arm.

"October's a long way off. Let's wait and see."

"Sure," Jeff said quietly. He looked at the floor and turned the glass in his hand, wishing that he had kept silent.

It was late when John and Samuel left. Jeff cleaned up the room and banked the fire and just before he blew out the lamps he looked over toward the corner where Buck's bed stood.

"I'm going out early in the morning," he said. "Before I go I'll start the fire and leave some tea on your table."

"There won't be anything open in town."

"I know—I've got something I want to do. If you can last on the tea for awhile I'll be home in time to get you an early lunch."

"I can last," Buck said. "You go ahead and do whatever it is you want to do. I'm sorry you've been penned up so close on my account."

"It's not that," Jeff said, as he blew out the lamps. "I just wanted to tell you so if you woke up and found me gone, you'd know."

The wind was high the next morning when he and the setter started for the east ridge. He kept his gloves on and rested the twelve-gauge in the crook of his arm, and before he had reached the pasture gate his ears were stinging in the cold. The setter whirled and leaped excitedly against his side until they were beyond the fence, and then with her tail streaming brightly in the wind she raced away through the long grass. Jeff had not been hunting since the day that Buck had fallen. Now he felt the excitement rising in his chest, and he beat his hands along his sides to keep them warm. If the birds were there and his luck held he would have a Christmas present for Buck by noon.

They had hunted for two hours before they found the covey. The quail were along the south flank of the ridge, away from the cutting edge of the wind. The dog stood stiff as a ramrod while Jeff walked in slowly, carefully, trying to hold his eyes open wide in the cold. And then as the sudden drum of wings rolled through the morning quiet he fired and saw his bird follow the quick arc to earth. And while he stood there, the shock of the firing still ringing in his ears, he saw the dog coming steadily and proudly through the grass with the bird hanging limp in her mouth.

The covey had flown with the wind down toward the creek, and it was there that Jeff did most of the rest of his shooting that morning. He winged his last bird just before noon, a single that he kicked unexpectedly from the grass as he walked up toward the house. It was a clean, straightaway shot that gave him his fifth bird, and the game bag at his back was pleasantly heavy as he came up through the blackjacks along the point. As he drew close to the fence he could see Buck sitting up in bed, his gaze fixed down the ridge toward the creek. Jeff waved to him and raised the gun, but there was no answering motion. And then he began to run while the wind cut at his face and the bag slapped awkwardly against his back. He ran full tilt to the kitchen door and flung it open and then he saw Buck looking out at him, smiling.

"I heard the shooting," he said. "How was the luck?"

"I saw you in the window," Jeff panted, beginning to laugh a little now with relief. "You didn't wave—"

"When you get the birds on, come in and sit down," Buck said. "There's something I want to tell you."

His hands, stiff with cold, worked slowly and clumsily but at last he had the birds cleaned and in the skillet. Then he sat down by the bed and lit a cigarette. "I was awfully lucky," he said proudly, and then he held up his hand.

"Five?"

"That's right."

"Was I right about quail or not?"

"You would have been," Jeff nodded, "except I don't think it can really be described. You gave it a good try."

Buck laughed and looked toward the graying afternoon. "There's something that's been on my mind," he said after a moment. "And it's just this. If anything should happen to me, this place will be yours. I've written it into the will, but I wanted to tell you about it. No strings, no qualifications—yours for whatever you want to do with it."

In the deep silence Jeff could hear the sputter of the grease in the frying pan, and then he put his hand to his forehead. "I don't know what to say, Hardin. My God, I—" but there were no words.

"Those birds'll burn, son, if you don't tend to them," Buck said softly.

CHAPTER XII

☐ By spring Buck could get around again although he still felt as weak and unsteady as a new calf. And it was good to see another spring, to see everywhere frail spears of grass thrusting through the shrouded earth, to see tall columns of rain that swept suddenly against the windows and scattered red bud petals in profusion along the fence. Every afternoon he walked slowly down to the point and sat there with his back against the dead blackjack, letting his mind grow dense with the stir and rustle of burgeoning nature until gently and easily he fell asleep. For there was a peace upon him now, bright and warm as this March sun, soft as these vagrant winds that rippled the new grass. There was a voice that seemed to be calling him, a voice that spoke to him in words he did not know but which somehow he understood. It was as though his body were already being translated into the myriad tongue of the prairie, and as for his spirit—he smiled and looked down the slope to the spot where he had fallen that bleak December day.

It was toward the end of March when one morning he arose and knew that this was the day. "I think you can go back to the farm tomorrow," he told Jeff casually at breakfast. "I'm strong enough now." In Jeff's eyes there was something like alarm, and yet it was as if Buck had reached some final quiet where the emotions of others could no longer touch him.

"Are you sure? I'm happy to stay unless—"

"I think it's probably time you got on back to Samuel, don't you? And then you'll want to be making your plans."

"Yes." The cigarette jerked in his fingers as he flicked it and he smiled fleetingly at Buck. "Well—I'll be packing my stuff then."

"Besides, I sort of cheated on you—you only promised to stay until quail season, remember?"

It seemed for a moment that Jeff would speak, and then he merely nodded and said nothing.

Buck swung round in his chair and glanced across the valley. "But before you go there's something you can do for me, son, if you wouldn't mind. The prairie chickens are dancing and I'm not up to driving yet. I'd like for you to take me over there—it's in the north section of the Miller ranch—and after that you can bring me back and go on. You've wasted enough time looking after me."

"Nonsense. And it's not as though I'll be leaving right away. I'm not going to let you work your way out of that deer hunt."

Buck laughed and reached for his tobacco. "You'd have to talk the doctor into that, and I'm afraid it's a little late. You heard what he said about how careful I'll have to be from now on."

At dawn the next morning they were in the car, driving toward the county road. It was a clear day, the sky without clouds, the eastern horizon scarlet with sunlight. From a sagging fence post a meadow lark sang briefly before gliding on stiff wings down into the grass, and along the road they passed two rabbits sitting bolt upright, ears raised, head turned toward the sun as though in morning prayer.

"You never talked much about prairie chickens before," Jeff said, yawning and rubbing the sleep from his eyes. "What's the matter, can't you eat them?"

"Some people do. I like to watch them dance."

"Actually dance? It's a little hard to imagine."

"Certainly. You'll see."

Buck leaned against the door, letting the breeze blow in upon him through the open window. Along the fence calves stood awkwardly on frail legs, chewing the new grass or turning in sudden apprehension to flee from the car with their bouncing, rocking-horse run. A hunting hawk circled the blue immensity of the sky while flocks of birds from their swaying perches along the telephone lines made the morning loud with song.

"It's a hell of a nice spring," Buck said musingly, looking out across the faint swell and dip of prairie. "I always did think men got the short end of the stick when this time of year came around. Everything else in the world has some special way to express it all, and we can't do anything but go around and watch."

"You're getting too old for spring," Jeff said jokingly. "You've forgotten. I used to like to run—still would, probably. Play catch, lie in the grass—I can still remember."

Buck looked at him for a moment and then looked back out toward the pasture. "Maybe so," he said. "Maybe that's what it is."

After they had driven on a ways, he pointed to a small hill about a mile and a half from the road. "There's a cattle guard a little further down. Cut off the road and just work on over to where the ground starts rising. We can tell from there whether we're in luck or not."

When they left the road the car bounced from side to side as Jeff drove over shelving rock and small bushes and trees to get to the base of the hill. Then Buck motioned for him to stop.

"Listen," he said, his voice hushed, almost a whisper.

For now through the still spring air came a deep booming, swelling in intensity until its rhythm seemed to flood the vast canyon of the dawn. Like the thudding of drums, it was felt as much as heard so that the listener seemed to hear magnified the pounding of his own pulse, to feel as though immersed in water the booming in the hollows of his flesh.

"They're up there all right," Buck said quietly. "Turn around and back up to them."

Jeff worked the car steadily up the hill until the rise began to level off. The ground here was flat, spiked with black stubble left by the fires of the previous fall and showing green where the new grass had lanced sunward. Parked here on the hilltop they could see to the blurred horizon in every direction.

"Cut the ignition," Buck whispered, and motioned with his head for Jeff to look out of the back of the car. There were twenty or twenty-five birds that they could see, birds that seemed about three times the size of quail and that were the color of dark sandstone. Where the ground was bare the males ran and danced in a peculiarly intense and concentrated aloneness while the females lay in the long grass at the edges of the open space. It was the females who looked on, contentedly letting themselves be courted and fought over, and it was for them that the cocks stamped with furious rapidity their fiery dance, their tails sticking stiffly into the air and their feet pounding pistonlike against the earth while from their swollen throats boomed the spring madness that laced their veins as each bird became the voice of urges beyond the reach of ordinary song.

As the emotion came upon them each cock in turn would rush quickly along the ground, stopping suddenly to drum a wild staccato while lowering his head and inflating into flaming orange globes of passion the sacs that lay along his neck. Often before he had finished dancing he would be charged blindly by some jealous rival and then a fight would ensue, both cocks crouching low to the ground before flying into one another with wings and legs and beaks driving desperately until one had retreated and the victor was left to boom and strut his prowess before his watching lady.

It was a ritual that Buck had seen many times before

but one of which he had never grown tired. For in it was so much of the necessity of life, its vainglory, its blind urge to perpetuate, its struggle, its victory and defeat. And all of this expressed in a frenzied and yet highly formal dance from which there was no variation and whose interest lay not in its suspense or novelty but in its simple inevitability, the noble and exalted and yet tragic inevitability of life reduced to the most elemental terms.

On that particular morning Buck was watching an old male which was trying in vain to gain dancing room for himself. The younger ones, knowing his weakness, harried him continually from side to side until finally in despair he fluttered into the air and flew a few yards down the hill from the dancing ground. Buck picked him up with the glasses and he could see him well now, the tiny feet working with incredible speed, the head thrusting suddenly forward and the orange sacs swelling until the booming, whistling song rolled softly through the morning. He was an old bird and he was alone and still he danced, still gave what was left of his strength before the altar of whatever blind gods he knew.

They had watched the dancing for almost an hour, Jeff nodding as Buck explained in a hushed whisper, when suddenly in perfect concord the birds rose in circling flight and were gone.

"Remarkable," Jeff murmured. "I wouldn't have believed it."

"I guess it is at that," Buck said. "But it's every year, come spring. Different ones, too, I suppose. And yet they always come back, same as the seasons, It's all tied together somehow, isn't it." For a moment he rested his hand on Jeff's shoulder before he turned around in his seat. "I think we may as well be heading back."

They spoke very little as they drove back to the house. Jeff seemed intent upon some thought of his own and Buck leaned limply against the car door, drinking in the morning. When they reached the gate, Buck was silent for a moment and then he turned to Jeff and held out his hand. "It was good of you to stay all this time," he said as he smiled into Jeff's eyes. "You know what it meant to me. They were good days, weren't they." And when Jeff looked away, he went on. "You look after yourself now, boy—and tell that old Pap of yours that everything was just fine."

He got out of the car and stood for a moment by the gate. "And don't forget what I told you about the house, hear?'

"I'll be over in a couple of days to see if there's anything you need," Jeff said thickly, but Buck was already walking up the road to the house.

By resting in between jobs Buck was able to get a lot done that day. He cleaned out his desk and burned all the loose papers that were still lying around the house. Then he oiled the guns and ran a rag over the books and straightened the old familiar pieces of furniture that stood at random about the room. Toward the middle of the afternoon he opened a can of spaghetti and ate it along with what was left of a bottle of wine. When he had cleared the dishes, he lay down and waited.

It was just before sunset when he got up again. He went to the gun cabinet and got his pistol and checked the magazine. Then he slipped it into his pocket and went outside, leaving the door open behind him. His feet were quiet on the new grass and the setter, sleeping in the shade, did not stir. As he walked slowly toward the point he could see the final flaming of the sun through the rigid lacework of the blackjacks. Something like thunder rumbled in his ears, and before his eyes the clear sky stretched distant and calm to the horizon. And now it was no longer a single voice that he heard but many, sounding a throbbing hymn of devotion that made the earth shake beneath his feet. He stopped for a moment and lowered his head, and of a sudden there was a trembling through him as though the spring wind had with sweeping fingers

210

plucked the strings of his soul. Then he rubbed his head once across his eyes and walked on in the fragrant twilight, his head erect and proud and dauntless, his spirit brimming with the peace of eternity.

PART THREE

As the leaves of the trees, so also are the generations of men. The wind scatters the leaves to the ground, yet in spring the forest blooming puts forth new leaves. And so it is with men; one generation passes away, and another is born.

Homer

CHAPTER XIII

□ It was another spring, and Jeff was back with him, and before long the preachers would be building the New Jerusalem in Grey Horse again. These thoughts hummed happily through Samuel's mind as he stood at the sink preparing breakfast for the hounds. Every winter now he could not keep from wondering whether he would live to see another spring, and this winter it had been worse with Buck down and Jeff gone most of the time. And besides, he thought to himself, in winter the preachers kind of went into hibernation and gittin' the spirit was a tough proposition, especially when a man couldn't read any too good. But spring was the time for shoutin' and stompin' and it wouldn't be too long now before the old brown tent would be pitched on the south edge of town and God would be walking among them again.

He was putting the feed in the pans when he heard the clatter of the cattle guard. He wiped his hands and walked to the window and then he could see White Eagle's pickup coming into the yard, the loose fender banging as usual. When John got out of the car he was glad that the old Indian closed the door quietly behind him, for Jeff was still asleep and Samuel wanted him to get his rest. Looking after Buck had not been an easy job and the boy had seemed more tired than usual the night before.

Samuel returned to the sink and was filling the last pan when he heard the scrape of feet at the step. He half turned, smiling, wondering what kind of foolishness had brought John out at this hour, and then the door opened in a burst of sunlight and White Eagle was standing there tall and straight. He was looking at Samuel, his face severe, but Samuel could read nothing in his eyes which seemed now hard as flint. After a moment John shut the door behind him and walked heavily to the kitchen table and sat down. Still he said nothing, made no movement, his eyes fixed upon his wrinkled hands which rested before him on the oilcloth; then at last he reached into his pocket and brought out a pistol and laid it in the light.

"That's Hardin's gun," White Eagle said gravely. "I come out this morning about some stuff for the museum. I found him down on the point about a half hour ago."

Samuel stared at the gun, frowning, trying to fit it all together, and then his face seemed suddenly to splinter into lines of pain. He looked at John and shook his head quickly. "No," he said softly, incredulously. "No. Not Hardin—" and then his voice trailed off as he continued to shake his head.

"It was in his hand," White Eagle said. "He's gone. I carried him up to the house and left him there."

Samuel turned away and walked over to the window. The skin around his eyes seemed tight enough to split and he ran his hands roughly up and down his legs. His body ached, and at his temples there was a knot of pain that blurred his sight.

"All right," he said hoarsely. "We'd better git goin'."

"I only got that pick up—just the one seat up front and the bed that I haul in."

"Yeah," Samuel said, rubbing his hand hard against his forehead where the pain burned like a coal. "O.K. We can take my car. The back seat's out in the barn but you can put it in while I feed the dogs."

"What about your boy?" John asked quietly. "I didn't see him anyplace around."

"Hardin sent him home yesterday," Samuel said. "He's still asleep and I don't want him along. Let's git started."

"He's got to know sometime."

216

"Not now," Samuel said wearily. "Not this way. Come on."

Somehow he got the dogs fed, his hands working almost automatically as his mind shrank into a cold and terrible darkness. When he entered the pen the dogs crowded around his knees and leaped up against him, but he pushed them away abruptly, hardly seeing them through the sorrow that masked his eyes. And still chilling his body was the same dull ache, as though winter had settled forever in his bones.

They were silent most of the way to Buck's place, Samuel concentrating on his driving while John stared out the window, rubbing his hands together in his lap. The sun was clear of the horizon now, and the day was filled with a soft and gusty wind that set the tassels of the black-jacks dancing. Huge puffs of cloud moved lazily through the sky, and scattered among the trees were creamy splashes of dogwood which stirred slowly in the full light. But for Samuel there was only the narrow yellow road on which his eyes were fixed and the quick trembling of fear in his stomach as he thought about Jeff and how he would have to tell him.

"I was goin' over myself this morning," he said, staring ahead at the rock-hard ruts of the road. "I was afraid there was somethin' wrong the way he sent the boy home yesterday. It didn't seem right."

"Jeff didn't say anything?"

"He acted like he didn't want to talk about it. I thought maybe he was just tired."

White Eagle nodded, not answering.

"Too bad he couldn't have had a better quail season," Samuel said after a while. "Bein' that it was the last one."

"He didn't have birds on his mind," White Eagle said sternly.

Samuel looked at him for a moment and then turned his eyes back to the road. "I reckon he didn't, at that," he said, his voice suddenly broken and resigned.

It was eight o'clock when they reached the house. As

they slammed the car doors, a flock of crows rose in a black cloud from the oak just beyond the fence. The silence was shattered by their raucous cawing, and they moved ponderously through the bright air like some dark portent of tragedy. Samuel and John had stopped at their flight, and now they went on through the gate and into the back yard as the crows faded into silence. They had gone no more than a few steps before they stopped again. This time it was the dog, Hardin's red Irish setter, facing them with the delicacy and power of a flame as her tail flickered slowly back and forth. Her muzzle was lifted high toward them, teeth bared to the gums, and her eyes, like the set of her body, were apprehensive.

"Biddy." Samuel knelt and put out his hand. The dog went limp then, lowering her muzzle and moving forward until her head rested in Samuel's hand. He let his fingers slide around her neck to the base of her skull; after a moment he straightened up and followed White Eagle to the door. As he walked through the yard it seemed to him that except for the strange quiet, everything was just as it had always been—the weathered fieldstone house and the rusted pump under the mulberry tree and the shower rigged up by means of rope and an old watering can. He even noticed how squarely the bricks were laid in the ground under the shower, bricks stained purple by the crushed mulberries of many springs. And he was remembering how Hardin would stand here singing and splashing himself as he took his bath in early morning, thinking how it was so exactly like Hardin not to wash out of a wash pan like everybody else but to fix up some kind of a contraption so that he could shower right out in the open where the water could pour over him like rain.

It was dark inside the house with the big front door on the east closed. The remains of the fire were gray in the fireplace and as Samuel's glance traveled quickly around the room, he noticed the faint gleam of light on the guns; he ran his finger down one of the barrels and then he knew that they had been freshly oiled. Unwillingly his eyes returned to where Hardin, wrapped in a blanket, was lying on the couch.

"I'll help you," he said as John bent down and lifted Buck in his arms, but John shook his head.

"Just get the gate for me," he said, his face strained and hard against the weight of Buck's body.

Hardin was limp, just as he had been on that afternoon when Jeff had carried him back to the house, that bleak afternoon that now seemed so immeasurably distant in the past. There was a dark, crusted line of blood trailing down one side of his face and one arm was hanging loosely out of the blanket. The way the fingers of the hand were crooked and stiff made Samuel think of the talons of a dead hawk.

John brushed past him, his face grim and his mouth a tight, thin line, and Samuel closed the back door tight and hurried ahead to open the gate and the door to the car. At John's heels followed the red dog, silent, nose lowered to the ground, her tail curved stiffly between her legs, and Samuel held her while John was laying the body in the back seat. Then after a moment he led her quickly around to the other side of the car, coaxing her into the front seat and talking low to her until they started.

"Let's take him in to my place," John said as the car dipped down into the pasture between the ridges. "Paul's wife is there but there's nothing we can do about that now."

"Sure," Samuel replied. He was looking out at the sky where there seemed just a suggestion of haziness, an almost invisible veil softening the outlines of the trees and fence posts that stood along the road. The air now was warm and limpid, but there was a wetness in the atmosphere which meant change, perhaps a storm. Thinking ahead to the funeral he hoped that the good weather would hold.

"I suppose you'll look after the funeral," he said.

"Yeah," John said as they drew near town. "He told me how he wanted it to be—I was out to the place one afternoon just before Christmas and he told me then. It won't be what he wanted, but it will be the best we can do."

"Chetopa?"

John nodded. "That was the way he wanted it."

Samuel gave no indication of what he was thinking, for if Hardin wanted a Chetopa burial, then John could take care of it in his own way. But he made up his mind that somebody would have to be along with a Bible.

"Jeff and I'll be there," he said.

White Eagle looked at him for a moment and then turned his face out toward the prairie again. "He wanted that, too," he said.

They came down the hill into Grey Horse, and just beyond the city hospital Samuel turned east on the road that led out to Indian Camp. The sun stabbed sharply at the windshield now and in the sudden silence after the dirt road they could hear the tires rolling along the blacktop.

"How you gonna tell the boy?"

Samuel had managed to keep his mind off Jeff until White Eagle spoke. Now he frowned and said nothing for a moment. "I don't know, John. I cain't rightly see that there's any two ways about it—it's just tell him and hope for the best."

"They were pretty close, I guess."

Samuel was still frowning, his eyes held fast in a web of wrinkles as though he were staring into the sun. "Jeff never had any dad to speak of. He seemed to think a good deal of Hardin. It's gonna hurt him pretty bad.'

John worked the wrappings from a cigar and glanced over at Samuel. "What do you mean about his not havin' any dad?"

"Jeff's dad shot himself, John. The boy never forgot it —it's been on his mind for a long time."

White Eagle's hands were motionless, still holding the

220

unlit cigar, and then he looked away out the window. "That makes it even worse, don't it."

"I reckon maybe it does, when you think about it."

It was with a feeling of relief that Samuel pulled into the drive that led to John's house. He stopped by the kitchen door and got out of the car and when he saw that John had opened the rear door, he whistled softly for the setter. It was the only way he knew to help, for John would want no one else touching Buck. And as he was stroking the bird dog's head, John's slick-haired and yellow-eyed pointer came swiftly around the corner of the house. He had the blunt, formidable, somewhat stupid appearance of most pointers and he slowed up as he saw the red dog, not bristling but merely approaching a little stiff-legged. Samuel held on to Biddy and talked playfully to the pointer. Then he picked up a stick that was lying nearby and threw it out towards the fence. As both dogs started after it, he turned and followed John up the steps to the kitchen door.

Paul's wife was holding the screen door open, standing there woodenly, her bleached hair stiff and uncombed and her eyes squinting sleepily against the light. In her face there was neither curiosity nor sympathy nor even interest, but only a kind of bleared disgust and weariness. Samuel stiffened when he saw her and lowered his eyes before the directness of her stare, for there was too much in his face that he did not want her to see. And when he passed her in the doorway, he swallowed and quickly lifted his hat and went on into the house.

She had said nothing to John and he had not even looked at her as he had carried Hardin into the house. When Samuel got as far as the living room, he saw that John had gone down the hall and into the bedroom and had shut the door. Samuel took off his hat and stood there in the middle of the living room, waiting uncomfortably, turning the hat in his hands. Behind him he could hear the slap of the girl's slippers as she came along the hall and then she walked by him, going over to a small table that stood before the artificial fireplace. She shook a cigarette loose from a pack, lit it, and smothered the flame with a stream of colorless smoke.

"What's the deal? Who's he got in the blanket, a drunk?"

"There's somebody dead," Samuel said coldly.

She turned toward him now, her eyes glittering and her face coming forward a little. "Who is it?" she asked harshly. "Who's dead?"

"Hardin Buck." And then he turned from her, sick at mentioning Buck's name before her eager eyes.

After a moment he heard the bedroom door being closed. John came into the living room and stood there for a moment, looking without expression at the girl. Then he motioned for Samuel to follow and the two of them went through the kitchen and out to the back yard again. They stood by the side of the car watching the dogs chase one another along the fence.

"I'll keep the dog here with me," John said. "She'll be all right with that one. Probably wouldn't do with your hounds."

"I reckon she wouldn't at that," Samuel said. "What about the pick up?"

John was silent for a moment. "I didn't remember," he said. "I can use Paul's car until I come out and get it. Keys are in it—put it someplace out of the way."

"And the funeral," Samuel said softly, his voice hoarse and thin.

"Thursday." White Eagle seemed to be straining his eyes to see off into the distance, and in the light his face was eroded and grooved as an empty river bed. "That will be Thursday, at his place. Down on the point was where he said he wanted it. Thursday morning."

"You'll take care of all that, then."

White Eagle nodded.

"Then I'll handle the rest of it," Samuel said. "Whatever else has to be done."

They stood there for a moment, looking at each other, and then Samuel pulled on his gloves and opened the car door. "We'll just have to do the best we can," he said.

"It's pretty hard, ain't it," and now for the first time the mask slipped and there were dark lines of pain around John's eyes.

"It is for a fact," Samuel said quietly. He pulled off his right glove and held out his hand to White Eagle. "Thursday, John."

They shook hands and Samuel climbed quickly into the car and started the motor. As he drove away he saw the red setter sitting near the gate, her head held high as though she were searching the air, while the pointer crouched beside her wagging his head in play.

It was after lunch when Samuel finished what he had to do in town, and the sky now was smoky gray and the air was turning cold. The wind pulled at his hat as he came out of the cafe so that he had to grab at it and shove it down hard on his head. Then he bent over a little and turned into the wind and started up the street toward the car. He had taken care of the sheriff and the coroner just to make sure that everything was cleared, and now he had one last thing to do.

He drove slowly on the way home, looking across the prairie to the northwest where the clouds were gathering in a cold, gray mass. The grass in the pastures was bent flat beneath the cutting wind and the cattle were beginning to bunch along the fences, sensing the storm currents in the air. By the time that Samuel was rumbling across his own cattle guard, the rain had already begun its solid splatting against the windshield. He parked behind John's truck and walked rapidly across the backyard to the kitchen door, and when he neared the house and raised his eyes from the ground he saw Jeff standing there in the doorway, waiting for him. In the boy's face there was a strained alarm, almost an accusation.

"Where's John?"

"He's home," Samuel said, stopping so that the rain slanted between them, and now as he stood there he realized just how hopeless it would be.

"Isn't that his truck?"

"Yeah. He had to leave it out here this morning." He looked at Jeff for a moment longer and then brushed by him into the kitchen. "That's a cold rain," he said. "But northers move fast. It ought to blow over by night."

"I didn't leave any wood over at Hardin's," Jeff said quickly. "Maybe I ought to go over and get some up for him."

Samuel put his gloves on the table and then he came back to where Jeff was standing and laid his hands on his shoulders. "You better sit down, boy."

"What's wrong, Pap?"

"I wish I didn't have to tell you. It's Buck—he's dead."

The silence was loud with their breathing and then slowly, almost unconsciously, Jeff sat down at the table, his mouth half open, his eyes stunned and helpless. "Oh, my God—how—why didn't you—" and then he buried his face in his hands, shaking his head from side to side.

"Yeah," Samuel said, patting Jeff's shoulder. "Go ahead." And now as he held his face tight he could feel the pain burning again in his forehead.

Finally Jeff looked up at him, his face wet with tears. "How did it happen?" he asked in a low, choked voice.

Samuel looked away, unable to meet Jeff's eyes. "John found him down at the point this morning—he was dead then."

"But what would he be doing down there?"

Samuel tried again to look at him, and still his eyes faulted as the lie lay dry as dust in his mouth. He shook his head abruptly. "I don't know. Nobody will ever know."

But now Jeff had shoved his chair back and was standing beside him, his face so close that Samuel could feel his breath along his jaw.

224

"You're not telling me how it happened, Pap." His voice was low, hard, jagged with grief.

Samuel moved his hands in despair. "Don't ask me again," he said, and his voice seemed to crack in his throat.

Suddenly Jeff grabbed his coat from the chair and ran out into the rain. For a moment Samuel could not move and then he followed him.

"Jeff, boy," he called after him, his voice broken and sobbing and his eyes blurred. "Come back—Jeff—don't—" but now in the storm that drove cold and hard against him his strength seemed to collapse and he leaned against the corner of the house, waving feebly and still calling as the car rushed by him and faded into the distance.

CHAPTER XIV

☐ By nightfall the rain had softened to slow mist and the lament of the wind was low and infrequent. The house was dark and silent, and then at last as night closed in Samuel rose from his bed and lit the lamps. It had been a long day since he had first heard John's pickup rattling across the cattle guard. A long and lonesome day, and now it was done. There was only the funeral to wait for, two days away, and the sharpness of Buck's image would be eroded by the winds and the waters of time until even the memory of him would be crumpled back into formless dust. For it had been that way with Samuels wife Maude, who had died on a spring day many years ago now. He could recall her only vaguely, not so much as she had been in flesh and blood as merely a general poignance that lightly touched the chords of memory, a feeling of absence, of sadness and of loss. And when he in his turn went into the ground, then she would be forgotten, as would Buck, as would they all. It was a hard and bitter thing to think on.

He ate more hurriedly than usual that night, and as he sipped his coffee the silence of the house pressed in upon him like a crowd of lonely spirits. And in such a silence, shrouded in raw and wind-haunted darkness, there was only one thing to be glad for—simply that Jeff would know now and that he would not have to lie to him again. He knew where Jeff had gone, knew that he would not stop until he had found Buck, had seen him, had looked with his own stunned eyes at the small black hole in Buck's temple. And then maybe he might know why Samuel could not tell him, might find forgiveness somewhere in his troubled heart. Because I've seen it twice too, Samuel was thinking. I've had to face it down two times myself.

From the pen out back he could hear the whining and the barking of the hounds as they shivered hungrily in the cold. He finished his coffee and fixed hot food on the stove and then he made two trips through the chilling mist, carrying the battered and steaming pans into the pen. The dogs bolted the food savagely with quick, violent gulps and stood trembling before the wind, talking to him in their short, whining yaps or simply looking up at him with eyes that would suddenly glow red in the light from the kitchen window. Two of the pups had bad feet and Samuel knelt down on the wet ground to inspect them and twice when lights appeared along the road he rose and stared through the darkness, looking for Jeff's car. Finally he slapped the pups roughly and called out of the pen the old hound who had been his companion in the kitchen on many a winter's night. And even though it was not winter that night, there was all of the somberness of December in the air, and Samuel felt less alone seeing the aged dog stretched out in the warmth before the stove.

In the light of the kerosene lamp he took care of the few letters that needed answering, scrawling his replies laboriously on the coarse and fibrous paper of a nickel tablet and glancing up quickly every time the wind pushed at the door. His correspondence was not large but it was steady, consisting almost entirely of letters from fox-hunting friends in Tennessee and Arkansas and Missouri as well as Oklahoma. Only a few days earlier he had written to the wife of a hunter who had died, and he was thankful that he did not have that job to do tonight.

It was still early when he finished and he knew that there would be no use in going to bed. Around eight he opened the kitchen door and looked out, but there was nothing there save the steady drift of mist through the pale light cast by the lamp. Jeff had been gone a long time, too long for comfort, and yet Samuel could do nothing but wait, pacing back and forth through the ghostly silence. He pushed the door shut and walked back into the living room, and as he stood there listening to the wind his eye fell upon the old picture of his wife, taken when they were first married. He went across to the mantel and looked at it for a moment and ran his hand across the back of her Bible which lay beside the picture. And there was a strangeness in it for him, just looking at the photograph and feeling the Bible which her hands had held so often, a strangeness and a sadness as well. For the face that looked at him out of the faded severity of the tintype was one that the turning years could not soften, and the image that he saw now in the dusty frame was that of someone listening with rapt intensity to some distant hymn.

And Maude had listened to that hymn all of her life, or so it had seemed to Samuel, for her face had never really changed. The words of the hymn had spoken of labor and of duty and of righteousness and most of all, of sacrifice. And Samuel knew the hymn right through; he had grown up to it and its words still rang powerfully in his soul, but there had been another kind of music for him and he had been helpless before it. It was the music of the wilderness, of a night-time world of clear creeks and forested hills where in the silence beneath the stars a man might sit in the firelight listening to the ancient cries of the chase and filling his eyes with the almighty vastness of the heavens. And hearing this music he had had to follow it, no matter where it led, hoping only that God in His boundless tolerance could find room for one who worshipped and believed all right enough but in whom there was little of toil, little of right-mindedness, little of duty, and even less of sacrifice.

As for Maude—well, her God was just not a hound man's God. Yet she had done her duty by Samuel and in many ways she had been a good wife. When she died he discovered what she had meant to him in ways he had never given thought to, and as he stood above her casket in the graveyard, listening to the clods thumping against the lid as the diggers began to shovel the earth into the grave, he had grieved above all for one thing, that she was gone and that now there would be no chance to say the things which he had never said in spite of thirty years of sharing a house and a bed, in spite of five children born and two buried. That was the hard part, and it was too late. And the grief was compounded by his sure knowledge that she had given him far more than he had ever given her in return. For in the way she had read her Bible every night, sitting by herself in the kitchen and working along with her index finger from word to word, in the way she had used it as explanation and as guide, as consolation and wellspring of peace, and even in the way she had painstakingly covered its flyleaf with all the names of the family for as far back as she could remember, he had gotten from her a sense of something continuing and enduring, something of which he and she and their children were no more than a brief part. When she was gone he had begun reading her Bible as though to recover something of her presence, and from that lonely beginning he had found the glory road that led to the revival tent and somehow it had all fused wordlessly within him, this stern and mighty God of hers and what he felt as he sat with his back against a tree, listening to the music of the night.

But his memories now were dark with too much death, and suddenly he wanted to get away from these things that had brought the past to life in him. He opened the back door again and the mist was coming down harder and he wondered if the boys would be over on the ridge with their dogs. In a moment he had his heavy coat on and was out whistling three of the hounds into the trunk of the car. Then before he started he went back to the kitchen and wrote a note for Jeff, telling him where he would be if the boy needed him, and yet knowing at the same time that there was no need which Jeff would feel tonight that anyone living could fulfill.

He took the county road as far down as Buck's cattle guard and then he turned off the road and followed a pair of soft and sandy tracks through the blackjacks until he emerged in a small clearing. There were four cars there which shone wetly as his headlights swept across them, and down through the trees he could see the fire. As soon as he opened the back of the car the hounds leaped to the ground and loped off into the darkness, and Samuel walked through the mist toward the small flare of flame. When he was close enough he could make out the forms which sat or sprawled in the flickering light, Virge, Sim, Will MacIntosh, and old man Hendricks with his son Lee. They all greeted him as he approached and sat down in the warm circle of light, and he greeted each man in turn.

"Any fox around?" he asked Virge.

"They ought to be some around," Virge answered, "cause we shorely ain't bothered them a hell of a lot this year. Good night, though."

"A mite wet but the scent ought to hold," Samuel said. "Haven't seen you out for a spell, Mr. Hendricks. Gittin' along a little better now?" He had raised his voice to penetrate the old man's deafness, and like all the others he mister'd him because the old man was going on ninety.

"Better," old Hendricks answered, his voice cracking a little as he laughed. His eyes were bright in the firelight, and Samuel wondered how bad the damp night air would be for him. "You bring that Fireball pup along tonight?" the old man asked.

"You bet I did."

"He's shorely one hell of a lot o' hound," Hendricks said, nodding his puckered face quickly and laughing without sound. "Mighty glad you brung him."

"He needs work or he'll be gittin' fat like that one," Samuel said, pointing to Virgil. "Too much sittin' around and a little too close to the trough."

The old man laughed and asked his son for the bottle. The thin cords in his neck trembled as he tilted the pint and then he passed it around to the others. When it came to him Samuel shook his head and returned it to Lee and they all sat in silence for a while, listening to the snapping of the burning wood. After a bit Sim got up and went out into the darkness. They could hear him in the underbrush and when he came back he was dragging a long, dead limb behind him. It was black with rain and when it began to burn the smoke was sluggish and heavy.

"I heard down at the smoke house this afternoon that Hardin Buck had died," Virgil said quietly after a while.

"That's right," Samuel answered.

"When did he go?"

"This morning."

"It's too bad. He was a good man."

"He was, for a fact." He did not look at Virge and his words were tight and controlled.

Will poked at the fire for a while with his stick and then looked over at Samuel. "Fella told me he killed hisself, Sam."

"That's the way it looked," Samuel said briefly.

"It didn't sound right to me," Will said, holding his small silver cup so that it shone in the shifting light.

"I don't reckon it sounds right to any of us," Sim said. "But there it is."

"First time that's happened around here in a long time," Lee Hendricks said. "That old boy that built that rock castle up back of the ice house—they claim he killed hisself though nobody was ever just positive about it. But he was crazy as hell. And Buck shore wasn't crazy, I know that much."

"They said you was one of the ones that found him, Sam," Sim said, his voice gentle and uncertain.

"It was John White Eagle that found him," Samuel answered. "I helped take him into town. I don't know any more about it than you fellows do."

They heard barking then, coming from the woods to

232

the south. The dogs had evidently nosed into a trail but it was cold or confusing because their voices were indecisive.

"Ain't found him yet," Virgil said.

"What's that, Virge?" old man Hendricks asked.

"I said they ain't found him yet," Virgil shouted. "The dogs has got onto a trail but it's cold."

"Cold," the old man said. "O.K., son."

Samuel wondered if old Hendricks ever heard the dogs at all any more. The old man sat there as though he were reading their faces, as though perhaps his memory supplied the voices of the hounds once he saw by their faces that the dogs were on a scent.

"Buck's place was right over on that ridge yonder, wasn't it, Sam?" Lee asked.

"Yeah," Sam said. "This was his land."

"I knew that. He did a lot of huntin', didn't he?"

"Birds, deer—used to go for bear up to Montana. He wasn't much for hounds."

"How come?"

"He liked to kill, I guess. But then it was a lot more than just the killing with him. He used to say that hounds didn't have enough pride, even though he liked to hear 'em sing."

"Pride?"

"That's what he called it."

"Funny thing to say," Lee said. "Who in hell cares about a hound's pride—all I care about is his voice, how loud and true he can holler."

"Well, that was the way he thought of it," Samuel said.

The dogs were just yapping now, noising their confusion, but it was a good sound even so.

"They must be down by the corner of the fence," Virgil said. "Old dog fox was probably lyin' down there this mornin' gittin' some of that sun."

"Scent ought to hold in the wet," Sim said. "They'll find him."

"Maybe," Virgil said. "But he's likely to be a long way from there once he hears that racket."

"Probably sittin' up on the other side of the creek," Will said, "figurin' out which dogs they is and whether they got any sense."

"Reckon he can tell?" Lee said.

"Course he can," Will said. "Ain't that so, Sam."

"I reckon," Samuel said. "Wouldn't be much point of chasin' him if he couldn't. If the fox didn't figure it out that way it'd just be a footrace, and who in hell wants to sit out in the rain all night for that."

"Maybe so," Lee said. "But if he can tell from just listenin' to 'em how much sense they got, he's better off than most people I know." He laughed and stirred up the fire with a stick. "Eh, Virge?"

"Go to hell, Lee," Virgil said.

"I always wondered if that was true or not, Virge," Sim drawled. "Did that trader from Little Rock really put a blind one over on you?"

"Blind or not," Virgil said, "the sonofabitch could shore as hell sing in the dark."

"Only trouble was," Sam said, "he couldn't rightly tell when it was day."

Old man Hendricks blew on his hands and hunched in closer to the fire. He looked back and forth at the faces as the others talked and when they laughed he opened his mouth and nodded, smiling as though he had missed the joke. "Anything goin' on?" he asked his son.

"Talkin' about Virge's blind hound," Lee said in his ear.

"Blind was he, Virge?" the old man said, and he shook his head quickly, laughing to himself.

Samuel looked across the valley toward the point of trees on the other side and thought how dark and cold Buck's house would be that night. The place had always been cold without a big fire in the fireplace, and there would be no more fires now for a long time, if ever again. He wondered what would happen to the place, what

Buck had planned to do with it. And then he wished that the dogs would pick up the scent and make the valley ring with the pealing of their voices, just so that something might go on the way it ought to go.

"I never could figure what a man'd want to do a thing like that for," Will said after a while. "I remember back in 'twenty-nine that a couple of lawyers killed theirselves. One of 'em sat in his car with a hose comin' up from the exhaust and the other one took some kind of poison. But that was different—ever'body was scairt then and them fellas hadn't only lost their own money but a lot of Indian money to boot. People said the government was comin' in on it and they just didn't see any way out. But a man like Buck—what would make him feel that way?"

"He wasn't any too well," Samuel said curtly. "His heart was bad—he didn't want to end up in bed. I might have done the same thing; you might have yourself."

"A man just don't quit like that though, Sam," Sim said, lowering his voice. "Look at that old coot—damn near ninety and out here on a night like this."

"He's different," Sam said. "He's got sons, people to look after him. Buck didn't have anybody. He was alone, don't forget that."

"Maybe so, but he wasn't so old. Early sixties, wasn't he? He coulda took care of himself and gone on for a good while. People just don't quit without reason."

"I reckon that came under the heading of his business," Samuel said softly.

"Course it did." Sim nodded. "I don't aim to be buttin' in or anything, Sam, you know that. It's just—well, it's just like he took off walkin' across the prairie yonder and nobody ever saw him again. A man would want to know why—you couldn't help wantin' to know what it was all about. He was your friend more than he was ours, but we all knew him and liked him. He belonged here and it's hard to see him go like that, that's all."

"You're mighty right about that," Virgil said. "Even if it ain't none of our business, you can't help thinkin'

235

about it. And if he hadn't been the kind of a man he was, maybe it wouldn't make so much difference. But he was special—no better than the rest of us, I don't mean that—but there was something about him that marked him out from the rest." He looked into the fire as he talked as did all the others, for these were not words that rode easily on their tongues.

"I guess it was just that he did pretty much what he wanted to do a good part of his life," Samuel said. "Like his house there. He wanted to build the place and live in it by himself so he did it, even though he had to sell the bank and other things that people in town got down on him for. He went about things like that straight and quick, and it made a lot of people mad."

"What in the hell did he do in that place all by hisself, Sam?" Lee asked. "Looks to me like a man'd get awful danged lonesome."

"He never wanted for things to do," Samuel said. "It was the time to do 'em in he lacked, if anything."

"But what would he do?"

"Oh for Christ's sake, Lee," Virgil said. "Sam didn't live in the house with him."

"Lately he was busy with the museum," Samuel said, "takin' that painter around to get pictures of the full bloods. But I couldn't say just how he spent his time."

"I guess he did what he wanted to do, all right," Virgil said. "But there was somethin' else, too. You said he went about things straight and quick—it was the look in his eye when he did it. It was a hard look—not unfriendly-like but hard. That face of his put me in mind of a red-tailed hawk."

"He was part Chetopa," Samuel said.

"I know. That would account for some of that wildness in his face. But the things he would do. You know that dog trader that comes down from Jeff City ever' so often. I happened to be lookin' over the fellow's dogs one day when Buck came along, and I watched Buck then, just to see what he would do. You can imagine how he looked standin' on the curb, big and easy, his hands in his pockets and him smokin' that curved stemmed pipe he always had in his mouth. Trader got so nervous after awhile that he couldn't hardly do his business. 'Fraid Buck would cheat him some way cause he could tell that Buck knew the dogs as well or better than he did himself."

"I've seen him like that at quarter horse auctions," Will said, reaching out his cup toward the pint that Lee was holding. "He had a funny way about him all right. And shoot? Jesus. It was worth goin' all day without a bird just to watch him."

"And yet he ends up like this," Sim said, his eyes narrow and hurt and puzzled. "It just doesn't seem to fit."

The dogs were still working out the trail down by the creek and Samuel shifted uncomfortably, wanting them to pick up the scent. A cold trail was bad any night but it would seem extra bad tonight. And he wanted to put from his mind, if only for a moment, what he had seen that day. It was a long time before anyone spoke again.

"I was kind of thinkin' about it," Virgil said finally. "It seems to me like we oughta do somethin'. I don't know just how to put it, but just a little somethin' that we could all remember."

"How do you mean?" Samuel said.

"Well," Virgil said. "Somethin' tied up with Buck was what I was thinkin' of. Just kind of one last thing, you might say."

The others nodded and sat huddled in the mist without speaking.

"Sure," Sim said, his face suddenly reflective. "Well, look here—this was his ridge, and we always had the run of it just like it belonged to us. How about havin' one last run and not big either; just the hunters around here that knew Hardin and used his land." He looked from one man to another, his voice tentative in the general uncertainty. "No fuss but easy-like, the way he would have done it himself."

"Yeah," Will said, looking over towards Samuel. "Why

237

not the night after the Indians open that museum. One last time."

Samuel looked at them now, at their faces hard and earnest and even eager. "He would have liked it," he said simply. "We'll do it."

And then they passed the pint around once more, leaving the last drink for old man Hendricks. He drained the bottle and tossed it out into the brush.

"Well," he said, wiping the back of his hand across his mouth, "there's lots o' talk up here tonight but the dogs is right quiet.'

"Cold trail, for sure," Samuel said to him, and then he looked at the others and his voice trembled as he spoke. "But I'll be on my knees between now and that night, and if the Maker takes any pleasure at all in hound music, He'll see to it that things go right." Then he got up and stretched and sounded his horn down the valley. "I reckon I've had enough for tonight. I'll leave that fox to you boys—looks like he's too smart for the kind of dogs I got."

"We'll give him bad dreams, anyway," Virge said.

"Yeah. The funeral's Thursday over at Buck's place. If you feel like it—well, I'll be there with my boy." He smiled briefly and waved his hand at them and walked into the darkness toward the car. After a moment the dogs scrambled noisily through the underbrush and he put them into the trunk once more.

On the way home he wondered if he had done the right thing in leaving the place that night, for it would not be good for Jeff to return to an empty house. And as the apprehension worked through his mind he pressed his foot against the accelerator, wanting to hurry, afraid and not wanting to think about what he feared. As his headlights swept into the yard and washed the darkness from Jeff's car he felt a quick sense of relief and then suddenly he noticed that the house was black and lifeless. Without bothering to let the dogs out of the back he half ran across the yard to the kitchen door and strode noisily into the dark kitchen.

"Jeff?" he called anxiously, staring around him into the darkness. "Where are you, boy?"

He could have wept when the voice answered him from the bedroom. "In here, Pap."

Samuel leaned against the kitchen table for a moment, breathing heavily, and then he went slowly to the doorway of Jeff's bedroom. In the darkness he could see the tiny orange hole that Jeff's cigarette had burned in the black. "I didn't know where you were, boy."

"I went to White Eagle's." In the dusty silence of night his voice was listless, broken, almost automatic, as though the mind and heart behind it had gone dead. "Buck was there."

"I hope you can let it go—my not tellin' you, I mean."

"Sure. It doesn't matter."

"Well," Samuel said thickly, and then he was silent. He reached over and touched the covers of Jeff's bed. "Maybe we can talk about it tomorrow. I reckon we can both use the sleep."

There was no answer, and Samuel backed awkwardly from the doorway. "We'll fix things, boy, don't you worry about that; we'll make things right some way." He ran his hand stiffly over his forehead and turned and went back out into the mist. And when he had put the hounds into the pen again, he stood and listened to the wind in the blackjacks and wondered how much more he could stand.

CHAPTER XV

☐ Jeff woke abruptly in the clear, chill dawn and stared about him as though someone had called him from sleep. The day was faint, more shadow yet than light, and the room was hushed and dim. He put on his shoes, and the bed springs jiggled and grated as he got up and dressed hurriedly in shivering silence. There was no sound in the house other than the occasional groan or crack of a board, and Samuel was apparently still in bed.

He waited until he was outside to light a cigarette and then he walked down through the lot to the curving road. There had been a frost during the night and the rime sparkled thickly on the grass, and as Jeff looked away across the cold and motionless prairie he could not help thinking that this was no place for a man in life or in death. A grave here seemed little better than having one's bones sanded white by the incessant wind as they lay in the glare of the sun, and rest, even in death, seemed unthinkable in this emptiness. Men were lashed by the rain and blunted by the sun until they might lie again in the dust and yet even then there would be no peace; the grass around them would bend and rustle in the wind and the clouds would scatter quickly across the reaches of the heavens and the dust itself would rise and spin and settle and then lie restless and haunted. And this would be true of Buck even more than of the others, for he would be buried this morning on high prairie where the wind moved always like a hunting dog in autumn and where the sun and rain and every weather found the land naked and open to their assault.

He went on down the road until he came to the bridge and then he leaned there against the railing, smoking, shivering a little, watching the modulations of the sky as bird song dinned through the creek bottom. There was something almost like surprise in his eyes as he watched the molten light hovering upon the horizon, as though he had not believed that the sun could return again.

It seemed so long ago that the girl had opened the door for him and the sudden heat of the kitchen had made it momentarily hard to breathe.

"Looks like a damned parade," she had said, shutting the door hard against the rain and returning to the kitchen table. She had some cards spread out before her in a game of solitaire and at the other end of the table Paul sprawled in a chair, a half-emptied bottle and a shot glass in front of him. "On down the hall," she had yawned. "He's in the bedroom."

He had heard the low, guttural Chetopa voices, and he could see the old men, the full bloods of the tribe, standing in the living room, the colorful silk shirts that they wore contrasting vividly with their dry and wrinkled faces. Then in the door of the bedroom he saw White Eagle, dressed in bright ceremonial clothing, and suddenly to Jeff it had seemed that White Eagle was no longer the man whom he had known but something beyond that, the embodiment, perhaps, of all the old men who stood in the other room and talked of death. White Eagle's eyes were remote and his voice deep and withdrawn. Jeff had looked at him in silence, nodding at his heavy words, until the old man stepped out of his way.

Buck was lying on the bed, his lean face forever still, the eyes gone out, the high forehead open at the temple. It had taken Jeff a moment to realize, for his attention had been distracted by the vivid blanket that lay across Buck's body and by the severe rigidity stamped upon his features. But there it was—the blackened flesh, the temple broken and empty. He stared wordlessly and then turned and looked into White Eagle's stern face.

"He didn't tell me that," he said, frowning as though he could no longer see. "He said he was dead, but not that, not—his own gun."

White Eagle nodded slowly and Jeff had looked back once more at the drawn face, hard and chiseled as the face on some ancient coin. Then he had bent his head and walked through the broken talk on down the hall.

He drove for what must have been hours until almost without realizing it he had found himself at the farm again. He went in and lay down in the silence and still he could not think about it. Suicide—the word glowed weirdly in the darkness of his mind, casting an aureole of misty light about the Janus-faced image of his father and of Buck. And when he asked himself why, the word rolled like a stone through the empty, echoing labyrinth of memory and there had been no answer. There had been no answer the next day when he had talked about it with Samuel. It was as though the sheer, brute fact of it lay beyond the range of reason.

Now he shook his head as though to clear away his thoughts and turned to look down at the sun-swept creek below him. The birds still sang in the trailing willow trees and the ancient cottonwood by the bridge would scatter its snow again and somehow he would grow used to it, find a way to live with it just as he had for all the years before. And yet this would be like growing used to a world whose sun had suddenly gone cold, or a world from which once again the voice of a father was missing.

The smoke from the chimney was twisting in the wind as he walked back up to the farm house, and the hounds, huddled together and trembling, looked at him sadly from the pen. Samuel was standing at the kitchen door when he got around to the back.

"Mornin'," Samuel said. He looked up at the sky and then held the door open. "Cold."

"Yes, it is," Jeff said softly, coming into the kitchen. He went over to the stove and held his hands over the burners. "Seems pretty cold for March, anyway."

"Well, we get this weather right on through to the end of April some years. You can never tell. How about some coffee."

"Sure."

"I got your breakfast there on the table. You go ahead and help yourself."

Jeff sat at the table eating, watching Samuel fix the food for the hounds. He had noticed something peculiar about the old man and now he realized that it was the clothes he was wearing. His white shirt had a high, stiff collar and he had on trousers of a hard, dark, faintly shiny material. The coat that matched the trousers was hung on the back of one of the kitchen chairs and Jeff realized how long it had been since he had seen his grandfather in a suit. The shirt was a little short in the sleeves and made Samuel's hands seem bigger than they were, and above the collar his face appeared more wrinkled and weathered than ever. Before he went outside he put on his coat.

"I figured I ought to wear my suit," he said, looking at Jeff.

He was awkward, standing there with the battered tin pan of dog food in his hands, and yet Jeff saw a strength and a gentleness in the old man's body that he had not noticed before.

"It looks good," Jeff said.

"It's kinda little. It hasn't been outa that closet for quite a piece. I bought it for your grandmother's funeral." He stood there for a moment and then he went to the door. "Be right back," he said over his shoulder.

Jeff blew the steam from his coffee and tasted it. Then he put in some more sugar and stirred it slowly, thinking how things always worked so that they were just a little different from what he had expected. Seeing Samuel this way had startled him, and yet here he was in the same kitchen, sitting at the old table where he had sat so often before. It might have been any of the mornings of the previous six months except that Samuel had a suit on now, and Buck was dead. This was the morning of his funeral, and Jeff had to keep reminding himself as though he could not yet really believe it.

"Be with you in a minute," Samuel said. He went on through the kitchen to the bedroom and when he returned he was holding a Bible in his hand. Jeff recognized it as the one that lay on the mantle beside the picture of his grandmother. "We can take my car," Samuel said. "Make it easier."

"All right," Jeff answered. He could not help feeling that the best thing for him would be to leave the place forever as soon as the funeral was over, but he could not let Samuel know it. He had hurt the old man enough as it was.

"What will it be like?" he asked as they drove out of the yard.

"The funeral?" Samuel said. "Well, I'm not sure. It'll be Chetopa—that was the way Hardin wanted it. I guess you knew he was part Indian."

"Yes."

"But not like the old time. They used to have a big dance the night before, mourning dance they called it. Some of the young ones would go out and get a scalp off of a tribe they would be fightin' with. Then they would ride the dead man on a horse up to where they was goin' to bury him and afterwards they would kill the horse so's he'd have somethin' to ride on to the next world. But this'll be different, of course. I think it was mainly that Hardin didn't want any preacher and he didn't want any graveyard. He wanted to stay on his own place and he wanted to go like his people before him had gone."

"It seems—well, a little strange," Jeff said.

245

"Strange?" Samuel said. "I reckon it is. But that was the way he wanted it. And I don't guess that it makes a hell of a lot of difference."

"What do you mean?"

"Just that if there's somebody up above who takes any notice of what's goin' on down here, I reckon he'll care as much about Hardin as anybody else, no matter how he goes into the ground."

The sun was well up and strong by the time they reached the house. The wind was stirring the leaves of the blackjack trees and a bluejay was talking loudly in the woods before the house. Several cars were parked just outside the fence, among them the pickup truck that belonged to White Eagle, and beyond the woodpile to the rear a pony was tethered.

"I guess White Eagle brought the horse," Jeff said.

"That would be John," Samuel said.

There were not many people in the yard and Jeff recognized most of them. No one was doing much talking and when he and Samuel joined the rest of the men there were short greetings and comments on the weather and then silence.

"Good day for quail," Samuel said.

Jeff nodded. "I'd like to go again," he said. From where they were standing he could see most of the country over which they had hunted, the east ridge and the creek and the valley as far west as the point where he had killed his first bird and where Buck had fallen. And thinking of it now, he wondered again what had really happened that day. The sharpest thing in his memory was the ringing shock of the twelve-gauge as he had fired without thought, almost without volition. "Maybe next year," he said, smiling briefly.

"Yeah," Samuel said.

Jeff looked over at him and the old man's face seemed lonely and tired. And suddenly he wondered if he would ever see Samuel again or whether this would be the

246

last time, and he wondered if his grandfather were thinking the same thing. "I'll have to be going before long,"
he said.

"I know. But then I hadn't figured on you stayin'
so long, anyhow."

Jeff clenched his hands in the cold and looked down
at the ground. There were so many things that should
be said and yet no way ever to say them. The moments
came and went and the loneliness remained. After
a while Samuel went over to speak to some of the fox
hunters who were standing in awkward isolation in one
corner of the yard. Jeff could see the quick smiles on
their faces as Samuel came among them and he felt more
alone than ever.

The pony stamped and whinnied and then the back
door of the house opened and Paul White Eagle emerged.
He was tall like the others but there was a soft heaviness
in his body which the old men did not have. The glasses
which he wore contrasted strangely with the vertical
lines of paint on his face and there was a jerkiness in his
movements that belied the blankness of his expression.
He hesitated for a moment outside the door and looked
around him and finally went on toward the gate. Jeff
could feel his discomfort and uncertainty.

"That's John's son," Samuel said, walking up to him
quietly. "I think we're supposed to follow him down to
the point."

The old full bloods went first, following young White
Eagle as he made his way south through the blackjacks.
Following them came the Chetopa women, walking less
certainly on their high heels, and then the hunters and
other white friends who had heard of Buck's death.
Beneath the feet of all of them the stiff grass broke and
lay flat, and as they came out onto the windy naked-
ness of the point they narrowed their eyes against the
painful light. The prairie gleamed in the sun like a massive shield and a great unbroken silence enclosed them

247

all as they stood around the stone barrow. Beneath such a sky their voices would have been as the chattering of sparrows. No one spoke.

White Eagle's son stood beside the barrow, facing the east. He did not turn when they heard the noise of the pony crunching through the silvered grass. Jeff, looking around, saw the men coming through the trees, one leading the pony and two walking on either side, holding Buck erect on the pony's back. White Eagle was following behind and Jeff could hear his voice raised in a wild and lonely lament. There was something unearthly about it all, the steady crunching of the pony's hoofs in the silence, White Eagle's voice high and grieving, and then Buck himself, tall as a god. beneath the trees, his body swaying with the movements of the pony. And Jeff was stunned, held fast in a dream from which he could not emerge, as Buck came riding down upon him, towering above them all, his face bright with red and yellow paint. He might have been alive save for the remoteness of his expression and the sculpted stiffness of his body, but in death he was dominant as no living man could have been. There was a magnificence in his figure that made grief seem small and insignificant, and he was irretrievably distant, beyond all their caring. Jeff wanted to look away but Buck filled his eyes; he felt a terror in his heart that he had never known before. For this was a death that was naked as the prairie, hard as the life of this empty, wind-searched land.

The pony passed beyond Jeff and stood now by the barrow; its ears were stiff and alert and the hair of its mane and tail lifted a little in the wind. One of the old men had taken a place beside the barrow and was now chanting a slow and minor song. White Eagle was singing, too, holding up his hands first to the east and then to the west, and as he turned, the pony shifted its feet and snorted. The feathers in White Eagle's long headdress seemed to bother the pony as they spun and fluttered in the wind, and he shook his head nervously until one of the men stepped forward and placed his hand above the trembling nostrils and quieted him.

Jeff looked around him and saw Virgil Sands staring up at Buck, his eyes wide and his mouth partially open. He realized that he had never seen Virgil really silent before and now there was something in his face that told of dreaming, of Virgil seeing perhaps himself in Buck's place, not dead but simply noble, mourned by men such as these. Further away Paul White Eagle was standing somewhat apart from the others, his body tense and his hands restless at his sides. His face was turned to the ground and he seemed to be listening to the intoned song of the men. He appeared young among the other men, who were all middle-aged or elderly, and yet his face was the hardest of all. It was as though he heard it all faintly from far off, for there was just the trace of a frown on his face. He did not look up until White Eagle was lifting Buck from the pony's back, and then in his face there was a desperate bewilderment; his body seemed to tremble a little and his shoulders surged forward; a jagged bolt of pain sprang suddenly across his face, and after a moment his eyes were upon the earth again.

White Eagle placed Buck in a sitting position in the barrow and continued to chant while the men who had walked beside the pony brought up the stones and laid them over Buck's body. Their faces shone in the sun and their coarse black hair stirred in the wind like the dark mane of the pony; the sun glancing off their silver ornaments filled their movements with light, and yet their faces were darkly still. They were painted with the colors of the earth as Buck had been, and they wore the same buckskin shirts and black silk trousers. The older men held their blankets tightly around them, bearing slowly the smaller stones to the barrow while White Eagle's son came suddenly forward and carried the larger stones as though he were glad for the work. Jeff wondered what White Eagle was saying but he could make

249

nothing of the Chetopa words. Yet without understanding them he could feel their grace and measured quality as White Eagle spoke, and he knew that the emotion which charged the old man's tongue was deeper and more universal than language.

Then beside him Jeff heard Samuel talking quietly, almost mumbling. He glanced at the old man from the corner of his eye and he could see his lips moving, saying something that seemed to be meant for Samuel alone. His glance traveled down Samuel's body to the wrist that shone whitely above the edge of the coat pocket into which his hand was stuffed. The pocket bulged thickly from his side, and Jeff knew that he was holding his Bible. The old man seemed oblivious of those around him as he continued to mutter whatever it was that he was saying, and there was a strained and determined reverence in his face as he squinted down to where the men were putting the last rocks on the barrow. He seemed to be hurrying, as though there were something that he must finish, and his face recalled to Jeff the face that one sometimes saw from a train window, a face from which memory seemed to be reaching out to clutch the fleeting moment. And then, feeling all at once the terrible finality, he turned again to the barrow and realized with a sudden chill of dread that it was all over. The last stones were in place and the chants had ceased. Already some of the men had turned back toward the house and White Eagle was talking to the man who was holding the pony. Jeff's first reaction was that there had to be more than this, that it was all too quick and stern and deliberate and that there must be more time. Yet all of them now were beginning to move up the slope of the point toward the blackjack trees. Jeff felt something growing tight within him and involuntarily his hands stiffened at his sides, and yet it was over and Buck was gone.

"Is that all?" he asked Samuel hopelessly.

"I reckon that's it, for us," Samuel said. "They'll be havin' a feast, John and the others. I don't think—"

But Jeff had turned away, shaking his head. When he looked up, White Eagle was coming toward them and he noticed that the paint on John's face was cracked across the many seams and wrinkles. The claw necklace at his throat made a dry clicking sound and the sun blazed on the silver disks at his waist. He spoke no greeting and his voice was remote.

"There will be a feast at my sister's place tomorrow," he said. "We would be happy for you to come." Then he nodded and moved away from them, following the others towards the house. Jeff could hear the soft rustle of silk as he walked and his moccasins were silent in the grass.

"Well," Samuel said after a moment. "I guess that's about it."

But Jeff was not listening. He was looking down at the yellow stones that rose high and rounded above the swell of prairie. Buck was there in the darkness alone, but Jeff could only remember him as he had looked riding down the point through the blackjacks, seeming as majestic and as noble as a god. The sun had found lights in the stones and now they seemed to burn as though a pyre had been kindled there, a pyre for some hero whose barrow would remain as a reminder for later men. Yet he was gone, and with him had vanished something sharp and keen from the lives of all who had known him. Not even the primitive glory of the sun and of the earth and of Buck himself could quite make up for it just now.

Jeff had not meant to go to sleep at all. They had come back from the funeral and eaten lunch and then when Samuel had gone out to make some deliveries, he had come into the bedroom just to lie down for a while. Now the day was gone and he lay in the darkness of the room, hearing the sounds of his grandfather in the kitchen. He rubbed his hand across his face as though he might brush away the night, and then he sat up and lit a cigarette. He had the sense of something thoughtlessly and carelessly lost, something which he could never bring back again, and in his mind was a stubborn anger which he could not control.

Samuel was standing at the stove when he came into the kitchen. "Git some sleep?" he asked.

"Yes, I didn't mean to—I just lay down to rest for awhile and I guess I dropped off."

"Well, you'll probably feel better for it. I got dinner about ready. It's been a long day."

Jeff sat at the table, smoking, and when Samuel had served the meal he ate in silence, only half listening to what his grandfather said. He could not shake off the effects of sleep or the dull remorse that seemed to lie heavy in his mind. He was still sitting there when Samuel had finished feeding the hounds, and he felt no desire to talk even when Samuel sat down opposite him again.

"I wouldn't let it get me down," Samuel said quietly. "I know how you feel, what with your dad and all, but—"

"It's not that," Jeff said quickly. He looked up at Samuel and then he frowned a little. "I'm still sleepy, I guess."

Samuel took his watch from his pocket and looked at it and then began to wind it. "It's a nice night," he said. "I thought we might take the hounds over on the ridge for awhile." He was silent for a moment and Jeff did not answer. "Frost ought to have made it just about wet enough to put that fox to his trumps. I kinda thought that maybe once more before—"

There was no way to refuse when he put it like that. Jeff sat up stiffly in his chair and rubbed his hands together. "Sure," he said. "Sure, that'll be fine."

But on the way over, he could not help being sorry that he had come. Samuel had hitched the horses to the wagon and had loaded the hounds in the back and now they were jolting along the road to the turnoff into Buck's land. The moon moved obscurely through ragged clouds and the road before them was dark, and in the wagon bed the hounds snuffed and thumped the boards with their tails.

"The huntin's been on the poor side, all right," Samuel said, apologetically. "Maybe we'll have some luck tonight. We're about due."

"I guess so," Jeff said. He was thinking of all the nights of the previous fall that they had come out like this, and to little avail as far as he was concerned. Cold trail, Samuel had called it, and he thought now that the phrase was a pretty good summation of all the time that he had spent here. It had been a long series of cold trails, culminating in Buck's burial this morning.

"I've had bad years before," Samuel said, "but I can't remember one like this one. Much longer and them hounds will forgit what they're supposed to be huntin'."

"I guess I picked a bad time," Jeff said listlessly.

"It puts me in mind of the first year I come here," Samuel said. "It was so hot that summer you could fry eggs on the side walk in town. Long time ago."

"Why did he ever come back?" Jeff asked after a while.

"What do you mean?"

"Buck—back here to Grey Horse. What made him want to come back?"

"We talked about it some once," Samuel said. "He was workin' out in California. He told me that when he got the wire about his dad's dyin' he walked around town until the liquor stores opened in the mornin' and then he bought a bottle of whiskey and drove until he was way out in the desert. He said he found himself a mesquite tree and sat in the shade of it most of the day, drinkin' the whiskey. He said that all he remembered was that it was real clear and that he could see a helluva long way. Then when it started to get evenin' he got back in his car and commenced drivin' again and he kept at it until he was home. He said that when he got back it was like he hadn't ever really been away."

"It's hard to imagine him in that bank," Jeff said.

"Oh, he ran it, all right," Samuel said. "Buck was a smart man—had a lot of schoolin', Hardin did. He didn't have any trouble with the bank."

"But then he quit."

"Yeah. I always figured it was kinda like the way I quit the grocery business."

"He was a hard man to understand," Jeff said.

"He had his ways all right," Samuel said. "The gate ought to be along here somewhere."

They turned off the road and followed the faint tracks to the ridge. When Samuel stopped the wagon, the hounds scrambled down to the ground in a confusion of yelping and barking and disappeared into the darkness.

"I guess they know where they're at," Samuel remarked, fixing the reins on the brake handle.

Jeff was glad that there was no one else on the ridge; he was in no mood for the usual humor that went on around the fire. He helped Samuel drag up a dead limb and they sat without speaking, listening to the cracking of the fire. From time to time they could hear the hounds working down along the creek.

"You know somethin'," Samuel said after a while. "I think Hardin died a happy man."

"That's not what they think about it in town," Jeff said.

"What do they know about it in town? What would any of them ever know about a man like Hardin?"

"All right," Jeff said. "But I think it's stretching things a little to call him happy." The certainty of his grandfather's voice had increased his feeling of irritation. Buck had shot himself—why not let it go at that.

"Put it that he had something settled, then," Samuel

said. "Something happened that put things in place in his mind."

"But what was there to settle? He didn't strike me as a man with many problems."

"It only takes one," Samuel said.

"All right—he was sick; his heart was bad. There wasn't any other way out. If that's what you mean by settling things, by being happy—" Jeff felt a necessity to stick to the few facts he had, as though Samuel's talk might lead them into regions of conjecture more bleak, more hopeless than ever.

"No, that was a little thing," Samuel replied calmly. "Whatever it was that was botherin' Hardin was a whole lot bigger than that."

"Maybe so," Jeff said. "What I'm getting at is that it wasn't settled. John White Eagle said that nothing Buck had done would be enough."

Samuel was silent for a while. He looked off toward the creek and then he held out his hands to the fire. "What do you mean, enough? Enough for what?"

"I don't know," Jeff said. "That was the way he put it. They were talking about the museum and White Eagle said that Buck was expecting too much from it and that no museum could ever be enough—something like that."

"What would have been enough?"

Jeff shook his head stubbornly. "That was what he said. He talked like Hardin wanted the museum for himself."

"That wouldn't make him any different from anybody else," Samuel said. "But it's all past now—who can ever give the answer to somethin' like this."

He looked away then as though he were anxious to end the conversation.

"I suppose," Jeff said. "Yet I had the feeling that White Eagle knew why it happened."

"Well, maybe so," Samuel frowned, poking the fire. "Did you ever notice that pickup of his, where the right fender's gone? He hit a culvert on that side and took the fender clean off. Hardin told me about it, said John was singin' and beatin' the outside of the car door like it was a drum. I guess he just forgot that he was drivin' a car. He coulda killed himself."

Jeff waited, but Samuel said nothing more. "I've noticed the fender," he said after a moment, "but what does that have to do with Buck?"

"It's just that birds like that know things sometimes. Like ever' now and then you find a preacher who can talk in tongues and heal—gets himself into a trance where he can see things that you and me wouldn't see. John's a little like that."

"I don't know about that," Jeff said dryly. "But he didn't act like he thought that Buck died a happy man."

"Then that was one time he was wrong, boy," Samuel said shortly. "He was just plain wrong."

There seemed no point in talking about it further, and yet Jeff could not help being angry at the old man's sureness. Why didn't he come right out and say it if he knew something that the rest of them didn't know? And Samuel seemed angry himself, now, that Jeff should question him. Yet Jeff felt that they must reach some conclusion, however unpleasant it might be. He had had enough of the vagueness and intangibility that seemed to characterize everything that had happened to him here. Some one real thing had to be established, beyond doubt, beyond supposition.

"You said he had something settled," he said bluntly. "What was it, then?"

Samuel looked at him quickly, staring at him for a moment, his eyes hard and furious. He kicked at the fire with his boot and his face grew dark with anger. "Goddamn it," he said. "Goddamn it to hell. Are you blind, boy? Didn't you see him that last day? Don't you know why he didn't shoot, why he ran like a fool for your bird? He was alone, do you understand? He had a bad heart and he was alone. He had something—he had his

256

house and this land—he knew he would have to go—didn't you just tell me yourself this morning that he had left it all to you? For God's sake, boy, don't you know what was in his mind?"

Jeff could see the tension in his face as he struggled for the words, could see his hands reaching out toward him, and then suddenly the darkness was alive with the clamor of the hounds. He heard their voices belling through the valley, clear and primitive and hot, and then he could feel the old man going from him. Samuel was still there, still looking at him, but his spirit was gone into the darkness, fleshed now in the music of the hounds. Sweat stood on Jeff's forehead and through his veins surged the fear that had come so powerfully into his body as his grandfather had shouted at him. With terrible intensity he saw Buck again as he had run up the windy slope that day toward the fallen bird until his body had become a silhouette of agony against the dusky sky. He remembered the tortured words that had fallen from Buck's lips, how later Buck had told him about the house and suddenly now his heart was flooded with a joy which he had almost forgotten. For without his knowing it he had become a part of someone again and he no longer stood alone. In the firelight Pap's face was old and remote, and yet Jeff knew that the blaze of anger had burned away the last barrier that stood between them.

CHAPTER XVI

☐ By the time he got back to the house, Paul White Eagle was cold and he needed a drink. The wind seemed to sing in his ears and he could still hear the voices of lamentation and now as he lit his cigarette the match trembled in his hand. He shook his head and rubbed his hands hard against his ears. When he listened again he could hear the blackjack branches scraping across the roof and the distant murmur of voices, and though the house was half dark and uncomfortably quiet, there were still too many people outside whom he did not wish to see. He had known that he should not have come, yet there had been no way to get out of it. And now it was over. Buck was buried and it was done, except that he could still hear the voices of the old men, the words that they had chanted, words that seemed to echo in the dark places of his memory, evoking things that he did not want to think about.

All the time down there at the grave he had felt that they were staring at him; he had wanted to run and then once he had thought that he would fall because the sun had hurt his eyes and made him dizzy and the words kept going crazily through his mind, making him afraid. Everyone seemed to want something of him, something that he did not have. Jackie was easy; she only wanted money and he could give her that. But his father and the old men who had stood there chanting, they wanted something else and the thought of it frightened him. I wish to hell I was white, he thought suddenly. Then they wouldn't expect nothin' of me. But he was lying and he knew it; what he wanted was what the old men had, the things they sang about, the things that made them dance, and he was afraid.

He heard the door open then and he turned around and his father was standing there.

"I guess they are all gone," John said, speaking in Chetopa to his son.

"I guess so," Paul said. "I got a little cold. I come inside." And although he could understand his father, he was embarrassed by the guttural formality of the old tongue.

"You did good," John said. "You looked like a Chetopa."

"Yeah," Paul said. "I got to get back to town."

John nodded. "I told Grimes I would hobble the pony out back. I said we would leave him there."

"I'll turn the car around," Paul said.

"Sure," John said. "I never could teach you anything about horses, could I."

"I'll get the car," Paul said.

They did not talk on the way back to town. Paul was uncomfortable on the hard seat of the pickup and he hoped that nobody he knew in town would see him in these clothes. He looked straight ahead until they were beyond the town and then he realized that they were not headed for the house. "Where you goin'?" he said. "You missed the turn."

"I wanted to go out to the grave," John said. "We haven't been there together for a long time."

"I told Jackie I would be back early," Paul said. He lit a cigarette and tried to hold his hands steady.

"I don't think she'll leave," John said.

He parked the pickup on the side of the road and Paul followed him up through the long grass to the top of the hill. The wind was blowing hard and they leaned into it, walking with their heads lowered until they reached the barrow of stones that marked the grave. Below them they could see the town and the hills beyond which merged gently into prairie.

"This is where I want to be," John said after a while.

"You told me that," Paul said.

"I want you to remember. Right here, next to him," he said, indicating the grave of his father.

"Yeah," Paul said.

"You have forgotten many things. I want you to remember this."

They were silent for a while and then John sat down beside the barrow. "Sit down," he said.

"Look," Paul said.

"Sit down. We do not get to talk much. When you are at home, she is always around. There will not be many more times."

"Don't talk like that."

"Sit down."

He watched the old man light a cigar and then he sat down beside him. His legs felt stiff and the ground was cold; he was still breathing hard from climbing the hill. The wind kept blowing and it was like the wind he had heard at Buck's. He was trying not to think of anything, but he could still hear the voices and they stirred in his blood like restless spirits. They seemed to be saying something to him and he did not want to hear it, and yet he had to listen.

"You were too young to remember him," John said, motioning toward the grave. And as he spoke the slow, deep Chetopa tongue the words throbbed through Paul's mind, reawakening the songs and talks that he remembered dimly from his childhood. "He was a warrior. He walked among tall men, and no one was taller than he. On his pony he was like a mighty wind in the front ranks of the fighters. He was a great one among the children of the earth. But when he became heavy with years, the young ones forgot the things that he had done and to them he was only an old man around the camp, an old man whose talk was of a time beyond their remembering. Our people had moved here by then, and the old stories were dying. Moving us here was like taking the past away from us, because the past stayed back among the hills and forests and creeks where we had lived, and it could not live here. We were among white men and in a strange land, and your grandfather was of the past and unremembered. Finally one night an owl came and sat on a blackjack limb above the old man's lodge and called to him down through the smoke hole. 'Old man,' he said, 'you are too long on the earth—the people have forgotten you, and your name is no longer in their hearts— there are no songs for you now and you will not be remembered. You must make a song for yourself so that the ones after you will know your name on their tongues. You must tell them what happened so that they will remember.' The old man heard the owl and he knew that the words were true. That morning at dawn he got up and painted himself and dressed in the buffalo robes and eagle feathers which he had not worn for a long time. Then he took his drum and went out into the center of the village and sat down. He began to sing, songs of the gods and of men, songs of games and of feasts and of victories, songs of the old time. It was the children who heard him first; they came and sat down around him and listened. After a while others started coming until the whole village was there, listening to him. Pretty soon two of the young men went out and caught their horses and rode away, and when they came back in the afternoon they brought with them people of the other tribes who lived nearby. People rode into camp all that day, and the old man went on singing. It was as though all his life was coming out in those songs and I was afraid. He was too old to have such strength, and yet he went on singing. By evening some other old men had joined him, sitting around him in a circle, beating the drums and singing the songs that they knew. He was making many songs himself, and then there would be only his voice

262

singing above the drums. We made fires then, and we danced. There were many people, and we danced all through the night. I was afraid for my father and I went to him and spoke to him but he did not answer me. He did not even look at me and I was ashamed. The dance went on all night and at dawn he stopped. He got up and went to his lodge and lay down. He lay there for two days and then he died. We buried him here. He had made many songs, and the mourning dance was beyond anything that even the old men could remember. I was young then and I have not forgotten it. The camp was filled with people and most of them are gone now."

He wants me to dance, Paul was thinking. He's telling me this because he wants me to dance when they open the museum. They will be dancing for Buck and he wants me to be there and I haven't danced since I was a boy, except once—he winced, remembering it. It had been on a summer's night, some years back. He had been at the drive-in with the usual crowd, drinking beer until he was thick-tongued and sweating heavily. There was nothing to do except drink beer or fight or just drive aimlessly around town, and in summer they usually drank beer; they could drive around in winter when beer didn't taste so good, and fighting was hard on clothes. And he was always there, night after night, sometimes sleeping in the car all night unless Jackie or someone else was good enough to drive him home. But on this particular night Jackie had gone off with someone else and there had been a fight and he had felt a little sick. He remembered that he had taken the road towards Tulsa and that he had just kept driving for what seemed a very long time. There was kind of a blank then—he knew that he had been driving the car fast and that he had ended up in a ditch and though the car had gone sideways hard, he had not been hurt. He remembered climbing out of the car and standing in the moonlight, looking at it and laughing. He felt as though he had accomplished something, something that the others would talk about for a while. He felt good about it. He looked up toward the moon and laughed, and then in the silence he had heard a steady, pounding beat, like a drum. He laughed again, following the sound through the field until he found its source, a little oil pump throbbing steadily through the darkness. He had given a whoop then and started to dance, singing the scraps of songs that remained in his memory. Twice he had fallen and got up, still laughing and lurching crazily around the pump until the third time, and then he could not get up. The ground had tilted under him and he had been sick and after a while he had slept. The sun hot in his face had waked him the next morning and he had walked to town for the wrecker. And he wants me to dance for Buck, he thought. Why can't he get it through his head?

"You did good this morning," John was saying.

"I only did what you told me to. I didn't have any right there. I shouldn't have been there at all."

"That is the way Hardin wanted it."

"He didn't want me."

"He wanted it right. That was the way it had to be."

Paul shook his head and looked down at the ground. "Look," he said. "You want me to dance. I'm not fit to dance, can't you see that? Why do you tell me these old stories? I don't belong to those people. You do, sure, but I don't. It don't do any good now—it's too late."

"Who will remember you, boy? Who will sing when they put you in the ground?"

"I don't care about that."

"You will."

"Nobody will want to remember me. You ought to know that better than anyone." And yet he could not forget how Buck had looked and how the old men's voices had sounded through the wind. More than anything else, it made him realize how alone he was. He had accepted nothing from the past, and he would have nothing to give. Everything that he was would go into the ground with his corpse. "Buck was alone," he said suddenly.

John looked over at him. "Yes," he said after a while. "He was. But there is the museum, and his place, and there will be a song And the young one was there."

"Who do you mean?"

"The one with Sam Beecher."

"What about him?"

"He was there," John said. "I don't know."

"Look," Paul said. "It's getting cold up here. I told Jackie I'd be back early."

"Yes," John said.

He went to church alone that night. He had wanted Paul to go with him, had even asked him at supper, but Paul had refused. The boy had started to drink as soon as they had gotten back to the house and by suppertime he had become sullen and mean. He had laughed when John had asked him to come with him to church. He laughed and shook the bottle in John's face until John knocked it from his hand, smashing it on the floor. The girl had cursed the old man then, had stood in front of him and cursed him until Paul hit her in the mouth and shut her up. When John left, Paul was wiping up the whiskey from the floor and the girl was standing at the sink, watching them, her eyes hard and without tears as she wiped the blood from her mouth.

So he had gone to church alone. Now he was sitting with the others in the sweat lodge, watching the attendant pour water upon the hot limestone, watching the steam rise like some suddenly released spirit and feeling the stifling air wash over him until all at once the sweat was bursting through his skin and flowing down his body in tiny rivulets of warmth. This was the beginning of purity, this evil emerging molten from the body, and now as always he thought of Paul and wished that he were here. But things had gone wrong with Paul, even from the start. He had been a late child, borne to him by his wife not long before the divorce. He had raised Paul by himself, believing it to be the best way, and he had failed. Somewhere along the way the world had changed without his knowing it and by the time he found out about it, it was too late to make any difference. He remembered when Paul had come home from school, saying that the teacher had told him that he needed glasses. John had tried to take him out of school then, and had found that he couldn't. When he learned this, it made him think that there must be some awfully strong reason why people should be in school, so he had spent much money sending Paul to a military school and then to the university. Paul learned how to drink and how to spend money fast and by the end of his first year there he had come back home to stay. But that was just one of the mistakes. In John's mind it all went back to the fact that Paul had not learned the old ways in spite of what he had tried to teach the boy. And yet he was still trying because there was no other way. That was why he wanted him to dance. Because the blood was there, if the old words could ever once reach his heart. And it had to be the heart; Hardin had known it in spite of the museum.

He drank the cup of buckeye-root tea which the attendant handed him and then he sat waiting. The pungent, bitter taste lingered in his mouth and after a while he felt his stomach move. He got up and lifted the flap of the lodge and went out, feeling with suddenness the night around him, vast and calm and clear. He bent to the earth and vomited, and now his body was clean. He went back into the lodge and after he had bathed and put on fresh clothing, he went to the church.

A cedar fire was burning on the crescent and the air was fresh and sweet. The Road Man was sitting at the head of the altar, and White Eagle nodded to him as he took his place among the men who sat around in a half-moon circle. He listened to the prayers being sung, each man shaping his own prayer as he was able, and he began to feel a song fluttering in his heart. He took up the

266

bead-decorated gourd filled with pebbles and shook it to the rhythm of the water drum, and through the chant his voice wandered like the wind. In his other hand he held a stick of cedar, the wood of eternal life, decorated with the long and graceful tail-feathers of the scissortail. When his song had flown, he passed the stick and the gourd to the man at his left and lit a cigarette so that his prayers might be borne upward by the thin line of blue-white smoke ascending through the prayers of his companions. He chewed the pieces of the green peyote button and drank much water and gradually he began to move into the world of his prayers, a world of vivid dreams colored by the power of the peyote. He sang of the greatness of his father, and of the failings of himself and of his son, and always his confession was strong and unsparing. And when at last his songs of failure had gone from him, he thought of what he yet could do; in the water drum he heard the rhythms of the dance and he realized that there lay upon him the responsibility that had lain upon his father. The evil had gone forth from his heart and from his body and now in his dreams he longed to create something as new and fresh and strong as the images that filled his mind. When the gourd rattle came to his hand again, he shook it slowly before him and it seemed to him that he was singing to the listening spirits of the dead, of Hardin and of his father. He sang of the opening of the museum and of the dance and of what he would do, how he would make the old songs live as his father had done before him and how he would make a song for all of them, Paul and young Beecher and Hardin and himself and Samuel as well. In his heart he was joyous and his mouth was filled with promises and he knew that he must do this thing. This was his obligation and he was glad of it. Light was coming in the door when his song was ended and he stayed in the church until it was empty. Then he went out and greeted the sun, grandfather of all things, and walked on through the dawn to his home.

He awoke at noon, tired and yet refreshed. The cedar

267

smoke still clung to his clothes and brought back to his mind memories of the church and of the prayers that he had made. He nodded his head, thinking of all that he had promised, for he knew that it was right and that it was a good thing. In his heart he felt a peace that he had not felt for a long time, a peace that came from knowing what he must do and knowing that he could do it. The dance at the opening of the museum would be a dance for many things.

He finished dressing and drove over to his sister's for the feast. The day was mild and clear and filled with light, and larks whistled their songs from the fenceposts along the road. It was the finest kind of prairie day, windless, the sky blue and hard and flawless, and the light so intense and all-pervading that it seemed to exist in its own right as something independent of the sun. The prairie grass was a soft green and the occasional blackjacks that stood in sharp isolation seemed to reach toward the sun like ancient men hymning songs of joy and thanksgiving. It was a day that worked on the nerves, playing among them like the wind among the blackjack leaves, and made a man dream of doing things that would express the majesty and harmony around him. As John drove along, he watched a hawk that was circling the skies ahead of him and after a while his hand began to tap the side of the car, drumming softly and steadily. He made a song of the hawk, of its strength and of its pride and of its great fortune in being able to look down upon the earth like a god. He sang of its prowess as a hunter, and then he sang of what it hunted, the field-mice and the cowering rabbit, and this made him laugh. It was a fitting song for such a day.

There were many cars parked before his sister's house when he got there. He could see the smoke rising from the yard and as he walked across the road he could smell the mingled odors of hickory wood and roasting meat. It had been a long time since he had seen so many of the people together. He went to his sister and thanked her and then he began to move through the crowd, greeting his friends. Some of them he had not seen for years; they were in Grey Horse now to talk about the opening of the museum. And many of them, old men like himself, were accompanied by their sons and their grandchildren, and it made his heart heavy when they asked about Paul. Yet it was good to see them, to talk of things half forgotten and long out of mind, and it was good to find so many children, to watch them as they ran wildly through the crowd, dodging in and out around the tables and past the pits of smoking beef. To hear the voices of the scolding women made him think of those days when he had run through the camp just as these children were running, being scolded for stealing pieces of meat from the spit. Seeing the old faces again made it seem that the years had passed without his really knowing it. And now as he ate and laughed with these men whom he had known for so long, he felt curiously alone. Perhaps it was merely that they had others of their own blood to look at so that they might always turn and find a part of themselves somewhere in the crowd, while he had only himself. It was a bad thing and he knew that the others realized it, but they did not speak of it; they spoke instead of whether the tribe stood to gain by repressuring the oil fields, of how payments might increase, of what the museum would be like, of things that came easily to the tongue The heart had its own ways and the tongue was not always good at handling them.

From time to time the talk turned to Buck, and John noticed that they always mentioned him with uncertainty and with hesitation. After a while he gathered some of the old men and went with them out behind the garage. They stood there in the sun, their emotions shaded by the stiffness of their speech.

"What is the matter?" he said, when they were away from the noise of the people. "What is it about Hardin that is bothering you?"

"It is the dance," one of them said. "We did not know.

269

It should be a dance of celebration, but we did not know after we heard the news."

"It will be a dance of celebration," John said. "He had a bad heart; he died the way he wanted to."

"We did not know," the man said. "We heard that he was dead and we were not sure how it should be."

"He would not want it changed," John said.

"That is a good thing, then," the man said. "We were sorry when we heard. He was a fine man. He did many things."

"He should not be forgotten," John said. "The dance must make him live in the hearts of the young ones."

"That is how it should be," the man said. He was silent for a moment then. "We wanted you to know that we are grateful for the meat and food which you will send to the encampment. All of us do not have the money of the Chetopa, and now the people will feast as they have not feasted for many years."

"The museum is for all of us," John said. "We want this to be a time to remember."

By late afternoon he was tired again and he wanted to be by himself. He went away quietly and by the time that he reached home the western sky was banked with red clouds. He sat in the grove behind the house, smoking a cigar and thinking of Buck, and there was a great loneliness in his heart. It was hard to believe that he was gone, and yet it was almost as if he had seen it coming, ever since last summer when Samuel's grandson had arrived and even before, when Hardin had gone to Kansas City to the clinic. He wondered if young Beecher would ever understand; it would be a hard and a strange thing for a young man to know. Perhaps none of them would ever understand, for Buck was gone now, and who was to say what had been in his mind? And yet John could not forget what Hardin had said to him that night at the house, the night that he had told him about his heart. Buck had asked him to explain it to the boy if anything ever happened, and now the obligation made John uneasy, for this was a thing that he could never explain with words. He remembered how desperate Jeff had been on the stormy afternoon, the day they had carried Buck's body to the house. That was the time for explaining if it could be done with words. But somehow the boy would have to see it himself in the dance, hear it in the drums and in the singing. For there was no other way.

He heard the leaves rustling behind him and suddenly his son was standing there in the half light.

"I looked for you at the feast," Paul said quietly.

"There were many people," John said. "I did not know you were coming."

"I hadn't planned on it," Paul said. "I wanted to see you. I wanted to tell you that I will dance."

John looked at him, trying to see his eyes in the twilight. "I am glad," he said. "It has been a long time."

CHAPTER XVII

☐ By the middle of April the days were limpid and fragrant. The grass had buried the bones of winter, and what rains came were gentle showers that calmed the dust and washed the world to brightness. And in the prevailing grace that attended April's arrival, Jeff's grief had gradually softened into an emotion compounded of pride and gratitude and nostalgia, an emotion that would steal upon him like the slow spread of twilight across the land. A familiar bird heard suddenly in the clarity of dawn, a train whistle fading in the distance late at night, just the feel of the wind in his face and the sweet new smell of the prairie—all these somehow evoked the sadness which chilled his heart. Yet the jagged shards of pain had been washed away and he could think of Buck once again, with a sense of loss, perhaps, and yet with a strange fulfillment.

He had postponed his leaving until the opening of the museum, and he spent the intervening days by helping White Eagle in whatever ways he could. There were many details to be handled at the last minute, and White Eagle was not particularly good at details at any time, and thus Jeff found himself needed and useful where before he had so often seemed no more than a casual bystander. And as he worked with John he grew to respect the old Indian more than ever for his rocklike strength that somehow weathered the waves of disappointment, of grief, of outrage which washed over him day after day.

To be faced with the wreckage of his people was sufficient shame, but to look upon the dishonor of his name and the dying out of his own blood was enough to turn his heart to dust.

But even though Jeff's days were filled with the problems of finding camping space for a tribe from the southern part of the state or of making sure that there was wood enough for the fires that would burn all week or of satisfying some hopeful politician by shifting his position on the program, still the nights were long and silent, and in the darkness his mind slowly revolved around the decision which must be made. Samuel would be whittling in the porch swing, talking about something that had happened to him long ago while Jeff, half listening and murmuring at the proper times, would be wondering where he would go when he left. He did not have much money, yet it was enough as long as his wants were simple. But when he thought of leaving, he could not help thinking at the same time that this was home, or what little of home that he would ever have. The land was bleak, severe, harsh beyond compromise, and he was not sure that these weathers could ever turn his skin to leather, that these skies could ever put the look of infinity in his eyes, that this earth could ever hold in peace his restless bones. Yet the barrow of Buck rose above these plains and here Samuel too would be buried, and if Jeff stayed he would walk among the memories of their deeds and he would be known by their names. There was much to forget, and for this it would be best to go; and yet there was much to remember.

The week end of the last week in April was the date which had been set for the opening of the museum. All week long the various tribes had been coming to Grey Horse, making their encampments on the level land which lay around the museum and feasting as they had not feasted within the memory of even the oldest men. In the daytime there were hand games and races and dancing and endless talk while the women prepared food and fended off the dogs and children who stood staring hungrily at the pots. And then at night there would be scattered fires, bright flowers in the darkness, and the murmur of many voices on the night wind. Everywhere there flowed a current of excitement as the brightly clothed people gathered around the fires, and the air was sharp with the keen tang of wood smoke and of cooking meat. Unseen dogs barked and occasionally a horse would whinny, and the darkness was rich with the immanent humanness of the camp, the strong laughter that rose above the leaping flames, the carcasses of beef suspended from the trees, the quick voices of the children, the narrow-eyed reminiscing over a glass or a bottle which momentarily fired the long-banked embers of youth. It was a time of well being, of contentment, of celebration, and the name of the man for whom they had come together was on many lips.

On the morning of the opening a parade was held in the town, winding along through Main Street and proceeding slowly up the hill to the site of the museum. Following this there were the usual speeches by town dignitaries and the afternoon was given over to show dancing by the younger men of other tribes. This dancing was colorful and intricate and somewhat abandoned, and it was pleasing to the crowds that filled the Round House, but the Chetopa did not dance and the old men sat on the benches along the wall, waiting until night. As the afternoon wore on the picture-takers and the officials and the merely curious gradually departed, leaving only a few white people and the gathered tribes for the dance of celebration which the Chetopa would hold that night.

Jeff and Samuel had eaten with White Eagle and his people and now they were sitting on the grass in front of the museum, waiting for the dance to begin. The museum itself was a heavy, square building made of yellow sandstone, seeming new and bare amidst the darkness of the trees, and yet it belonged there, housing as it did the mementos of the tribal glory which had long since passed

275

away. As Jeff looked at it he realized that it was a triumph in its way, a solid and massive resistance to time, a victory over the certain decay and disappearance of the tribe. It was Buck's triumph partly but more than that it was the triumph of a way of life, for it stood for the memory and even the continuity of a heroic existence that men too easily forgot.

"How do you like it?" Samuel was looking at the museum, his hat pushed back on his head.

"Everything's going well," Jeff said. "Tonight will be the best part."

"The damned thing ain't much for pretty," Samuel said, "but I reckon she's hell for stout."

"The museum?" Jeff smiled. "What do you want it to look like—a store?"

"You're just like the others—always talkin' about groceries. I meant to tell you—closed the deal with Virge this morning."

"You mean you're buying back into business?"

Samuel shook his head and laughed. "Virge is scared to let me out o' his sight. Remember last fall when we went over to Four Corners—that pup he wanted to buy off me? It's the same one. I told you how she got goin' real good when Virge and I were out the other night. Well, he caught me down town this mornin'—had the check in his hand. He won't quit worryin' for a year now, 'fraid the dog'll drop dead or go blind all of a sudden. I reckon I'll be huntin' with him every night now for awhile; he won't rest easy 'til he finds somethin' wrong with the dog and he'll want me there to prove it by."

Jeff smiled, remembering the way Virgil had looked that day in Four Corners when he had held out the check to Samuel. He recalled too his own sense of annoyance and disappointment, his discomfort standing there in the dusty street beneath the sun while the men had stood silently looking at the dogs. But that seemed a long time ago now, and many things had changed in his mind.

"You still planning the hunt for tomorrow night?" he said, looking over at Samuel.

"Yep. Think you'll be there?"

Jeff looked away. "I'm not sure," he said. He lit a cigarette and let the match blow out in the wind. The night was closing over them swiftly while they talked and now the museum loomed indistinct in the darkness. The fires stood out myriad and clear, and borne on the night winds came the thin jangle of bells. "I hope you weren't counting on my staying."

"I don't guess I ever really thought you would," Samuel said. "Got your mind set on goin'?"

Jeff started to speak and then he was silent.

Samuel carved a small rectangle of tobacco from the plug and then flipped the knife blade closed and looked over at Jeff in the dusk. "I asked you when you first come, son, and you didn't act like you wanted to say. What was it you come here for? Why did you come in the first place?"

It was a while before Jeff answered. "I guess maybe I thought I had left something with you to keep for me and that I needed it. It wasn't that I didn't want to tell you—I just never have found the words."

"Somethin' like the pony?" Samuel said.

"Something like that," Jeff replied quickly. "Like the pony, the hounds, like just being with you."

"Well, it takes a while," the old man said. "I reckon I was savin' them all right, but I don't guess I rightly believed that anybody would ever come. Funny how it turned out." He pulled his hat down tight and got up. "Look—Virge and me got things we have to do tonight. I'm just gonna stand on the edge of the crowd to hear John and then I'll take off. I wouldn't be surprised if Virge didn't have a posse out gunnin' for me now."

"You go ahead," Jeff said. "Virgil would be twice as nervous if I was along. I'll see you tomorrow."

"You're comin' back out before you go," Samuel said, looking at him closely.

"I'll be out. I'll see you tonight if you're back when I get there."

"Sure. In the morning, anyway."

He walked away and Jeff watched him until he was hidden in the darkness. Something in him seemed to follow after the old man and he knew that he should be with him on this last night. Yet even more strongly he knew that he must be here at the dance, for it would be a part of that memory which must suffice for him always.

He and Samuel had been sitting some distance in front of the museum on the slope that overlooked the town, and now as he walked back toward the Round House he could see that the grounds were crowded with people who like the spokes of some great wheel were converging upon this light-filled hub in the center. Most of them were Indians, thin and poorly dressed, and only a few wore rich and heavy blankets across their shoulders. Their faces were big-boned and stolid and in the movements of their bodies there was a visible remnant of wild grace and natural dignity. Many of the children who walked at their sides were grave and wide-eyed as though they had been instructed in the solemnity of the occasion. For this in some ways marked the acknowledgment of something that was gone for all of them, a freedom, a fierceness, a life eager and immediate as the currents of the blood. What was left to them was the blight of a way of life for which they had not been made and whose corruption showed now in so many of these scarred and bloated bodies. And yet, imperfectly seen in the darkness, there was something once again of the old nobility in their faces as they gathered through this April night in commemoration of a monument which a man and his will had created for them.

The Round House toward which the crowd was moving consisted of a frame of tall poles roofed by arched and brush-covered saplings. Fronting the inner walls were stands for spectators and in the very center was a small circular seat row large enough for eight or ten

278

men. The earthen floor was hard and unyielding as though it had been stomped into firmness, a dark clay oval in the midst of so many faces that were themselves the color of the earth. And while the building grew dense with the color and the motion of the crowd, there was a strange quiet that hovered in the air like smoke.

The drummers were coming in by the time that Jeff had found a seat. They arranged themselves on the circular bench around the drum, six of them, dark-faced men wearing tall hats and brightly-colored silk shirts and ordinary trousers. Except for the shirts, they were dressed like the men one might find any day of the week leaning against the front of the bank. Some of them had cigarettes in their mouths, their eyes squinted against the smoke as they tapped tentatively on the great drum or talked back and forth among themselves. Occasionally they would laugh with a peculiar suddenness and their words would fly quickly; then just as suddenly their faces would be still again. They paid no attention to the people sitting around them in the Round House.

After a while Jeff heard the faint jangling of bells, distant at first and then coming steadily closer until finally the dancers were filing into the enclosure and taking seats on benches that stood at the edges of the dance floor. The bells fastened to their ankles and wrists rang with every movement while the air was pierced by shafts of reflected light cast from the silver disks and mirrors and the bells themselves. Like a great flock of brilliantly-plumaged birds they settled themselves around the dance floor and now their heavy male voices rose like the voice of the sea. There was much noise and movement and quick laughter and yet gradually the atmosphere grew taut as a stretched bowstring. Suddenly the noise subsided as quickly as it had begun. There was only the faintest clashing of the bells as one of the dancers got up and walked heavily to the center of the floor. Jeff recognized the walk first and then he knew that the man was White Eagle. His face was striped with paint and the light played in the folds of his silken clothing, and around him the bells rang rhythmically until he stood tall and stern in the middle of the dancing ring. In his hand he carried a long feathered stick and he held it before him until there was silence. When he spoke his voice was deep and the words seemed chanted and prayerlike.

"We dance tonight to celebrate the opening of the museum. To those of you who have come from far off to help us, I give thanks. The Chetopa welcome their friends, hoping that their tables will be filled and that their hearts will be light. It is a time of joy and of celebration." He stopped for a moment and looked around at the people sitting in the stands and then went on. "This museum is here because of one man. The idea came into his mind and it was a good thing to him because it was a way of making the old things be remembered. There were some of us who did not want to see that the museum was good but he made us listen and open our eyes. Because we knew him to be brave and strong and true we listened to his words, and in our hearts we knew that he was right."

And now his voice rose higher and seemed to tremble as though in song. "I do not want this man to be forgotten. His name was Hardin Buck. Little Owl, and his name must remain in the mouths of the Chetopa as long as there are Chetopa left to sing. This dance is for him as well as for the museum, a dance of celebration for his spirit that is gone. For he was a man who stood tall among us, and his spirit moved greatly in our hearts, and his name must not grow strange to our tongues. His honor will live in our songs and in the memory of this dance, for it will be a dance such as the dance my father made, a dance about which stories will grow long after our children are as old as ourselves. This is his dance; let your hearts fill and overflow with remembrance of him. May his spirit hear us, wherever it stands in the night, and may its strength remain always in the hearts of those to whom it has spoken."

He stopped then; a hush had fallen upon all the people who sat watching him and listening to his words. The air was still as though hardly a breath were being drawn, and suddenly one of the men around the drum threw back his head and began to sing. His voice was savage and driving, seeming to hover and dip in the air with the flight of a swallow, singing alone until the other men around the dum joined him and their voices moved in broken unison while their arms rose and fell as one above the drum. Singly at first and then in small groups the men moved onto the floor and began to dance. The old men moved gravely and deliberately in a slow circle around the drum, and further out the young ones whirled and stomped in the fullness of their feeling, their feet pounding patterns of quick grace upon the earth. The air grew thick with sound as they danced, the bells ringing with harsh clarity through the heavy thudding of the drum and the wild flight of the voices soaring above.

Presently Jeff began to notice individuals among the mass of moving color. One old man was dancing as though he were all alone on the floor, pawing at the earth with his feet and shaking his head loosely from side to side in imitation of the buffalo. Occasionally he grunted and swung in a half circle and then continued on around the drum. Another man was dancing with quick, nervous motions, whirling with his head thrown back and suddenly bending over from the waist as though searching the ground with his eyes. In his hand he carried a feathered stick like the one which White Eagle had carried, and he trailed it along the ground at his side. The first song lasted only a few minutes; with a sudden loud pound of the drum it ended and the men walked back to the benches, all save the tail dancer, who danced on alone for a moment after the others had ceased. Boys passed before the benches carrying buckets of water and dippers from which the men drank. After a short interval the singing began again and once more the drum pounded strongly through the Round House, throbbing forth the theme around which the dancers stomped their variations.

Not all of the dancers had left the bench during the first song and some of them did not dance during the second. Jeff could see that many of them were boys, their arms smooth and thin and their eyes frightened. Gradually, as the dancing went on, they joined the elders, coming out self-consciously alone or one following another and then dancing on the inside near the drum as though to hide behind the men. But there was one man who had come in among the last and who still sat on the bench, and there was a slackness in his body that was apparent in spite of the magnificence of the clothing which he wore. Jeff watched him for a while, trying to remember, and at last he realized that the man was White Eagle's son, whom he had seen at the funeral. He wondered why he was not dancing, and then he guessed what must be going through his mind.

One song after another was sung, again and again the dancers returned to the benches and came back to the floor to dance, and slowly as the hours wore by the dancing grew in majesty and power until it seemed to Jeff that he could almost feel the tempo increasing with each song. And it was more as though the quickening of the tempo were in the surge of his own blood, for the drum seemed to drive heavily onward, unvarying in its measured beat. And then at last he saw White Eagle's son rise and begin to dance, alone at first and not going far from the bench and finally moving in among the others, dancing with them until he seemed to blend into the flashing colors and blood-darkened faces and become a part of the song that was being created.

They danced long into the night, for this was a time of pride and of glory for the Chetopa. For many years they had followed no trail together and now they were unified once more in homage to their forefathers. Jeff, looking around through the throng, saw many an ancient face thrust forward, lost in profound absorption, and presently some of the women began to filter down through the crowd until they had formed a circle almost entirely around the dance floor. There they danced with a tiny, sidewise step of the feet, moving around the edge of the ring, the heavy fringes of their shawls swaying from side to side, while in the center the men whirled and drove their feet against the earth as the songs rose above them toward the stars. And this was no exhibition; every person in the place seemed caught up in the emotion of this night, and it was as though one great central heart beat for all of them there in the middle of the floor, one massive heart which drove the songs through all their veins. It was a night of controlled frenzy, of primitive exultation, a night whose throbbing Buck's spirit must feel, no matter where it might stand in the darkness.

Jeff had felt his heart tightening from the first moment that the singers had seated themselves around the drum. When White Eagle had spoken, he had been almost unable to breathe as he had listened to the old man's intoned words, seeming half song, half prayer, and his mind had gone back to the thoughts he had had while he had been looking at the museum earlier in the evening. The museum had seemed to him to embody a kind of triumph of continuity, and now White Eagle and his son were dancing to the same rhythms, hearing and expressing the same songs of the past, parts now of the same movement, the same progression. And as he watched them dancing there together, something started to come full circle in his mind; rapidly and without his willing it, all of the half-comprehended moments of the past six months seemed to well up within him and he was aware of a sudden, almost terrifying sense of the pattern of all that had happened. Once again he saw the bird falling and Buck running up the slope, and then Buck swaying loosely on the pony's back as he rode down the ridge toward his grave. These and other images passed before him, and in his ears were the voices of those who had spoken to him, the voices of Samuel, of White Eagle, and of Buck, Buck's voice quiet and casual and lightly edged with laughter. And then it seemed that the words went through his mind and beyond and there were no longer words now but merely sounds. The voices of the singers became the thin, cracked wailing of the coyotes and the resonant pealing of the hounds, and in the bells of the dancers he heard the ringing chant of the cicadas, the rusty song that had made the long fall nights seem hotter and more breathless than they were, and then he heard the drums and in them was the pulse of the earth itself and the unceasing drive of his own blood, and finally in the dancers themselves he relived for a blinding moment that last dawn that he and Buck had shared together. Before his eyes danced White Eagle and his son, treading the earth in celebration of another man's spirit, and he felt as never before the ancient dream of immortality, the unending rhythm of the cycle that was imaged in the heart and its seasons, for Buck was dead and he himself was alive, and yet the things that stirred in him now had flowered in the dark earth of Buck's dying.

It was late when he got home that night and he was glad that Samuel had gone to bed. He yawned as he opened the window, realizing suddenly how very tired he was, and then he knelt to look out once more at the soft shimmer of the stars. In his heart the drums still throbbed with all the beauty of a quail's beating flight, and in his mind there was no longer any question.

When he awoke the next morning he hurried into his clothes and began at once to pack his suitcases. And when he came into the kitchen, blinking against the light, his face still lined with sleep, Samuel put down his coffee cup and stared at him.

"You seem to be in one hell of a hurry," he said, looking at the suitcases Jeff held in his hands. "You don't make it out this way but once about ever' thirty years— at least have some coffee before you go."

Jeff grinned at him and set the bags down. "Remember what Virge said about you having to learn to bark? I wouldn't want that to happen to a relative of mine. And I'm hurrying so that I can be ready in time."

"Ready for what, goddamn it? What are you talkin' about?"

"Ready to help keep Virge off your back tonight when he finds out about that dog."

Samuel stood up and looked at him. "You're not goin'?" he said quickly.

"Only as far as Buck's," Jeff said. "Somebody's got to look after things over there, and I guess it might as well be me."

"I always told 'em those hounds would git in your blood," Samuel said, shaking his head with happiness.

And then they both laughed, their eyes filled all at once with gladness and with pain.

By late afternoon Jeff had settled in the stone house and now he was standing in the front yard, watching the shadows flow down the valley toward the creek. A squirrel scampered suddenly across the roof behind him and sat up nervously on the ridgepole, cursing him furiously. Jeff smiled and threw a stick at him and then walked out through the gate and down to the point. Against the sunset were banked long blue islands of cloud, and the prairie that stretched to the dark curving of the earth was green as jade. And there at the point the barrow blazed in the dying light, already weathered, already a part of the vast harmony which enclosed it.

When dusk blurred the trees in darkness and the twilight air was quick with veering swallows, he returned to the house and fixed his supper in the soft glow of the lamps. He had been up much too late the night before and now he was sleepy, and when he had finished washing the dishes he lay down to take a nap before going over to the ridge.

He did not know how long he had been asleep when he woke suddenly with a start. He was fully awake and frightened and listening intently until at last he realized what had sung him out of sleep. He got up and walked out to the moon-washed porch and then on the east ridge he could faintly make out the restive gleam of the fire. As he stood there the sound broke against his ears again, hound music swelling up from the creek bottom, and he knew that this night, too, would sing for Buck's spirit, in whatever darkness it lay. Then he stepped into the moonlight and set out across the yard toward the ridge, for they would be waiting for him there by the fire where he belonged.

FOUR OUTSTANDING
WESTERN NOVELS
FROM CURTIS BOOKS

CURTIS
BOOKS

FOUR BOOKS BY DEE BROWN
BESTSELLING AUTHOR OF
"BURY MY HEART AT WOUNDED KNEE"

CURTIS
BOOKS

☐ GRIERSON'S RAID   (01024—$1.25)
The minute by minute account of what General Sherman
called the most brilliant expedition of the Civil War in which
Colonel Grierson showed what could be done within an
enemy's interior without a base from which to draw supplies.

☐ ACTION AT BEECHER ISLAND   (01008—$1.25)
Here is the bloody saga of the Battle of Beecher Island—
nine days of starvation, mutilation and hell that changed
the history of the American frontier.

☐ THE GIRL FROM FORT WICKED   (01007—$1.25)
"The heroine of the title is the eldest of nine girls, traded off
by her father at the Fort for a barrel of flour. . . . The special
quality of this Cavalry-Indians novel becomes evident . . .
and the many aspects of the frontier are deftly made part of
the plot."—*The Roundup*

☐ CAVALRY SCOUT   (01016—$1.25)
This novel of the Indian Wars brings together John Single-
terry, a civilian scout, Marisa, a half-breed Indian girl who
loves him, and Medicine Woman, a witch of the hunted and
harried Cheyenne tribe. These three have a rendezvous with
destiny at a battle called "Comstock's Last Stand."